REVENCHE

LLOYD INGLE

authorHOUSE®

AuthorHouse™ UK
1663 Liberty Drive
Bloomington, IN 47403 USA
www.authorhouse.co.uk
Phone: UK TFN: 0800 0148641 (Toll Free inside the UK)
UK Local: 02036 956322 (+44 20 3695 6322 from outside the UK)

Published by AuthorHouse 01/07/2021

ISBN: 978-1-6655-8419-7 (sc)
ISBN: 978-1-6655-8420-3 (hc)
ISBN: 978-1-6655-8418-0 (e)

Print information available on the last page.

CONTENTS

1

"I have a little job for you, Andrew!" Andreas Bosworth's heart missed a beat as soon as he heard those words. Knowing that Vivien Bailey, his business partner, mentor and friend, only *ever* addressed him by his given name when something serious was involved and being aware that the problem would be far removed from *little*, it would also be one that *he* would not ordinarily wish to be associated with. Andreas responded fractiously, "If it involves travelling, the answer is no. Lu is due the baby any day and my intention is to be *with* my wife when she goes into labour. There is also the small matter of a law degree I am studying for, that seems to have conveniently slipped your mind!" Viv, as he was known to his small circle of friends, smiled and walked towards the office door, "Don't worry!" He remarked nonchalantly; intentionally failing to disguise the underlying rationale in it's submission, "It's not operational-immediate old chap, please forget I said anything!" "You crafty bastard!" Andreas shouted as the door quietly closed behind his friend and on the other side of the the door, with his back against the large oak portal and a self-satisfied smirk played across his elegant features, Viv was now secure in the knowledge that his colleague was hooked and ready for being reeled in. Walking jauntily to his office, he scarcely resisted the temptation to laugh out loud at his artifice.

Sitting down ill at ease, Andreas tried to revive his interest in the building site file, that he had been perusing before being summoned to Viv's office and finally losing patience with his inability to concentrate on the matter at hand, he pushed the file away angrily, spilling the contents of a half emptied, cold cup of coffee into the saucer. "Damn the man!" He muttered, as he headed angrily for a confrontation with his mentor and foregoing the courtesy of knocking, he entered Viv's sanctum, strode purposefully to the desk and placing both hands on the veneered surface, he demanded an immediate, detailed explanation of the required task. "Well now!" Viv remarked, disentangling his hands from the back of his head, "It's taken longer for you to lose your patience than I'd anticipated; sit down and I'll explain *exactly* what is required!" Leaning forward with the semblance of a smile, Viv began his exposition, "Two years ago, the figures for investments and returns from our offices in Australia began not to tally; nothing substantial you understand but enough to raise concerns. This year however, there is a *significant* amount unaccounted for, thereby making a solution to the problem more critical!" Pausing for a moment, his face became more stern, "It *could* be just human error but the more logical explanation is that the money has been embezzled!" Andreas sat back in the chair, staggered and annoyed too at Viv's trickery in whetting his appetite for mystery and drama. Viv continued, "The trip would *not* take place until you have taken and hopefully attained your degree, which will give you ample time to prepare!" Responding warily, Andreas asked, "I haven't *agreed* to anything yet and what kind of preparation do you envisage?" "Oh I don't know!" Viv replied airily, "I *suppose,* anything you would deem necessary for a journey into the unknown!" Andreas's response was swift, "You know very well that this will turn out to be a hazardous undertaking, so perhaps you could tell me *why* I should leave my family, to travel to the other end of the globe, to sort out something that is so clearly a matter for the local *gendarmerie!*" Looking grimly at his colleague, Viv pushed forward a file that had been lying on the desk since the start of the conversation, "Discretion is the name of this particular game old chap and *that* sadly, is a commodity that the long arm of the law does *not* possess. *If* you require motivation for *your* involvement in the matter, you need look no further than this file, where you will find that the lion's share of misappropriated funds is from *your* account!" Not for the first time during the brief exchange, Andreas was struck dumb but regaining his composure somewhat, he paused briefly and remarked fatalistically, "I guess I have little choice and I *suppose* I have to be grateful that at least I will have *some* time to prepare!" Rising from his chair, Viv put an arm round his friend's shoulder and said, "I'm sorry old chap but for this particular task, there is no one in the firm that quite fits the bill the way that you do. However, it is not all doom and gloom, for at *my* request, the brothers have sanctioned the addition of a travelling companion and I urge you to choose your associate very carefully; he should be one who can be relied upon to assist in bringing this matter to a rapid and successful conclusion. Andreas's mind kicked into gear and controlling his emotions, he said slowly, "God only knows what I'll be facing if it *isn't* just an error!" Then pausing, he breathed deeply, "So I don't consider it being *over* cautious in requesting firearms and martial arts training!" "Of course, of course!" Viv answered. "Anything you deem necessary will be underwritten by the firm and I'll leave *you* to organize that!"

Returning irritably to his office, Andreas experienced difficulty in concentrating on *pedestrian* duties but as needs must, he diligently applied his nose to the grindstone, albeit it pausing every now and then to appraise the new change in circumstances. During one such lull in radical thought, he was interrupted by the strident ringing of the phone and waking from his semi-conscious state, he heard Ma's dulcet tones. "I've managed to get the *lautari* for the party!" She informed him gleefully, "Now is there anything else you'd like me to do?" In truth, Andreas had completely forgotten about the party that he had been coerced into organising, with the minutiae of the arrangements, commemorating completion of all building work at the new housing estates, being delegated to family members. Ma had predictably come up trumps ahead of the rest and being relieved at having something other than financial problems in Australia to think about, Andreas replied, "That's great news Ma, at least that's the entertainment sorted and I don't *think* there's anything else needs doing but if you believe there's something I've overlooked; run it past me ASAP!" Lounging back in his chair, he clasped his hands at the nape of his neck and suddenly realizing that it was an annoying mannerism he'd acquired from Viv, he hastily unravelled the digits. Deciding to contact Jimmy's gymnasium club to check on the availability of the club rooms for the celebration, *before* he was asked to shelve the task in favour of other little problems that Viv may have suddenly found for him to solve and finding that all would be well, he organized a tab behind the bar, before that too had been deferred and forgotten. Smiling, he sat back in his chair, like the cat that got the cream, congratulating himself on the all-round success of his own meagre contribution.

Unconsciously threading his fingers once more at his nape, he slipped easily into a nostalgic, Antipodean-free subliminal thought process, pondering on all that had happened since Ma and Pa had adopted him. They had almost certainly saved him from death by stepping in when his evil cousins, to whom his guardianship had been entrusted, were on the point of selling him to a Scotsman called McAvoy who, they discovered, was subsequently sent to prison for infanticide. A few years down the line from that time, Andreas inherited a fortune, when both his itinerant birth-mother *and* his guardians had died within weeks of one another, leaving him an extremely wealthy young man. The firm of Mowll and Mowll in the shape of Viv, had been entrusted with guardianship of the estate and with an innate eye for a good deal, Andreas had persuaded the firm to purchase on his behalf, vast swaths of land from old farmer Davies's estates. Under his mentor Viv's guidance, the sizeable acreage had been developed into profitable housing estates and with the homes now ready for occupation, it had been decided that a celebration of the success was in order and being entrusted with the arrangements, he had immediately but very much against Viv's wishes, extended an open invitation to all his Romany connections; in the faint hope that old grievances and vendettas were now buried in the past. *Jimmy's* gymnasium club had been selected for the shindig, being the only local venue large enough to house the potentially high number of guests and with Andreas owning the club, no problems were anticipated nor indeed *were* encountered. Lounging in his chair, he realized that the gathering was now almost upon them, with little if anything having been achieved by him personally and with the *lautari*, a band of itinerant musicians and singers, having now been engaged by Ma; the party was good to go.

The day of the celebration duly arrived with everything set fair for a gathering of mammoth proportions but unfortunately Andreas's sister Vee had to pull out at the last moment when her daughter, Lily-Ann, suddenly developed a terrible head cold. That unforeseen cloud had a double proverbial silver lining however, with Vee offering to have the two boys at her house for the night, fortuitously saving him the expense of a babysitter *and* allowing the couple the rare opportunity to get ready for a night out in peace. Arriving at the club early, Andreas took careful note of the fact that Lu's care and attention to her appearance had really borne fruit; standing a little apart from him sipping a chilled Sauterne, she looked ravishingly beautiful in spite of, or perhaps *because* of, the advanced stage of her pregnancy. Moving closely to her side, Andreas took advantage of the absence of guests by gently grasping her left buttock, before moving his hand, possessively to her now ample waist but his shenanigans were curtailed however, with the arrival of early guests and smiling coquettishly, she began to circulate among the crowd, catching his eye every now and then, portending a deeply carnal end to the night; Andreas smiled archly in anticipation.

With salutations having been exchanged and the first drinks supped, the assemblage were ushered to their designated seats at the vast tables and the *lautari,* ceased their hauntingly beautiful rendition of an old Romany melody to make way for the speeches. Andreas's address, scheduled to be last on the agenda, had been delegated, along with a few other minor tasks, to his brother Gunari and several times during the run-up to the event, Andreas doubted the wisdom of entrusting Gunnar, as he was more widely addressed, with such an important chore but the oration in all fairness, was received to great acclaim and far removed from the debacle that Andreas had feared, albeit with a strangely shy and nervous host faltering over a few of the words. With its brevity signalling an early start to the meal, a somewhat more diminutive than anticipated, cauldron of Ma's legendary rabbit stew was wheeled in, later being judged by all to have been the perfect entrée. The smaller-than-usual offering being explained away with Ma's usual aplomb, reasoning that overconsumption of the potage would leave insufficient room for all the other sweetmeats arrayed on the tables.

All was going well until midway through proceedings, when Lu began tugging on Andreas's sleeve and finally gaining his attention, she explained that the baby was on the way and would certainly *not* be waiting for the second course. Andreas swiftly caught Ma's attention and she who knows everything, had certainly *not* foreseen *this* turn of events. However, taking immediate control of the situation, she rang for an ambulance and the waiting trio were speedily borne to the hospital within five minutes of being summoned. Despite Andreas's concerns, a wailing Rosemary announced her arrival to the world, half an hour after arrival and with her customary adherence to the old ways, Ma arranged for a cab to take Andreas back to the club to impart the glad tidings and celebrate in the time-honoured

Romany fashion with his male counterparts. He was *expected* to adhere to protocol but dreading Lu's wrath, he expressed a wish to remain with his wife and daughter; nevertheless his purely perfunctory protests fell on deaf ears and a cab soon arrived to deliver him to the club.

Jimmy's gymnasium club had been named as much in homage to Jimmy Kelly, its former boxing trainer and now club manager, as it was as an intended pun of its former function and when Andreas arrived at the club in the cab, Jimmy was the first to greet him. Putting a solicitous arm around his former protege's shoulder, Jimmy led him into the hall and announced the birth, thus denying Andreas the opportunity to execute the task himself. The premature proclamation however, heralded a level of celebrations never experienced before at the old club and with Pa as head of the family and Ma's brother Riley orchestrating proceedings, the drink flowed copiously, even *though* Riley's habitual Rabelaisian behaviour was somewhat stinted by the watchful presence of his wife Dolores. Having no such inhibitors, Pa and Andreas became almost permanent fixtures at the bar, being joined from time to time by Gunnar, *when* he was able to tear himself away from his partner Pearl's apron strings. The tab was soon exhausted and taking out his wallet in order to create another, Andreas felt a presence at his right elbow; spinning round quickly, he found a smiling Viv at his side. Andreas exclaimed with a grin, "My God, your timing is impeccable!" Viv replied quietly, "I've spoken to Mr Mowll Jr and he assures me that in the circumstances, your presence will not be required in the morning!" Being a green light from heaven, the good news allowed Andreas to indulge his thirst a little more freely; a rarity in recent times but non-stop drinking and the trauma of having witnessed Rosemary's arrival, soon began to take it's toll and feeling the need for a little peace and quiet, he sneaked away to the relative peace of the new conference room.

Deeming the moonbeams shining brightly through the vast skylight to be sufficient light, he walked unsteadily to the large table and sitting at its head, he looked upward towards the vast glass ceiling and sentimentally reflecting on his life once more, he called to mind just how fortunate he had been to have been adopted by Ma and Pa, even if life had not *always* run smoothly. Having fallen in love with Lu in his early teens, his heart was shattered on learning that she had been promised to his arch-rival Lupe Scamp in their early childhood. Having believed that there would never be a time when *he* and Lu would not be together, the hurt and anger was actually softened somewhat, on learning the sad story of how the arranged marriage came to be. Ma and Pa had been destitute when work dried up and with the family almost at starvation level, Bill, the head of the Scamp tribe stepped in to bail them out; duly setting the money as a traditional *bride price.* Having little choice, it seemed a scant price to pay at the time; little dreaming how unhappy it would make their little girl in the future *and* their adopted son. Being forced to witness the union when the day finally arrived, both Andreas *and* the bridegroom were ignorant of the fact that the son she carried at her wedding, was in fact Andreas's child; as was the brother, born two or three years down the line and having always suspected that he was *not* the boys' father, Lupe began systematically beating Lu, until one day he went too far and savagely beat her to a pulp in a drunken rage. The aftermath was that in order to right the wrong inflicted on his sister, Gunnar challenged Lupe to a fight and after the two men had gone toe to toe for over an hour, a pyrrhic victory was finally achieved when Lupe was unable to pick himself from the floor and was banished from his clan forever for his loss of face.

After a respectable interval, Andreas and Lu were wed in the little Gypsy church situated between the two camps; in a marriage that had been predestined before they had even been born and starting their new life together in one of the houses built by his company, Andreas promised to take Lu on a round-the-world cruise when all the work at the sites had been completed. Now however, he faced the problem of informing her that the cruise would have to be deferred once more, *until* the problem in Australia had been resolved, realizing that the consequences of failure in the task he had been set, could result in his housing empire crumbling. With that dreadful outcome being a distinct possibility, his faculties suddenly cleared of alcohol-induced confusion and making his way back to the bar, he noticed that Pa and the family were still wetting the baby's head as if there were no tomorrow. Smiling at the heart-warming scene, Andreas joined Gunnar and Viv, sitting just beyond the far end of the bar and with familiar affability, Gunnar demanded, "Ho, Gadjo, where have *you* been hiding?" Replying with a grin Andreas remarked, "I wanted a little time away from looking at your ugly mug, so I went to the conference room for some peace and quiet!" Incautiously raising the subject of the trip to

Melbourne, Viv asked Andreas if he had thus far made any preparations for the journey and noting the astonishment on Gunnar's face, Andreas explained, "After my finals, I'm off to Australia to sort out a little problem for the firm and barring complications, I should be back within a month or so!" Gunnar declared excitedly, "Wow, Australia's a fair old distance; the only one in the family *ever* to travel abroad was Pa and that was to fight at a horse fair in France!" Viv raised his eyebrows, sat back in his chair and smiled archly, " I think that would possibly have been before passports had been invented!" Laughing at his own attempted humour, Viv turned once more to Andreas, "Perhaps you could come into the office tomorrow afternoon so we can discuss at length what we touched on this morning!" Before any more could be said, Pa and Riley joined them, pointing out that their sobriety had become a matter for concern among the guests, with the result being that the young men rose from the table to rejoin the fold and began quenching their thirst once more. Andreas and Viv however, did *not* over-indulge, knowing they would need to be at their sharpest for their meeting the following afternoon and with the party finally drawing to a close, Andreas opted to forego the luxury of a taxi. Staggering home to an empty house, he wearily flopped onto a cold, empty bed and looking upwards to the ceiling he grinned, *not quite the end I'd planned for the night but having a baby daughter more than makes up for that!* Falling asleep minutes later, he was disturbed in the wee hours by Riley and Dolores noisily arriving for their prearranged sleep-over and laying in the dark, silently cursing them for interrupting his sleep, he castigated himself for having agreed to the arrangement.

2

Before leaving for the farm later that morning, Andreas woke his sleeping guests with a steaming mug of coffee, cordially inviting them to make themselves at home while he picked up the boys from the farm and hastily escaping the stench of Riley's bodily emissions, he drove with the windows down, only ridding his nose of the noxious odour as he neared the farm. Taking a deep breath as he drove into the yard, he came to the conclusion that the beasts in their stalls, possessed a somewhat sweeter smell than that of his uncle when he had been drinking or indeed, even when he had *not* been at the golden liquid. As he stepped from the car, Vee dashed out of the house to greet him, wearing what appeared to be a new blue dress and being topped by a flour flecked matching pinafore, it portended a bag of *dainties* for his evening snack. Walking behind his sister into the farmhouse, he was greeted by the children rushing downstairs, desperate to learn all about the baby and with Vee disappearing into the kitchen to make coffee, Andreas's youngest son George said excitedly, "Will we be able to bring him home with us today Daddy?" Andreas smiled and enlightened his young son, "It isn't a *him* George, it's a little *sister* you have and no, she will *not* be coming home today!" George's blank stare demonstrated that he had evidently not reached the stage where he would appreciate the difference but he seemed satisfied with his father's response nonetheless.

Vee placed coffee and a plateful of freshly baked scones onto the table, whereupon Andreas remarked with a grin, "I hope I'll be taking a bag of those with me when I leave?" Smiling Vee replied, "*That* has already been attended to!" Shaking her head, she remarked, "I hope you don't mind me saying Andreas but you look as if you've been dragged through a hedge backwards, *hardly* a fit state to go visiting your wife and new daughter!" Opening his arms wide in supplication, he asked, "What's wrong with me?" Vee looked disgustedly at him, "You haven't even run a comb through your hair!" Impatiently ruffling his dark locks, he remarked, "Is that better? Not that she'll notice anyway!" Shaking her head, Vee responded, "Oh, she'll notice all right, you may be sure of that!" Playfully poking out his tongue at his sister, Andreas asked Michael's whereabouts. "He's gone over to the Jones farm to check on the price of stock!" She replied, "Business has been so good lately that he wants to extend the grazing land and increase the size of the herd!" Andreas frowned, "I hope your husband realizes that Mowll and Mowll have the right to veto *any* purchase of cattle; tell him I'll be over as soon as I can to discuss the matter!" Reassuringly he commented, "Don't look so worried Vee, there will likely be no problem but everything has to be done properly and after all, it *was* his father's dying wish that *I* look after that side of things. I'll pop over tomorrow and take you to see the new baby; perhaps I can catch up with him then but for now, I have the task of taking the boys to see their mum and baby sister!" The matter of the intended extension was temporarily deferred and giving Vee a kiss, he asserted, "Don't worry Vee; everything will be fine!" Handed over a bag of still warm scones, she recoiled in disgust, "For God's sake, do something about your breath, you smell like a barman's apron!" Andreas laughed as he opened the car door for the boys, "No kisses for me then!" No words were necessary, with her face betraying her abhorrence.

As soon as they arrived at the hospital, he made sure that his first task was to purchase a packet of chewing gum from the small hospital newspaper kiosk and inserting two sticks into his dry mouth, he entered the ward, in hope more than certainty, that she would be too tired to notice his halitosis. Smiling, he leaned over to kiss her cheek, *instantly* receiving a broadside for smelling of alcohol and shaking his head, he muttered, "You get more like your mother every bloody day; for God's sake, stop nagging and give me a kiss!" The boys climbed onto the bed; an act that was in all likelihood against regulations and looking at Rosie sleeping in Lu's arms, Andreas declared, "She'll break a few hearts in the future and capture a few along the way, I shouldn't wonder!" Noticing that far from looking haggard by the ravages of childbirth, Lu was radiant and leaning across to kiss her cheek, he gazed lewdly at her scantily clad body; feeling a familiar movement in his trousers, his trembling hand wandered across her hip but assertively removing the offending limb, she declared with a smile, "You can forget *that* for a while, my old sunshine; there will be a *NO ENTRY* sign pinned to the bottom of the bed!" The half-joking manner in which the put-down was delivered, left him not knowing whether she was in earnest or not but the bell signalling the end of visiting time began to ring out harshly, dispelling all thoughts of carnality *or* enforced abstinence. The boys were unhappy at having to leave and with their father cajoling the duty nurse into allowing them a further twenty minutes visiting time, they were actually asked to vacate the premises after thirty and exiting the hospital via the swing doors, provided an amusing ten minutes distraction for the boys *en route* to making their way back to the car. George asked his father, if they could go to Ma and Pa's on the way home and with Victor pleading for chips too, Andreas prudently decided to accommodate both entreaties. Driving directly to the chippie, he recorded his second sighting of Walthaar's latest conquest and happily receiving the news that there would be nothing to pay for the meal, gave him the thought that fish and chips could become a regular treat, if Walthaar's relationship continued. Heading for the nearest lay-by, they ate the repast with fingers plunging in and out of the newspaper-wrapping at a rate of knots and the result of this cardinal sin, was being told on arrival at Ma's that they would all have to go to the bathroom and wash their hands before being allowed to sit down. Declining Pa's offer of a *swally*, Andreas averred, "I'll have to give that one a miss Pa; don't forget I have a meeting with Viv *and* I've got to drive the boys home after that!" Pa nodded and was immediately prevented from partaking more alcohol himself by a warning glare from *She Who Must Be Obeyed*, "Don't forget that *we* are visiting Lu and the baby later!" She informed him and judging by his slurred voice, he had already imbibed a flagon or so of cider and his whingeing plea to be allowed to toast *Rosie's* arrival fell on deaf ears but his garbled drink-induced mispronunciation of Rosemary's name, had unwittingly bestowed a name on the babe, that would become hers for life. Deciding that it was time for him to leave for the meeting, the already excellent day got even better, with Ma *insisting* that the boys remained there until his return from the office.

Leaving the house in a buoyant mood, he parked just as Viv was just leaving for his lunch break, "I thought the meeting was for later in the day but I guess that preparations for the trip can just as easily be discussed over lunch!" "That will be fine by me!" Andreas replied with a grin, "If I'm not mistaken; I believe it's your turn to pay!" Ignoring the broad hint, Viv remarked, as they set out on the short walk to the Green Man, "The brothers are not too happy about the training courses, especially the one involving firearms!" "In that case!" Andreas retorted, "The brothers will have to find someone else to sort out the mess. I will *not* go into this business unprepared!" Ordering what they believed to be the safe option of fish and chips; it took two minutes of eating tasteless *pap*, for them to come to the conclusion, that they would have been better off sitting in the park with a second meal from the chippie. "Don't worry about the brothers!" Viv assured him, "I'll tell them that a weaponry course would only be a precautionary measure; have you any other thoughts on the trip that you want to discuss?" "I haven't had too much time, what with running back and forth to the hospital and worrying about a scheme that Michael has for extending the herd!" Viv stopped eating his spotted-dick and custard, "I think it will prove to have been a wise move of yours to have the farm protected legally by the brothers and *luckily,* it was all organised while the old boy was still alive!" Andreas explained the gist of what had been said thus far on the subject and finishing his drink, he concluded, "That will have to do for now Viv; I've got to pick up the boys from Ma's!"

Suddenly becoming weary, due in no small measure to the excesses of the previous evening's late finish *and* having his sleep interrupted, the short journey back to Ma's was onerous but being well aware that there would be a surfeit of caffeine waiting for him at Ma's, Andreas smiled and put his foot down. Three mugs of coffee later, he was sufficiently energized to hit the road once more and after dutifully kissing their hosts, the pilgrims progressed homeward. The excitement of the day's events however, proved a bridge too far for the sleeping pair in the rear of the car and the short journey was conducted in total silence. Arriving home, he successfully managed the seemingly impossible task of negotiating key to lock while carrying two sleeping children and after putting his boys to bed *without* a bath *or* clean pyjamas, they were soon in the land of Nod. Andreas sat spread-eagled in front of the television, drinking a flagon of cider, while intermittently devouring Vee's delicious scones, to which copious amounts of cream and jam had been added. Comfortable though Andreas was, Michael's plan for extending stock and grazing land, persistently niggled at his mind and finally giving up trying to concentrate on the programme he was merely half-watching, he switched off the set. *Jesus Christ* He thought angrily, *On top of all the worry of the Oz trip, I've now got bloody Michael complicating my life even more!* He sat back in the chair to begin drinking in earnest and when two flagons of golden cider had been emptied, the *minor* concern of Michael's planned purchase of more stock and the major worry of the trip to Australia had vanished completely and with the effects of *apple-juice* finally taking command, his bed began demanding his presence.

3

Rising early the following morning, Andreas showered and breakfasted before waking the boys, then sitting in his favourite chair, he noisily sipped a *cheap* whisky laced coffee, *it always tastes better when you slurp it*, he observed profoundly but when the drink had been consumed *a fortissimo*, to the final, delicious drop, his thoughts once more unerringly turned to the unwanted distraction of Michael's intentions. Although there seemed no *obvious* problems to the scheme, Michael would have to realize that the business side of things was now under the protective mantle of Mowll and Mowll and schemes for expansion would have to be sanctioned by *them*, even though the final decision would actually be Andreas's alone. Setting up a training regime in preparation for the Australian trip was now his principal concern, so Michael's plans would have to take a back seat and gathering the boys together, he left for the farm. Cramming a couple of chewing gum strips into his mouth to prevent Vee nagging about the smell of whisky on his breath and smiling at his artifice, he arrived at the homestead, to find a scowling Michael waiting in the yard, ready to address the matter of stock right there and then. "What's all this nonsense about my not being able to purchase cattle and extend my own land?" He demanded. Sighing deeply Andreas explained, "Michael, your father legally put the business side of things in *my* hands and *I* decided to protect the farm by placing the whole caboodle in the hands of Mowll and Mowll. That means that legally, you cannot buy stock *or* extend grazing land without their say-so; now it does *not* necessarily mean that you *cannot* make changes; you merely have to submit your plans to the firm!" Taking note of Michael's crestfallen face, Andreas put an arm around his brother-in-law's shoulder adding, "Don't take it to heart; I'm sure everything will be fine but it *has* to be done correctly and there really is no *need* for haste. Rest assured that I will *certainly* raise the matter with Viv as soon as I see him!" Andreas hated being pedantic but having the strangest feeling that for some strange reason there was something not quite right about the scheme, he suggested, "If you give me the number of beasts you wish to purchase, the price and cartage costs, I'll see what I can do!" Michael stormed off back to the house, leaving Andreas shaking his head in dismay.

Getting back into the car, he had to wait a good fifteen minutes for Vee to appear, and when Lily-Ann was safely ensconced in the rear of the car with the boys, Vee got into the front passenger seat, with a face like a smacked arse. Turning to her, Andreas explained, "Look Vee, I know that Michael is not happy with the situation but his father tied up everything legally to prevent him from embarking on wild schemes, as he is wont to do. On paper, the scheme seems practical enough but it will do no harm to bide a while just to check that everything is *kushti!*" Sensing however, that she too was far from happy, he said no more on the subject even though, legally there was nothing they could do about it anyway. They arrived at the hospital, where the boys were left to play with the swing doors, while he led a saturnine Vee and her excited daughter to the maternity ward. Lu was busily feeding Rosie, so Lily-Ann had to wait patiently until the bairn's appetite had been satisfied, before she was permitted to sit on a chair and nurse *Rosie*. The two sisters chattered away nine to the dozen about this, that and nothing in particular and when visiting hour was almost at an end, being confident that his breath would pass muster, Andreas fondly kissed Lu, leaving the girls to talk over the more intimate details of the birth.

Michael's plans were not mentioned on the journey home and on arrival at the farm, Vee purposely denied him the customary kiss in bidding him farewell; shrugging his shoulders he headed for home, temporarily postponing a seemingly inevitable confrontation. Two days later however, while on a visit to his parents, Ma asked him if he'd had any further thoughts on the plans for buying more cattle and guessing that Vee had approached Ma to intercede on her behalf in the matter, Andreas asserted, "I have not seen Viv *or* the brothers since my conversation with Michael and no decision will be taken until I do. I have the strangest feeling about this thing Ma and even though it's irrational, something tells me that all is not well with the scheme!" "You could be right!" Ma replied. "It would not be the first time that young man's hasty decisions have had unfortunate consequences and my advice would be to trust your instincts!" Kissing Ma's cheek he added, "I could be wrong but it will do no harm to wait a while anyway!" There was however, a set of circumstances afoot that would make them *all* grateful for him erring on the cautious side.

Returning home, he decided on another tranquillizing whisky-laced coffee and sitting down with the *Times,* he turned on the radio to hear the latest news; taking a sip of the elixir, he began to slowly unwind and was at ease with the world, *until* he heard an item of news that caused his body to jackknife into a more attentive posture. The newscast had been interrupted by a flash, concerning an outbreak of foot-and-mouth in Wales. His immediate reaction was one of gratitude for having stalled on Michael's plans but when the implications of what had happened dawned on him, he dropped everything and drove directly to the farm. Michael panicked when told of the bad news but focussing Michael's attention *away* from negative thoughts, Andreas ordered him to send for the vet immediately, "If the cattle are in the clear, we will have to take measures to ensure that they remain so and whatever the result, the farm will have to be isolated, which will mean the shop closing; we cannot have people traipsing about all over the place!" Understandably concerned for the future of the business, Michael said, "I *can* see the sense in that but the shop has become such a vital part of our existence, I fear that closing down the shop, would permanently harm the business!" "We have no choice Michael but leave it to me!" Andreas replied, "The owner of the mill owes me favours and I'll arrange for the ground floor to be used as a temporary shop!" The vet arrived within ten minutes of being informed and after giving all the animals a clean bill of health, he accompanied Andreas to Ma's, where Pa's horse Silver was also given the all-clear; considering it advisable to stable the horse at the farm, Andreas covered the horse's hooves with sacking and led him to the relative safety of the farm. Speed being of an essence, Andreas rang the firm that had built the fencing on the housing estates, asking for emergency barriers to be installed around the whole perimeter of the farm and a call to the firm that had installed the existing grilles, guaranteeing that the farm would be surrounded by grids within two days. Having now organized the most urgent measures, he left Michael to prepare for the shop relocation move, while he drove *post haste* to the mill and in next to not time, he had arranged for the two storerooms on the ground floor to be cleared of clutter, to make way for the resettlement of the shop; being surprised that not one person had thought to question his authority. With all the essentials now in place, he returned home and sitting in his favourite chair, he breathed a deep sigh of relief; *until* he realized that he was late in picking up Lu and the baby and speeding to the hospital, he found Lu standing outside the main door, angry and impatient. "Been drinking again?" She asked sarcastically. "No I haven't!" he answered and explaining the reason for his tardiness, Lu was suitably mollified, pointing out, "The farm has been the life blood of folk around here for years; let's get home quickly and find out the latest news!" Considering the precious cargo he was carrying, they made excellent time and rushing into the living room, he phoned the farm for an update. Sounding somewhat calmer, Michael informed him, "Work on the fencing will be finished in the morning and with the grid installations also expected tomorrow, things *are* looking a little better!" Andreas hung up and allowing himself a moment of relaxation with a mug of coffee, he turned on the television, learning that his worst fears had been realized; the disease had spread across the border.

Ma arrived to check out Lu and the baby and after she had rocked Rosie to sleep in that age-old way that only women are privy to, she demanded to know everything about the virus. Andreas told her the little that he had learned and when he had finished, Ma asked, "Is it possible for humans to become infected?" Andreas replied, "Apparently it's extremely rare but it *is* a possibility!" Ma immediately became concerned for Vee and Lily-Ann's well-being and conceding that he *had* actually overlooked that particular danger, Andreas suggested, "Perhaps Vee and Lily-Ann should stay here with us until it's all over!" Lu interjected, "It might be a good idea for you to stay at the farm with Michael; you *could* become a carrier by walking around here both places!" Andreas protested, "My place is here with my family!" Supporting her daughter's suggestion, Ma asserted, "Lulu is right. It *would* be the best thing all round *and* you would be on hand to help in the running of the farm!" Although he knew it made sense, Andreas was reluctant to be away from his family at such a critical time but Lu persisted,

"Look at it this way Andreas; we were apart for quite a while before finally getting together, so a little more time apart will be neither here nor there!" After much discussion, Andreas finally conceded that it actually would be for the best and packing a case with essentials, he headed for the farm, where initially he had trouble convincing Vee that it would be best for her to leave but *finally* seeing the wisdom of the standby measures, she packed a few things and was driven to the safety of Andreas's house. Returning to the farm after dropping his family at Andreas's, Michael brought up flagons of cider from the cellar to fortify himself and Andreas against the dawn of a new and worrisome chapter in their lives.

Clearing out a drawer, to make way for his underwear, Andreas came across a pack of cards and an old rifle butt, that had the markings of a cribbage board burnt into it and cajoling Michael into learning the noble art of cribbage, eventually paid huge dividends, with many an evening being spent in the time-consuming pursuit. Quickly settling into a routine of sorts, Andreas ministered daily to the mill, while spending the rest of the time in the back-breaking task of running a farm and acquiring the habit of taking turns at phoning their loved ones every evening, Andreas found that during *Michael's* contact evenings, the spectre of Australia hung like a pall over his senses and knowing that the task was in the not-too-distant future, did little to make its imminence any less of a headache.

Minor adjustments were constantly being applied to the safety measures and one evening while out walking the perimeter, Michael asked, "Do you think we ought to reinforce the gates to keep away *four-legged* visitors?" Andreas replied, "That's a bloody good idea and perhaps while we're at it, we should get rid of all the unwanted creatures *already* living on the farmland!" So early the following morning, one of the gates was left open, the grilles boarded over and the pariah smoked out of their lairs; once the bolt-holes had been sealed, the dogs made sure that few vermin remained but stragglers that managed to escape the jaws of the hounds and terriers, were shot and used to supplement their food rations. Once the task had been discharged, they removed the boards and began the task of reinforcing the gates, nailing warning notices to the fencing as they went along, hoping that the new security measures would give them, at least an outside chance of defeating the scourge. Having little time to rest on their laurels, they spent the next day harvesting apples to replenish the dwindling stock of cider and once that, too, had been accomplished, they deemed themselves to be sitting pretty; *until* a few days after the completion of the back-breaking chore of fruit gathering, when Michael rushed into the stable where Andreas was mucking out, "All our efforts have been in vain!" He screamed, "One of the pregnant cows has the disease!" Accompanying Michael to the field, Andreas perceived the distressed animal coughing and sneezing; leading the animal to a large shed near the perimeter of the field, he muttered sombrely, "Hopefully none of the other cows are infected; I'll inspect the rest of the herd while you call the vet!" Finding no other animal with symptoms, he returned to the farmhouse to impart the good news, finding Michael however, sitting at the table in a distressed state. Andreas joked, "Wait until the vet has been before you cut your wrist; for the time being, no other cow is infected, so we'll see what he advises!" The vet came straight away and after examining the hapless creature, he delivered mixed news, "The cow has BRSV, or bovine respiratory syncytial virus, which *can* be serious but at least is *not* foot-and-mouth. She should soon recover and give birth quite naturally but keep her isolated to prevent the virus spreading!" As predicted, the cow *did* make a complete recovery, giving birth naturally after a further few weeks and being a weakling, the calf should have been slaughtered but its life was spared by Michael, who earmarked it as a pet for Lily-Ann.

The vet's weekly visits always brought the fear that somehow the disease had managed to penetrate their defences and complacency was a luxury they could ill afford, knowing that potential disaster lurked behind every corner. Finally however, their diligence was rewarded when, after a nine-month confinement, it was announced that the virus had been completely eradicated and feeling as if a great load had been lifted from their shoulders, they rewarded their industry and perseverance with a celebratory drink, effectively exhausting the new reserves of cider. The vet arrived later in the morning and giving them the all-clear, he imparted the news that theirs had been the only farm in the county to have survived the holocaust without losing an animal. Had there been any cider left, they would have celebrated that fact but instead they began to tidy up the mess from their nine months confinement and remove their cars from the garage in preparation for a journey that, at times had seemed a bleak prospect. Michael called across as he got into his car, "Do you think the place is tidy enough?" "Trust me!" Andreas said, "Even if you had it looking like a palace, my sister would *still* find fault!" With Andreas leading the way, they drove along the well-worn road for the first time in nine months and pulling up in front the house, the pair were greeted with open arms. With the rest of the family joining them in the evening, an impromptu party was soon in full swing and taking advantage of the fact that everyone was up dancing, Andreas remarked slyly to Michael, "The way things are looking, I'll be building an extra room in another nine months!" Michael laughed but Lu, who had heard the remark, sidled up to Andreas and remarked, "You've got another think coming, sunshine; you'll be getting sod all!" Adding with a cheeky grin, "Well, not for the next few days anyway!" When the party finally broke up and the couple retired to bed, he found Lu intransigent over the Roma code of not having sex during a monthly visit; but being philosophical about that fact, he thought, *oh well, I have to go to the office in the morning anyway*!

4

Waking early and being well aware of how crabby Lu could be when she was having a period, Andreas crept from the room and quickly showered. Rousing his sons, he informed them that after breakfast, they would be accompanying him to the office, the gym and then on to the garage; *in that order*. Viv's mother was a Mowll by birth, which meant that Viv would inherit the business when his uncles passed away and because it had been hinted that Andreas would be offered a partnership at some time in the future, it seemed only fitting for his boys to be introduced to the machinations of the company at an early age. Andreas had already widened the firm's horizon by investing money in the business and *in re-inventing* their role to encompass investment, they had become more than *just* a firm of solicitors. Walking proudly through the portals with the boys, he strode into the reception area, where Viv suddenly appeared and shaking Andreas's hand, he commended his successful defence of the farm against the disease. Pointing out that although he and Michael *had* played the major role, the regular examinations by the vet and the speed at which the local tradesmen had responded to their cause had also played an integral part. As the group walked into Viv's office, Andreas was informed that arrangements had been made for him to resume his studies after the Christmas break, "You'll have some catching up to do and it will entail a lot of hard work but I have *every* confidence in your ability!" Looking at his watch, Viv told his colleague, "I am due in court in twenty minutes, so any further business will have to be conducted at another time!" Andreas was delighted with the news that all his earlier efforts would not be in vain but disenchantingly he grumbled, "I really wanted to discuss the

Australian trip but *if* you're busy, I suppose it will have to wait!" Viv replied impatiently, "Yes, yes. Spend the rest of the week making whatever arrangements you deem necessary, then return to work. We'll find time to discuss everything then but at the moment we are snowed under with work; *entirely* due to your absence, so a little assistance *sometime,* would be appreciated!" "I'll be in on Monday!" Andreas promised with a smile.. Viv dashed off with his cloak flying all ways, calling over his back, "We *will* have that chat; I promise!" Andreas shook his head and leaving the insipid coffee untouched, he instructed his sons, "Come on lads; let's go to the gym!"

George complained bitterly about having to be strapped in the car again, instantly reminding Andreas of Walthaar's dour disposition but the cloud lifted the moment that their indulgent *daddi* bought them hot rolls and butter from the mill. Jimmy was thrilled to meet the boys for the first time, smiling broadly as Victor wandered over and began pounding the heavy punchbag, albeit without managing to disturb its inert state. "A chip off the old block there!" He suggested. "Who knows!" Andreas replied with a smile, "He *could* be even better than I was!" "He would almost certainly be a little more dedicated!" A voice commented from the doorway and spinning round sharply, Andreas saw his old sparring partner Reuben standing in the doorway. The two young men had surprisingly hit it off from the moment they had met, in spite of the fact that Reuben was Lupe's brother. Shaking hands, Andreas asked Reuben if he was still boxing and ruffling George's hair, Reuben replied, "No but I do train but with no *real* purpose in sight, I'm thinking of giving *Gypsy* fighting a shot, as you did in Stow!" Looking Reuben over and appreciating the fact that his friend would now be *more* than a handful for anyone, Andreas warned, "It's tough, brutal and unlike any fighting you will ever have come across *but* if you're serious, I'm sure that between us, Jimmy and I can knock you into shape. Andreas felt a warm hand thread its way into his and looking up at his father, George said, "Daddy, are you and Uncle Reuben going to fight?" Andreas laughed, "No son, when I said knock him into shape, I meant that we'll help prepare him for gypsy fighting; if Reuben and I fought, we'd probably end up killing each other!" Reuben put a hand on his nephew's shoulder, "Your father is right but we wouldn't fight anyway because we are friends and even when *true* buddies fall out, the bond they share would not allow them to fight each other!" Watching Reuben disappear down the stairs, Andreas smiled and thought, *I think I've just found the ideal companion for the Melbourne trip.* The remaining trio watched Victor punching the bag until he tired of the exercise and turning to Jimmy, Andreas said, "Jimmy, it's time we made a move. I promised to take them to the garage to see their Uncle Gunnar!"

Gunnar was overjoyed to see the boys and as he lifted them up to kiss their faces, grease and oil from his boiler suit found its way onto their already butter stained clothing. Andreas rebuked his brother, "Your sister will not be happy with the mess you've gotten them into!" Gunnar grinned, "Oh well, you'll just have to sweet-talk her again won't you and presuming that there's an ulterior motive to this visit, I can tell you categorically that there will be no freebies; not now or at any other time in the future!" Andreas said mischievously, "That's a shame, I only came over for a free car wash!" "You've got no bloody chance!" Gunnar retorted. "You'll pay just the same as everyone else; this is a profit-making concern, not for cheapskates like you who think they can just wander in and get something for nothing!" Andreas laughed. "Okay, okay you've convinced me; now where have those two boys gone? I want to scare the shit out of them in the car wash!" George sat in the rear and Victor in front but sadly for Andreas, his prank did not have the intended effect, as both boys squealed with delight when the brushes rolled noisily over the bonnet of the car. The car emerged from the wash and Gunnar remarked, "Don't you think it's about time you had a new car? This one's just about given up the ghost; I'll see if I can find you a nice little runner!" "As long as it's cheap and I get a good trade-in price, you're on!" Gunnar shook his head, "You'll *never* change, will you?" Replying with Ma's oft-repeated adage, Andreas said, "Take care of the pennies and the pounds will take care of themselves!" Gunnar laughed, "Hmm, I think I may have heard that one somewhere before!" Pulling out onto the forecourt, Andreas sped away before his brother discovered that actually he *had* managed to obtain a free car wash.

Still having time in hand, Andreas decided to visit Walthaar but when they arrived at the square, the visit was temporarily deferred when the boys, noticing the market, promptly demanded candy floss. Watching them with the pink mess all over their faces reminded him poignantly of his late sister Lala, who could never get enough of its sweetness and with the boys' clothes being in an even worse state by the time they had finished eating, it became a nailed-on certainty that Lu would be having her husband's guts for garters. Admitting them to the flat, Walthaar remarked on the state of the boys' clothes, "I see you've been to the garage *and* the market!" Andreas began laughing, "You forgot to mention the melted butter from the mill. Is there any chance of you putting that bloody kettle on, I'll bet you aren't so remiss when you're eating free fish and chips!" Walthaar answered with a grin, "When she's here, I don't bother with coffee *or* food if it comes to that!" "You horny little bastard!" Andreas commented and seating himself in the most comfortable chair, he wondered why, within seconds of meeting one another, the brothers *all* honed their razor-sharp wit upon the others and supposing it to be habit more than anything else, Andreas thought, *but woe betide anyone else that tries it on.* After a further hour of barbs being thrown from one to the other, Andreas noticed George's head beginning to nod, trying desperately to delay the inevitable and experiencing difficulty in rising from the comfort of the chair himself, Andreas said, "Come on, boys, we'd best get home now and face the music!" Helping Andreas take the boys down the steep stair-case to the car, Walthaar remarked, "Got your hands full there brother and I dare say you'll be knocking another one out any time soon!" "Funny you should say that!" Andreas replied with a grin, leaving the sentence unfinished.

Arriving home, Andreas lifted the still sleeping George from the back seat, instantly becoming aware that he had wet himself and knowing that Lu would be getting the kids ready for bed straight away, he archly decided *not* to tell her of George's accident. Kissing Lu's cheek, he handed the sleeping infant into her care as carefully as he could, hoping that she wouldn't notice his wet pants until he had left the room but in a second Lu had launched into an unsparing diatribe, "Don't tell me you didn't realize what had happened and just look at the state of them both. Grease and oil all over them, more to the point, what the *hell* are those pink stains on their shirts!" Lying through his teeth, while finding it difficult to contain his amusement, he asserted, "Sorry, dear, I really hadn't noticed!" Calling him a liar and bringing his parentage into question, she stomped into the kitchen. Feeling somewhat guilty Andreas thought, *I'll make it up to her later* and when the children were tucked up in bed, he began to sweet-talk himself out of trouble once again. Telling Lu of the day's events over a couple of cherry brandies, made just how she liked them, he kissed her lips between each word and recalling Gunnar's prophetic words, he smiled, *oh yes I do play this game so well!* Being pleased to learn that Viv had been impressed by his part in the handling of the crisis, she was not quite so pleased when he enthused over the fact that Victor had been working on the punch-bag. Pulling a face he began to nibble her neck, then being absolutely sure that he had been completely forgiven and *only* after his artifices had reached their predictable, satisfactory conclusion, did he allow himself the luxury of a cider. Laying on the floor, with the constant, flickering firelight their only source of illumination, they began to speak of the need to return to normality, with Andreas announcing, "I'll check on the progress of the farm *and* the shop tomorrow!" Lu looked up and suggested, "You know, it might not be such a bad thing if the shop *never* returned to the farm!" Andreas looked askance as she continued, "There is nothing to say that this disease will *not* raise its ugly head at some point in the future and if the safety measures you have in place were removed, you may not enjoy the same successful but extremely fortunate outcome!" Thinking over her words and deciding that her take on the situation was logically sound, he promised to have a word with Michael the following morning and having other issues needing to be addressed, notwithstanding a new supply of cider, it became apparent that a visit to the farm would be required the next day. With his departure to Melbourne drawing ominously closer with every succeeding day, it was imperative that everything had to be in place, ready for his return.

5

After having just a couple hours of fitful sleep, Andreas roused the house, in readiness for the scheduled visit to the farm and leaving as soon as breakfast was over, they arrived just in time to find Michael and Vee polishing off what was left of their breakfast. Immediately broaching the serious matter of the farm's future, the two men withdrew to the parlour, where Andreas instantly relayed Lu's suggestion of the shop becoming a permanent fixture at the mill. Agreeing that the suggestion had merit, Michael added, "Being at the mill has certainly kept the business afloat and it *would* save a lot of trouble if it were to remain there but would the owner of the mill be agreeable!" Andreas replied, "That will not present a problem; it suits him to leave things the way they are and with the mill's proximity to the new housing estates, both businesses, should prosper!" Andreas continued, "I have a few ideas for the farm's continued freedom from disease that I'd like to run past you!" Pausing for a moment, he began his suggestions, "The whole country has suffered because of this outbreak but by taking sensible precautions, we lost no stock at all and believing that the days when livestock roam the land *will-nilly* are over, I'll outline my plans!" Michael nodded his approval and after clearing his throat, Andreas resumed, "The fencing we installed is still in place, so essentially we have an inner and an outer farm, each separate but interdependent on the other. If that set-up were a permanent arrangement, the inner farm could be utilised to house *only* livestock and with no hunting or farm shop, there would be little chance of contamination. The outer farm contains a small orchard but very little else, so there is ample room to grow crops, either to be sold on or used for our own fodder, which would certainly be a far cheaper *and* safer option than importing!" Michael thought for a moment and said, "I agree with *everything* you say and our excellent reputation for uncontaminated cattle, means that we'll be selling even *more* produce. With most of our competitors going to the wall, the future has never looked brighter but surely we *will* have to purchase more cattle to keep up with demand?" "That is already in hand!" Andreas asserted, "Before leaving this morning, I put plans in place to import a disease-hardy bull and six cows from Argentina to breed with our own stock. It has taken all this time for us to realize how much space has been wasted over the years and now we're going to put that right *and* stay safe too!" Then smiling he remarked, "I've been here twenty minutes and I'm yet to be offered a cup of coffee?" "I'll get Vee onto that right away, unless you'd prefer a flagon or two?" "God, I haven't had a session on that stuff since the crisis but unfortunately I have to drive home!" "Why don't you stop here for the night?" Michael suggested, "The children can sleep in Lily-Ann's room and you and Lu can use my father's old room?" Being informed of the plans, Lu was all *for* the chance to celebrate together in the age-old manner and with the drink instantly beginning to flow, Vee called Lu to the kitchen window, where both mothers watched in amazement at Lily-Ann and the boys frolicking with the pet calf.

The youngsters readied themselves for bed after lunch, while the impromptu celebration continued apace for the grown-ups, until tired and slightly inebriated they called a halt to proceedings. Judging the time ripe for explaining that the family trip to Australia, would in fact be a solo, hazardous undertaking; Andreas realized that the only problem was how to break the news gently. Snuggling up to her backside later, he tentatively broached the subject and just when he was on the verge of telling her the bad news, she pre-empted him, "I hope you don't mind Andreas but I really do not want to go to Australia just now. Rosie is too young to be travelling that far and perhaps we could all go together one day, when the circumstances are different!" Slyly he conceded, "That's okay love, you're absolutely spot on as usual; I really hadn't thought about it like that and thank you for bringing it to my attention!" Smiling, he kissed her chastely on the cheek and rolling over, he proceeded to fall asleep, wearing a huge grin.

Discovering himself alone in the bed a few hours later, Andreas rose, showered, and going downstairs, he found Lu busily feeding Rosie in the living room. Staggering past the peaceful scene to make coffee, he made *two* mugs, wordlessly placing one beside Lu and returning to the kitchen for *his* first sup of the day, he had just taken a long delectable slurp of the ambrosial liquid, when a whirlwind blew into the room in the shape of Lily-Ann, who announced her presence by instantly firing a mountain of questions at him, *rat-a-tat-tat* like a machine gun, scarcely pausing for breath, "Did you and Daddy sort out the farm? Did Mummy get drunk? Can I help Auntie Lu feed the baby? Did you like Daisy?" Managing to parry most of her questions, although possibly not in the same order as they were delivered or indeed at the same speed, he replied, "No, mummy did not get drunk, yes we sorted out the farm, I absolutely adore Daisy and you *can* feed Rosie when she's a little older!" Swiftly she exclaimed, "Oh yes of course, I forgot that she's still being breast-fed!" Sipping his coffee, he smiled in amazement at her speed of thought processing, while wondering *why* the calf had been called Daisy; he was *sure* that the animal had been a bullock. Continuing the conversation, he found her surprisingly well advanced for her age, with a vocabulary extensive enough to enable her to converse with many adults on a similar level. She was in the middle of explaining about the machinations of the shop and its importance to the farm, when Andreas felt compelled to interrupt by asking if there was anything he could get for her; if only to halt the flow of words. She said with a frown, "No thank you, Uncle 'Dreas; Mummy always sees to me. *She* says that men can't be trusted to look after children properly!" Andreas laughed, "Mummy's probably right but I'm sure that I could pour a little milk into a glass for you!" After deliberating that conundrum for a moment, Lily Ann smiled and answered, "Okay, Uncle 'Dreas, I suppose you *could* do that for me!" Shaking his head he went to the fridge, only just avoiding being flattened by the kitchen door as Vee rushed into the kitchen, "You can sod off out of here while I'm cooking!" She ordered, "I'll get things done a damn sight quicker without *you* under my feet!" "Yes ma'am!" Andreas replied, "But first let me first prove to your daughter that I *am* capable of pouring a glass of milk!"

Rosie was sleeping when Andreas re-entered the living room carrying a tray of coffee and home-baked biscuits; looking up from his newspaper, Michael said, "We'll go through to the parlour until breakfast is ready!"

Picking up two of the coffees from the tray, Andreas followed on and pouring a decent measure of rum into each from his cache in the Welsh dresser, Michael declared, "This is my sanctuary but I'm afraid Lily-Ann *does* invade from time to time!" Andreas laughed, "She's as bright as a button and talking to her is on a par with talking to most adults; in fact, you'd probably get more sense from *her!* She will do well at school and if I were you, I'd get her in as early as possible. I'd tutor her myself but sadly I cannot seem to find time to do *anything* these days and if you think she would benefit from early tuition, don't worry over the cost; I'll make sure that it's paid for!" Michael looked at him quizzically while pouring even more rum into the coffee, "Where on earth would you find that kind of money?" Startled at his slip of the tongue, Andreas hastily recovered, "Don't worry about where it comes from; I found it for the farm, so I'm damned sure that I can find it for my niece!" At that point Andreas was thankfully saved having to explain further by Vee knocking loudly on the door, telling them that breakfast was ready.

With Vee's cooking being at least the equal of her mother's, the whole company demolished a fair sized breakfast and with everyone having eaten to excess, Andreas volunteered to wash up, with Michael being guilt-tripped into drying the dishes. Andreas asked him if there was anything to be delivered to the mill, telling him not to make it too much, as he had to find room for some of the flagons of cider that he'd perceived were almost ready for drinking. Michael had a knack of brewing tangy cider that was, if anything, superior to that of his father and Andreas wondered idly if there might be a niche in the drink industry for tasty cider, *without* fizz; another problem for Viv to solve. Further thought on that subject was deferred, when the two kitchen skivvies had to satisfy the ladies' demands for more coffee and turning to Michael, Andreas responded resignedly, "No peace for the wicked!"

With Michael's coffee reserves having been severely reduced, Andreas told Lu that he would take her and the children to Ma's before going on to the office and thanking their hosts, they all set forth for Ma's place, laden with milk, yogurt, fresh cream and of course cider. Lu hardly spoke on the journey and suspecting the Australian trip to be responsible for her dampened spirits, he kissed her chastely on the cheek. Opening the car door for her on arrival, he waved to Ma and Pa, promising Lu that they would have a chat on the subject, *after* he had seen Viv and with his wife now somewhat placated, he got back into the car, waved once more and headed for the office. Thinking of his work situation *en route, he* appreciated the fact that even though Viv was *technically* his boss, he could be a tad *too* domineering at times but appreciating the fact that Viv was an excellent tutor and with Andreas still having much practical legal doctrine to assimilate, keeping a still tongue was essential. On the business side of their partnership, Andreas himself identified the properties he wanted to purchase, while Viv smoothed the path with the brothers and together the principal protagonists contributed in their own way to the successful ventures. On a personal level too the two colleagues were close friends, with childless Viv doting on Andreas's children, while they in turn *adored* him. The Australian affair however, had been rather thrust upon him by Viv but being fully aware that he really *was* the only man in the firm for the job, Andreas was quite prepared to go to any lengths to achieve a successful outcome and hopefully with Reuben Scamp by his side, the task could be accomplished with the minimum of fuss and bother.

Arriving at the premises of Mowll and Mowll, Andreas headed directly for Viv's office and getting down to the nitty-gritty right away, he asserted, "I've had some thoughts concerning the forthcoming trip to Melbourne and I believe it would be advantageous *not* to tell them of my visit until I'm actually on the way, giving them little time to cover their tracks or to prepare a hostile reception. You can inform both senior partners that I've also decided to take them up on their offer of a travelling companion and I'd like to take Reuben Scamp along for the ride; *if* he agrees that is!" Viv nodded. "It's up to you whom you take, as long as he is up to the task!" "There are no worries on that account!" Andreas replied, "He is a real handful and cunning with it, like all the Scamps!" Awaiting the arrival of refreshment, Andreas changed the subject to that of his idea for Michael's cider, "I've had a notion for producing Michael's cider on a commercial basis; what do you think?" Viv remarked, "Well, I'm glad that your brain does *not* need the exercise that your body plainly does!" Andreas growled, "Sarcasm is the lowest form of wit!" Realizing that he had touched on a sore point, Viv ignored the menacing snarl, "I'll look into that for you and if it *is* viable, we can go into it more deeply but I've a feeling it will not come cheap!" Being aware that Viv's judgement on his fitness was probably an accurate assessment and for a trip that was beginning to look *far* removed from the pleasure cruise he'd planned for Lu, he would certainly need to be a lot sharper. Suddenly remembering the goods he had in the car, he rose quickly, "I'll have to shoot off Viv; I've got stuff from the farm in the boot!" When Viv learned of the goods in the boot, he remarked, "You'd better get a move that sort of stuff won't last long in the boot! *He's right about that,* Andreas thought, *cider doesn't travel well in the heat!"*

6

Being aware of the need for haste, Andreas drove quickly to the mill and after delivering the dairy produce, he headed homeward, applying even more pressure to the accelerator. Walking through the door, he instantly sensed a less-than-convivial atmosphere and judging Lu's smacked-arse face to be a harbinger to the kind of displeasure which would not be abated instantly, he decided to let *her* raise the subject of Melbourne first and *that* was not long in rising to the surface. Dishing rabbit stew onto his plate, she said sarcastically, "I suppose you're all set to leave us now?" Refusing to rise to the bait, he told her calmly of all that had transpired at the office, realizing instantly by her dour features and the diminutive offering on his plate that she was not best pleased. Raising his voice slightly, he asserted, "Lu, this trip will not happen until my finals are over and believe me, *I'm* not happy about the situation either but we cannot spend the little time we have left before the trip in constant wrangling; our children *and* our marriage would suffer as a result!" Saying nothing, she walked back to the kitchen and pushing aside the half-finished stew, Andreas rose angrily, going to the shed to see just how much work would be required to restore the yellow peril to its former glory. The bike was set to become an important component in his quest for fitness but having dragged the cycle from its retirement home, he sat on a log dismally sipping the dregs of his coffee, realizing that like his body, the cycle was in dire need of a complete make-over. Deciding to get it serviced by an expert, he emptied the boot and with great difficulty squeezed the bike inside; arriving at the garage, he told Dinky, "I'd like it painted blue when it's road-worthy again!" Looking across at Gunnar, he added with a grin, "Then I think

I'll call it the *Blue Flash*!" Gunnar characteristically shrugged and said with *more* than a hint of sarcasm, "You wanna get Dinky to put a bigger saddle on the bloody thing while he's at it!" Andreas smiled but the barb had struck home and having little time to prepare, his fitness regime would have to be conducted, between studying and his preparation for Australia. Returning home and still smarting from Gunnar's brickbat, he informed Lu of his intention to kick-start his fitness at the gym, asking if she could remember where he had put his gear. She replied sullenly, "You left it at the gym six months ago, so it probably won't fit you now!" Deftly dodging the cushion that had been hurled across the room, she ran into the kitchen, almost tripping on a toy crane that George had left on the floor. Following her into the kitchen, Andreas put his arm around her waist and said, "Lu, please don't let's fall out over this; this matter *has* to be sorted out and I'm the only one in the firm capable of rattling cages!" Smiling in conciliation, he added, "I'll be seeing Reuben later at the gym and will be asking him to accompany me!"

After kissing her shoulder he walked to the gym, hoping that the exercise would serve as the first step on the rung to his former vigour but arriving at the gym in a state of near collapse, he asked Jimmy if Reuben would be coming in. "Yes!" He answered, "I've been training him all week for the trip to Stow; he's doing well but needs the kind of training that *I* cannot give him!" "Don't worry!" Andreas said, "Starting today, I'll be in the gym more often!" Looking at his former pupil quizzically, Jimmy asked, "What are you up to Andreas? You've got a strange faraway look on your face!" Andreas said soberly, "It's better that you don't know the details Jimmy but I need help in a certain matter and Reuben appears to be ticking all the boxes!"

Reuben appeared in minutes and as they descended the staircase to the changing rooms, Andreas said that he had an important matter to discuss with him and taking the bull by the horns, Andreas said, "I'd like you to consider the possibility of embarking on a matter that will involve more than a hint of danger *and* travelling abroad!" Being naturally eager to learn more, Reuben asked, "It sounds great but what's it all about!" Seated on a bench by this time, Andreas briefly outlined the problem, "Money has been disappearing at regular intervals from accounts in Australia and I have to go and sort it out. It's highly likely that it has been stolen and if it has, the thieves will not give up such a honeypot without a fight. There are reasons why you cannot be told more at this stage but *I* will have to go whatever; it's almost certain that we will face violence and there is more than a possibility of having to fight for our lives. I don't need a decision right away, so there is plenty of time for you to think the matter over!" Wide-eyed, Reuben answered loudly, "Australia! Count me *in!*" Andreas asserted hotly, "I've just told you that I don't *want* a rash decision; I want you to consider the pitfalls as well as the travel and excitement. I'll give you a few facts that may help you decide. If you agree to accompany me you would receive firearms and martial arts tuition as a precaution against violence that will almost certainly be coming our way and the money for your part in the enterprise would be enough to enable you to do or become whatever you choose but I *must* strongly urge you to consider *all* the options before giving a decision that could very well endanger your life!" Andreas got to his feet and said with a smile, "Come on; let's get ready for Stow!

At the end of their first pre-Stow session, with sweat pouring profusely from every orifice, Andreas reflected once more on how unfit he had let himself become and deciding to go for a dip in the stream after the session, he jogged to the river, dived in fully clothed and gasped as the initial shock of the cold, swift-moving water, forced the air from his lungs. Soon becoming inured to the temperature however, the cool purl of the stream removed all thoughts of the worrisome trip and having forgotten how refreshing it could be wallowing in the cool stream, he lay on his back, splashing the water with his feet but all of a sudden, it occurred to him that the stream running right through the middle of the farm, *could* be a possible chink in their protective shield. If it proved to be so, he would have to find a way round the problem before leaving for Australia and deciding to talk the matter over with both Viv and Michael, he lay on the bank in the faint hope of returning home dry. Looking around the spot, he saw the potential for commercializing the site and considered that being hidden from the new housing estate, it would be an ideal location for fishing. He visualised a fishing pier, bait shop and further downstream, maybe even a lido/boating area; nodding in approbation, he thought, *this whole area could very well turn out to be another nice little earner.* With the prospect of adding more cash to the already bulging coffers, the scheme also had the fillip of creating more problems for Viv to solve.

Walking home, he felt fitter and fresher than he had for some time and finding a meal lying ready and waiting on the table for his delectation, he wondered if he had finally been forgiven for having the temerity of swanning off to Melbourne. Sitting down at the table, he applied himself diligently to the peace offering, if indeed that's what it was and hearing her moving about upstairs, he wondered if he should go up and thank her properly for the offering but knowing where that would lead, he opted instead to resolve the problem of the stream, before he could even *contemplate* carnality. Ringing Michael to discuss his fears of the stream being a possible contamination carrier, he declared, "As the stream serves no real purpose, it ought to be relatively simple to divert the flow and although it would be a *huge* undertaking, it *is* a project that could possibly safeguard the farm's future!" Michael thought for a moment. "A scheme of such dimensions would entail an almost unaffordable outlay *and* we would have to get the owner's permission!" Andreas replied, "Expense need not necessarily be an issue; Ted owes my firm big-time for all the work that's been thrown his way and with the equipment still being handily placed, the cost would not be over-the-top; leave the owner *and* Viv to me!" With the re-routing of the stream almost settled, Andreas sat on the settee and with the boys joining him, he realized that at times he spent less time than he should with his family.

Viv interrupted his train of thought by ringing to arrange a meeting for the following morning and using the opportunity, Andreas mentioned his plans for turning part of the stream into a recreation area while diverting it away from the farm. Viv said, "There should be absolutely no problem in commercializing the stream, with small outlay and the prospect of rich rewards, the scheme has potential but I'm not so sure about diverting the stream; is it *really* necessary?" "I believe it is!" Andreas replied. "We have to plan for the future and if another scourge comes along, the stream *could* prove a potential risk. The equipment is ours and more or less on site, so it's just a matter of getting a decent price from Ted, keeping in mind how much he owes us and after all, the stream is only meandering through the countryside doing sod all!" "Hmm, a bit like you then!" Viv said with ill-concealed sarcasm, "Leave it with me; I'll look into it to see if there are any obstacles likely to arise!" Returning to the living-room, Andreas discovered that the children had gone to bed and Lu had just changed channels to watch a documentary on the dwindling numbers of pandas in China. After ten minutes of *that* and finding himself too tired from the day's events to watch, he retired early.

7

Deciding on a refreshing cold shower before breakfast, in readiness for what Andreas suspected would be a busy day, he let Lu sleep late while he attended to the children, finding that changing Rosie's nappy, always a potential disaster, did *not* have the most satisfactory outcome. Giggling at his father's discomfort, Victor passed wind, which sent his father reeling from the room amid howls of laughter and when the lady of the house finally deigned to honour the chaos with her presence, Andreas rushed from the house, still gagging from the pong and once he was far enough away from the miasma, he took a deep breath of fresh air and drove to the garage. Filling up with petrol, he drove across to the car wash and was told in no uncertain terms that there was not a hope in hell of getting away with another freebie, Gunnar averred, "I've got my beady eye on you!" Quitting the wash, Andreas pulled out onto the forecourt and after paying for the wash, Andreas told Gunnar of his plans for the stream. "Good idea!" Gunnar conceded, "Why don't you make the lido free for children of a certain age; it might induce more *adults* to use the facilities!" "That's a great idea, Gunnar; I'll keep that in mind!" Andreas asked, "Is the Blue Flash ready yet?" Without a word, Gunnar walked to the rear of the garage and wheeled out the old bike, looking as if it had just rolled off the assembly line and Andreas remarked as he stowed the machine into the boot, "God knows what we'll do when Dinky retires, because *you're* no bloody good!" Andreas rolled up the window of the car and after paying for the repaired bike and car-wash, he pulled out onto the road and smiling archly to himself, he wondered how long it would take for Gunnar to realize that he had left without paying for the petrol. The constant one-upmanship between the pair was, in all reality, just a game, with Andreas believing that he was constantly getting one over on his old friend, although in fact it was the other way round. *Always* being aware of Andreas's artifices, Gunnar played the stooge to perfection and as he observed to Ma, "He thinks he's getting the best of me but actually he's only cheating himself, seeing that he *owns* the bloody garage!"

Wondering idly if Reuben had decided one way or the other to accompany him to Australia, Andreas considered that Reuben's fighting prowess would definitely be an asset and with his lightness of heart contriving to create the ideal travelling companion, he was confident that together they would present a formidable front. Andreas was dreading having to search for another companion if he declined the offer, knowing that he would be hard pushed to find another who had even *half* the young man's attributes. *I just hope he is giving the matter a great deal of thought.* On that score, he need not have worried; Reuben had thought of little else since the request had been put to him. "What ails you, boy?" his father asked. "You've hardly spoken a word for days!" Reuben answered with the trace of a tired smile, camouflaging what lay beneath, "I'm sorry, *daddi*; I've got a lot on my mind!" Lying to his father, he declared, "I'm going to Stow to fight at the fair, with Andreas *and* Jimmy training me, I ought to be making better progress than I am at the moment!" His mother, ever the silent partner was well aware that he had lied but his father commented innocently as he poured more rum into an emptied glass, "Jesus, is that all? I thought you'd gone and killed some bastard; you should have come to *me!*" He slurred, "I've forgotten more than they will *ever* know about fighting!" Reuben said wearily, "I know that but Andreas is experienced at *this* type of fighting, I want to be better than best to make you proud of me!" That was the only element of truth he had spoken for days and after kissing his parents fondly, he made his way to bed, taking note of the suspicion in his mother's eyes.

Lying on his bed he stared at the ceiling, turning over every aspect of the conundrum he had been set; the money would make him richer than any Scamp had *ever* been, enabling him to buy a proper house, a car and all the things he had ever dreamed of. Maybe he could even get himself a classy woman like Lu, with whom he had fallen in love, the moment she had entered the encampment on the arm of his brother. Having to settle for worshipping from afar, he hated the way Lupe had treated his object of desire and had been glad when Gunnar thrashed him when Lu had returned to the Bosworth home with evidence of the latest beating on her face. The fact that Andreas and Lu had been destined to ride off into the sunset together did not however, prevent Reuben from coveting his friend's wife and resolving to meet *someone* worthy of him one day, he had the thought that having money might make him seem a better prospect. However, being killed in the execution of the task ahead was the other side of the coin and one that would leave his parents mourning the loss of their remaining son. The situation was proving to be a real quandary, one that would have to be settled one way or another *very* soon; with his mind tiring of mental tennis, he fluffed up his pillow and turned over but bordering at the gates of slumber, he suddenly sat up in bed, declaring loudly, "How could I *ever* live with myself if Andreas went ahead on his own and got himself killed?" Aware in that instant that he had finally reached the decision he sought, he rolled over and slept soundly for the first time in days.

Reuben went through for breakfast with a smile on his face and old Bill remarked, "You've come to a decision then!" Realizing that he had been fooling no one, Reuben answered with a smile, "Yes *daddi* and I believe it to be the right one!" Electing to walk into town to tell Andreas of his decision, he had the unusual experience of his parents standing at the door, watching him stride confidently down the road and returning his wave from the entrance of the camp, they remained on the step until he was out of sight. Dreaming of the trip on which he would soon be embarking, the beep of a car's horn sharply wakened his tranquillized senses and running across the main road, he got into Andreas's car. For the first few moments not a word was spoken, then Reuben said slowly, "I've decided to go with you to Australia if the offer still stands!" Andreas smiled and without taking his eyes from the road, he replied, "Of course it still stands; Welcome aboard!" Pulling up in front of the office, the duo entered the large double-doors and the incessant *clack-clack-clack*ing of type-writers, caused Reuben to hold his hands over his ears. "You *do* get used to it!" Andreas assured him and walking into Viv's empty office, he said, "Help yourself to a magazine; he shouldn't be too long!" Viv strolled in after a five-minute hiatus, unshaven and looking distinctly dishevelled, prompting Andreas to remark sarcastically, "Good *afternoon* Mr Bailey; Kate been sleeping on your shirt-tail *again*?" Viv grunted and disregarding the sarcasm, he mumbled, "How far have you got with your plans for the trip?" Introducing his soon-to-be comrade-in-arms, Andreas announced, "Let me introduce you to Reuben, he is the young man that I mentioned as being my choice of travelling companion!" Shaking hands, Viv was instantly impressed by Reuben's firm handshake, despite first impressions of the lad being too young for the task. "I'll be going to Bristol this afternoon to organize weapon training!" Andreas continued, "When that's done, I will be calling in on Jimmy, who is organizing a course in unarmed combat for us!" Frowning, Viv remarked, "I've been thinking of your plans in that direction and I'm in agreement with the brothers that it is way over the top!" Andreas said resolutely, "Do not forget that an awful lot of money is missing, so you can be sure it will not be given up without a fight! We know no one there *or* what the situation actually is and I will *not* leave these shores unprepared!" Viv leaned back in his chair and sighed resignedly, "I suppose you are right but absolutely *no* unnecessary violence!" Andreas smiled grimly, "I'm hoping that it won't come to that but I have the feeling that it is a probability rather than a possibility and my hunches are not usually wrong!" Looking over the top of his glasses Viv commented, "I think the less I know about what you are up to, the better but you *are* right; it *is* a sizeable sum of money involved and it *does* have to be sorted as quickly as possible!" Andreas averred, "We'll get the job done as quickly as we can and return home, hopefully unscathed. Weaponry will be provided and disposed of by our Roma counterparts in Australia and hopefully I can organize that before we leave but for God's sake, do not let Melbourne know we are coming until we are out of the country; I want these robbing bastards stirred up without them having time to cover up!"

Addressing Reuben for the first time, Viv asked, "Now you've learned a little of what is involved, do you think you will be up to the task? We cannot afford any slip-ups!" Reuben answered firmly, "I am capable of handling any situation that is thrown my way!" "Hmm, I just hope you're right!" An unconvinced Viv declared, "I'm afraid I have to ask you to leave now; I'm in court at ten and it's a quarter to already!" Sweeping from the room with his gown billowing behind him, he shouted over his shoulder, "We'll talk about the stream another time!" Reuben asked, "What's he on about the stream for?" Andreas replied, "Don't worry about that; it's company business. I'm off to Bristol now, do you want to come along or shall I take you home?" "I think I'll tag along!" He replied, "I wouldn't mind a shower first though; I didn't have time this morning!"

Going straight to the bathroom when they arrived, Reuben left his father making coffee and placing two steaming mugs on the table, Bill Scamp added a tot of rum to his own and growled at Andreas, "No rum for you boy; you're driving and my son is your passenger!" Slurping the hot, sweet liquid Bill declared, "Ah, just how I like it!" Staring malevolently at Andreas, he snarled, "I've been wanting a word with you for some time!" Slurping the mixture noisily once more, Bill looked at the mug rapturously, "It tastes so much better when you do that!" Andreas thought, *my sentiments exactly*, Bill continued, "I've had the notion all along that *you're* the one responsible for all the changes that have happened hereabouts and for that I thank you Andreas but you will *always* be just a *Gadjo* to me. Suspecting that whatever you two are up to will be dangerous, I'm telling you that if anything happens to Reuben, I will feed you to my dogs; because of you, Lupe is lost to me forever and I don't wanna lose the only son I have left!" Pausing for a moment, he jabbed his index finger an inch from Andreas's face, "Lupe was a good boy and would *never* have treated Lu the way he did if *you* hadn't come between them!" Andreas spoke softly, "Bill, I can't ever see the two us being best friends and although I respect you; what happened cannot be undone. Reuben and I will be leaving for Australia, embarking on something that will almost certainly be dangerous but *if* we are successful, he will have more money than you or he would ever have dreamed of. I promise you one thing: if he dies, I die too and *if* the worst should happen, the money he would have received will be placed in an account in his mother's name *and* she would be well looked after by Mowll and Mowll for the rest of her days. We begin training soon for what we have to do and after my exams, we will be leaving for Melbourne but if he changes his mind about going, he will be released from his commitment with no strings attached and I will go alone!" Continuing in a more genial manner Andreas asked, "There *is* something that you can do for us!" Bill leaned forward expectantly and Andreas grinned, "I'd like you to contact your kinsmen in Melbourne and ask them to supply any weapons we may need!" Bill looked at his adversary and sighing resignedly, he averred sternly, "I'm against what you're doing but *that* much I will do!" At that point, Reuben re-entered the room, "I thought I heard raised voices. I hope you two haven't been arguing!" "Not at all!" Bill said, "Just clearing the air!"

8

With only light traffic hindering their progress, they reached Bristol just after midday, managing to register for clay pigeon shooting at a sports equipment shop within the first ten minutes. "Job done!" Andreas exclaimed. "Let's eat, I'm starving!" Perusing the menu of a nearby eating house, Reuben remarked, whimsically, "Pity they don't have squirrel stew!" Andreas replied with a grin, "Yeah, these Gadjos really don't know what they're missing!" Sitting at a table in the hostelry a short while later, Andreas said seriously while munching on an unwholesome chunk of gristly steak pie, "I know we'll be using heavier weapons in Australia but this course is designed to speed up our reactions and not knowing what we'll come up against, speed could be vital!" After the wholly inadequate lunch had been digested, they walked around the city until it began to spit with rain, "Bloody city!" Andreas exclaimed, "It's always the sodding same when I'm here. Come on, let's get out of here!"

Sitting in the car, waiting for someone to manoeuvre into a space, Reuben asked tentatively, "Would you ever consider driving me and the old man up to Stow? It's a hell of a way and I'd like to get there in one piece!" Andreas said, "I don't think Lu would wear that; being away nine months during the foot-and-mouth and shooting off to Oz in a wee while, Stow would be a bridge too far!" No more was said on the matter but an idea popped into Andreas's head, prompting him to suggest, "How do you fancy having a proper meal, Reuben? I've got to see Jimmy, so why don't you come *with* me, then have a nosh-up at my place after!" Reuben looked at him. "Would your missus be okay with that?!" Bearing in mind how kind Reuben had been during her loveless marriage to Lupe, Andreas urged, "It will be fine; instead of coming to Jimmy's with me, I'll drop you at your house so you can let your mother know and as soon as I'm done at Jimmy's, I'll come back and pick you up!" Driving into the car park at speed and braking at the same rate of knots, he sprayed grit across the wall of the gym, leaving a six-foot long furrow across the tarmac. Jimmy emerged from the doorway and standing with arms akimbo, he instantly administered a sharp rebuke. "Why the hell do you youngsters do that? You of all people should know better!" "Sorry, Jimmy!" Andreas said shamefacedly. "I was in so much of a hurry I just didn't think; I'll be more careful in future!" Following Jimmy into the gym, he said, "I've just popped in to see if you'd managed to fix up a martial arts instructor for us!" "Yes!" he muttered, "She has excellent credentials *and* is available immediately!" "That's great news; could you arrange for me to meet her tomorrow morning?" Jimmy retorted, "I can but I do not want a repeat of *today's* parking!" Severely chastened, Andreas drove carefully away but as soon he was out of sight of the gym, he put his foot down. Reflecting on the fact that their instructor was to be a woman he opined that as long as she was good at her job, she could come from Mars for all he cared. Reuben was waiting at the gate and as he got in the car Reuben asked with a grin, "All sorted?" Andreas replied, omitting to enlighten his friend that the instructor was a woman, "Yes, it's all sorted!" Turning the ignition key he asked Reuben, "Why are you grinning?" Reuben laughed, "Because my old man told me to wait outside for you, as he didn't want a bloody Gadjo at his door twice in the same day!" Andreas joined in the laughter and nearing the house, he declared, "I have a plan in mind that might enable me to drive you to Stow, so when we get my house, just go along with everything I say!"

Entering the house, Reuben was welcomed like an old friend and Andreas smiled archly, believing that having Lu in a good mood was essential to the success of his plan. Andreas breathed in the smells wafting in from the kitchen, alerting the dormant taste buds to the promise of delights, "Ah my darling wife, that smells delicious!" Being served up in minutes, the piping hot stew and dumplings was swiftly devoured, necessitating a second helping and followed by strawberries from the garden and cream from the farm, the memory of the *city* fare was soon cast into oblivion. Complimenting Lu on the feast, Reuben averred, "That was *even* better than my mother makes!" Smiling, Andreas sat back in his chair, broke wind and emptied his glass of cider, then heading for the kitchen for reinforcements, he asked Reuben in passing, "Is your father still driving you to Stow?" Reuben look puzzled for a second but realizing suddenly that it was all part of the plot being set in motion, he replied, "Yes, if he can keep his eyes open that long!" Lu looked askance, "He's too *old* to be driving that far?" Pausing at the kitchen door, Andreas remarked, "Oh I'm sure he'll be okay; he's fine for his age!" Half-closing the door, he removed a flagon of cider from the cupboard and pressing his ear against the door, he heard her say, "Why don't you ask Andreas to drive?" Andreas grinned as he heard Reuben answer, "He's got so much on his plate these days; I hardly like to ask!" "Leave it to me!" she said, "I'll ask him later; he'll be like putty in my hands after he's had a few more ciders!" Assuming an innocent air, Andreas returned to the room. "I'll have to pop over to the farm tomorrow love; I'm running out of cider; will you phone Vee later and ask her to have some ready?" Smiling Lu winked conspiratorially at Reuben and turning down the offer of more cider, Reuben thanked his hosts and told them laughingly that he had better make a move, "My mother will be thinking I've left home!" Thanking them once again, he set out on the long walk home, with Andreas and Lu waving to Reuben from the door and when he was out of sight, Andreas put an arm around his wife's shoulder and guided her to the warmth of the lounge. Snuggling up to Andreas on the settee, Lu asked, "Why don't *you* drive the boys to Stow; it really *is* too far for Bill to drive there and back!" Flatly refusing, he said, "Stops can always be made; they usually do anyway to accommodate Riley's bladder weakness and seeing that I'm not long since being parted from my family, it's hardly fair to expect *me* to swan off to Stow with Melbourne, on the horizon!" Lu insisted, "Love, you've been so busy lately that you *need* a break to recharge your batteries!" He refused point blank but after having his arm corkscrewed continually for a good ten minutes or so, he finally acquiesced but only at her insistence *and* the promise of a reward in bed for his beneficence.

Collecting Reuben from home in the morning, Andreas waited patiently outside, not wanting to subject Bill to the ordeal of having a Gadjo in his house two days in a row and walking towards the car grinning, Reuben said, "You're a devious bastard!" "Clever Reuben; not devious *and* it worked!" Andreas exclaimed. "Come on, let's go and meet our trainer!" Arriving at the gym, he parked the car carefully, not wishing to incur Jimmy's wrath again and on being told that the trainer had already been and gone, Andreas tutted in frustration. Jimmy smiled, "Fortunately for you, I presumed to arrange for the first session to take place tomorrow evening!" "That's great, Jimmy!" Andreas said. "Thank you for that!" As they were in the area, Andreas decided to show Reuben the clearing earmarked for development and sweeping his arm in an arc, he proudly indicated where the pier and bait shop would be located, "This is all part of what Viv was referring to yesterday and further downstream, the river will have to be diverted away from the farm, as a defence against another foot-and-mouth outbreak!" "That'll cost a few *bob*; has someone come into money?" Reuben asked. Andreas smiled. "Well, it's a big job all right but the cost will be covered mostly by favours; come on, I'll give you a lift home!" As they got into the car, Reuben remarked, "I wonder what this trainer is like!" Andreas replied casually with a knowing smile, "One trainer is very much the same as any other!" Reuben found out the following night however, that this statement was not strictly true, as meeting Claire for the first time, Andreas could tell immediately that Reuben was smitten. As he told Lu later, "I thought his type of woman would have been a little more feminine!" Adding as an afterthought, "Someone like you!"

Weeks flew by with Reuben attaining a fair proficiency in all the disciplines, while Andreas alas sadly lagged behind, having more on his mind than trying to impress a female trainer and always trying to catch up with schoolwork, he was also running two businesses *and* trying to get fit for the Australian trip; all contriving to make a wearying chore out of what should have been an enlightening experience. Fortunately, the exams came and went in a blur, with the relief at their completion being supplanted by the worry of whether or not he had managed to attain the degree he had worked so hard for. With Rosie's imminent christening adding to the stress, he found that he was now looking forward to the Stow trip, *appreciating* the fact that subterfuge had been employed to secure his presence on the jaunt. With training nearing completion, Reuben began doubting his worthiness for the hazardous journey to the other end of the globe but pouring a balm on troubled waters, Andreas pointed out, "You have always been an excellent shot Reuben and don't forget that if we do have to shoot someone, that person would not be as small as a clay pigeon or be breaking the bloody sound barrier; the combat side of things will easily be honed at Stow!" Reuben smiled, knowing the truth of his friend's words, "Stow should be a relaxing time for you too, now the worry of your exams is over!" "Fat chance of that!" Andreas answered, "I've got to sort out a car capable of carrying all of us to Stow and Viv wants me in the office first thing tomorrow. I *had* hoped that Stow would be a relaxing break but with Pa, Riley and your father on board, that will be highly unlikely!"

Finally finding the time to visit the garage, he asked Gunnar if he had a car capable of holding four normal-sized people plus Bill Scamp; Gunnar informed his brother, "I've got a people-carrier out back, that could be made ready to drive away tomorrow if you like, *at a price!*" Andreas asked, "Would my family discount and the one I always get for paying cash be included in your estimate?" Playing the role of the offended lamebrain to perfection, Gunnar said, "Oh, for God's sake; you rich bastards are always wanting something for nothing! Never fear you'll *get* your decent discount!" Andreas left the forecourt and walked to the rear of the garage to inspect the car and was distinctly underwhelmed; the rusting hulk had once been brown or red and possibly any colour in between, when it had rolled off the assembly line some considerable time before. Knowing that Gunnar's magic touch would transform the wreck but feeling unable to pay his brother the ultimate compliment because of the stupid mind games they played, he remarked tersely, "I'll pay you when I come back from Stow and don't forget the discount!"

Returning the following day, he found that his confidence in Gunnar's ability to transform the derelict shell of a car into something special had not been misplaced, with the car being totally unrecognizable from the heap of the previous day. Having been returned to what in all likelihood was its original shining, deep red colour and being certain that everything under the bonnet would be perfect, Andreas passed a rare complimentary remark, "Whatever the charge Gunnar, it will be well worth it!" Gunnar's face was immediately lit up by a wonderful smile and Andreas thought sadly, *Why the hell don't I do that more often!* He had further cause to thank Gunnar for his choice of car later in the day, when Jimmy informed him that he *would* be going along on the trip after all. Andreas was beginning to regret agreeing to the onerous task of wet-nursing a bunch of adolescent

47

old men, knowing full well that he should *really* have been spending the few days left until the trip with Lu and the kids but with the die now cast, he had been left *hoping* that there would be enough time to spend at least a *few* days with Lu and the children before leaving for Australia. However, he was made aware of just how long he *would* have with his family, when he called in at the office to give Viv the date of their return from Stow. Viv smiled, "Your flight has been booked for exactly two weeks after your return from Stow and I will wire Melbourne the day after you leave to let them know you are coming, so you can expect trouble more or less straight away!" "Thank you for that, Mr Bailey; perhaps I can do *you* a favour sometime!"

9

It seemed as if the entire Romany populace of the county had turned out to see Rosemary Radu Bosworth being baptized in their small local church; with a few being requested to participate in the grounds, with a public address system barking out proceedings. Pa was soberly dressed and surprisingly, sober too but as soon as the ceremony was over, he and Riley wasted no time in wetting the baby's head with flagons of cider, which they had somehow smuggled into the church. Hurriedly ushering the crowd from the church when Riley tried to involve the pastor in a session on the liquid, Andreas led the procession to the Green Man, where a banquet had been prepared. Taking him discreetly to one side, Ma administered a warning to Andreas, absolutely forbidding *any* skinny-dipping in the stream, "I know what you're like after a few ciders!" However, calling the warning to mind later in proceedings, Andreas persuaded Lu into coercing Ma and Pa to have the children for a sleepover, becoming aware that his prayers had been answered when he saw a smile on Lu's face and sidling up to her, without Ma noticing, he whispered his intentions into her *shell-like*. Grinning like a pair of naughty schoolchildren, they judiciously left the celebration via the back door, with Andreas casting a furtive look over his shoulder, noticing the ghost of a smile on Ma's swarthy countenance. Racing to a secluded spot in the stream, they hastily stripped off and dived into the cool water. Racing her to the other side of the river, Andreas allowed her to win, knowing the reward he would receive later for doing so and smiling, he thought, *Reuben was spot on; I am a devious bastard.* Letting her lead the way back too, he was treated to the sight of her shining wet buttocks bobbing up and down in the water, instantly awakening his baser instincts and with her body being even more exposed when they reached the shallows, he could contain himself no longer and grabbing hold of her, he assumed the missionary position and exploited her body brutishly, while the gentle flow of the stream played across their bodies. Carrying her up the bank after mutual satisfaction had been achieved, he laid her on the grass and watched her shudder as a cloud blocked out the sun. Propping himself on one elbow, he plucked a blade of grass and began teasing her sensitive parts until she could stand the exquisite agony no longer. Pulling him on top of herself, she returned his loutish abuse and when the deed had been consummated once more, he declared, "We won't be able to have sex here once the lido has been built!" She looked up saucily, "Well, we'll just have to find somewhere else then!" He smiled archly, "Actually, I was thinking of fencing off a plot of land further upstream to create a nature reserve but I suppose it *could* be used for other purposes!" He began nibbling her ear, "No more, no more!" She cried, "Too much is enough!" Dressing quickly, they walked homeward and Lu asked, "Have you anything organized for tomorrow? I could do with a shopping spree?" "You'll have to go on your own then; I'll be busy paying bills!" Reaching home, Andreas yawned, "I think we'll have an early night. It's been a tiring day one way and another!" "I hope you're not *too* tired!" She said, "I haven't finished with you yet!"

Waking the following morning to the smell of frying bacon wafting up the stairs, he thought, a*h, my reward for being a good boy; at least I think I was good!* Andreas quit his bed, opened the window and going downstairs, he found his wife showered changed and wearing a green and yellow floral dress that he could not remember having seen before. She was jumping around, trying desperately to avoid the hot fat spitting forth onto the dress and ever the gentleman, her adoring husband offered to take over, "Off you go now, we can't have you going to Bristol with fat stains all over your nice, clean dress!" Kissing her cheek, he helped her don a matching cardigan and as she rushed from the house, he shook his head with a light-hearted grin on his face, tossed the bacon between two slices of bread and began to consume the wholly unhealthy but delicious fry-up. Washing it down with a whisky-laced coffee, he got ready for his meeting with Claire to settle the account for their tuition.

Arriving at the gym early, he went into the office, joining Jimmy in an alcohol-free coffee and reaching the grouts, they heard a car pulling into the park. The pair went outside to greet Claire and handing over an envelope crammed with high-value notes, Andreas proffered his hand in gratitude for a job well done. Smiling, she took his hand and before he had time to react, he was on his backside, laying beside the furrow he had created the previous day. "You really ought to have seen that coming!" She remarked, "I thought I'd taught you better than that!" Getting up, he dusted himself down and red-faced with embarrassment at Jimmy's obvious amusement, he grinned, "You may be sure that I will *never* make that mistake again!" Following the encounter, he headed for Bristol to settle up for the shooting tuition and taking great care in circumventing the shopping areas, he managed to arrive at the small-arms shop without bumping into his wife. He handed over another large envelope to the owner of the shop, who extended his right hand in the time-honoured fashion but smiling, Andreas shook his head, turned on his heels and left without saying a word, leaving the perplexed shop-owner with his unshaken hand still extended. Returning quickly to the car park, he decided to utilise the remaining time by visiting Ma and putting his foot down, he shaved a good ten minutes from the record for a Bristol to Ma's journey; walking breezily into the house, he dutifully kissed Ma on the top of her ever-increasingly grey head. "What time will you be picking him up?" She asked with a smile. "I thought about eleven!" He replied, "There's no need to leave quite so early this time, as I'll be doing the map reading!" Putting his arm around her shoulders, he grinned conspiratorially, "Get Dolores to check Riley's inside pocket for a bottle of whisky; they're bad enough on cider without that stuff!" "Okay, son!" She replied with a wink, "I know what a handful those two buggers are but *do* try to keep an eye on them if you can!" Andreas remarked, "It's worse than looking after a bunch of kids but okay Ma, I *will* keep an eye on them and I suppose you'll be packing his case for him as usual?" Shrugging, she smiled resignedly and after being brought up to date on family affairs, Andreas finished his coffee and kissing her cheek, he left for home.

Entering the house, Andreas sensed instantly that something was awry, being way too quiet and with his mind immediately slotting into alert mode, he crept along the passageway to the living room door, with his back pressed flat against the wall. Gently turning the handle, he gingerly eased himself into the darkened room and deciding to inch his way to the kitchen using the wall, he took the first step. All of a sudden, the light was switched on and being stunned for a moment, he heard, *Happy Birthday to You*. With realization dawning, he thought, *how the hell could I have forgotten my own birthday*. Putting her arms around him, Lu kissed him a little too warmly and he whispered, "Later, darling, later!" The embrace was cut short when Lily-Ann began tugging on his jacket to hand over her present and lifting her aloft, Andreas said, "Thank you, Lily-Ann. I'll open it just as soon as I've had a drink!" With Ma and Pa arriving ten minutes later, the family was complete and Viv remarked, "You didn't have a clue, did you? This was all organized weeks ago!" Andreas replied, "No I didn't and there was no card from Lu this morning to remind me!"

For a few hours, Melbourne, the exams and most of all Stow, were all forgotten in the joy of having his family around him; with perhaps *not* the biggest surprise, Reuben standing hand in hand with Claire; walking across to them, Andreas said, "I'm sure you'll forgive me if I don't shake hands!" Reuben's laughter was a giveaway that he had been informed of Andreas's gaffe. The party went on into the wee hours and with Lily-Ann falling asleep, she was laid on the spare mattress in Rosie's room. When everyone else had gone home and the kids tucked up in bed, Andreas began to get undressed, promising himself to make it up to Lu for his trickery in getting her to ask him to drive the gang to Stow. Spending the whole night atoning for his sin, he finally managed to extricate himself from Lu's arms and going quietly downstairs, he made *madam's* breakfast, serving it up on a tray. Returning downstairs to cater for his children's needs, he immediately had to remove a soaking, stinking nappy hanging from Rosie's hips like a Hindu dhoti and with the task having been completed, he ascended the stairs once more to retrieve the breakfast tray. Lu was sitting up in bed half-naked, still consuming the more-than-adequate repast and sitting on the edge of the bed, he watched her slowly masticating the manna with a coquettish grin playing across her mouth, then with each dainty mouthful being slowly and carefully chewed, he became seriously interested. "For God's sake woman, will you cover yourself up? I've got things to do later and haven't time to dilly-dally with your stinking body!" Cocking her head to one side, she put the tray to one side, ran her finger over her moist bottom lip and cast aside the sheet that had been serving as the last vestige to her immodesty. Rising from the bed, Andreas closed the door and turned round, "You minx!" He whispered throatily before hurriedly divesting himself of his clothes and not hearing George's accession to the room, they were blissfully unaware of his presence until they heard him say, "Why are you two wrestling on the bed?" Andreas kept the laugh confined to his throat, while Lu said calmly, "Why don't you go downstairs and watch the television, there's a good boy? Tell the rest of them that Mummy said that you are to have on whatever you want!" George waddled towards the door and Andreas said softly to his son, "Would you mind closing the door on the way out?" Hearing the click of the door being closed, they tried to resume where they had left off but finding that with the spontaneity disappearing, a void had been left, rendering their earlier passion incapable of being rekindled. Lu said, "Come on, babe; we may as well go downstairs!" Rising from the bed, Andreas grinned and remarked, "That'll be two showers I've had this morning and it isn't even nine o'clock yet!"

Lu took an age showering and dressing, a necessary aberration in the circumstances, making her long-suffering husband behind time for those really important tasks that he had planned for the day, like visiting people whose welfare had been placed in his capable but unwilling care, to inform them of the departure time and remind them to take spare underwear. Leaving the house as soon as Lu appeared downstairs, Andreas carried out each visit with alacrity, making him realize that the trip would probably not be the wished-for rest cure, prescribed by Lu as a possible panacea to his exam hangover and the troublesome Australian expedition. Beginning to regret volunteering his services at all and feeling fractious, he left Riley's house, the last visit on the itinerary and with the morning's exertions finally taking their toll, he returned home in low spirits, which fortunately were quickly dispelled by a meal and a flagon. During the ensuing peaceful evening with his family, he decided to let the children stay up later than usual, as it would be the last such night for a week and finally retiring for the night, being certain that the children were sleeping, Tarzan and Jane atoned for their coital frustration of the morning, finding that the meat actually *was* sweeter for the waiting but it still left Andreas feeling lethargic and unfulfilled, so promptly taking advantage of his half-sleeping but receptive spouse in the early hours, he rid himself of lingering lassitude. Creeping from the bed feeling much better for the exercise, he went about the business of getting ready for Stow as quickly and quietly as was humanly possible; a quick breakfast and coffee later, he left to pick up the gang.

10

It would not be a trip to Stow if *everything* went to plan and the complication occurred right at the outset when a detour was deemed necessary to accommodate both Jimmy being picked up earlier than arranged and the fact that *no-one* wanted to miss the spectacle of Riley's habitual grovelling to his wife. Immediately arriving at Riley's caravan, Andreas ran to the door to give Dolores a kiss, an act that was guaranteed to bring a smile to her sallow face, which was quickly supplanted by a scowl, the moment her husband emerged from the door carrying his old, battered suitcase. "Bye darling!" He said, attempting to kiss her heavily rouged cheek. "Don't you *darling* me, you good-for-nothing useless bastard!" She snarled, averting her face. Turning to Andreas, she smiled sweetly, "Be sure to have a nice time, Andreas!" "I will thank you Doll!" Andreas answered, being *well* aware that she adored him calling her Doll, which in her besotted mind had connotations of an intimacy, yet to be consummated. Sensing the malicious glare being cast in his direction, Andreas grinned mischievously in Riley's direction and placing the carelessly discarded case into the back of the car, Andreas took his place beside Jimmy in the front. They had been on the move for only fifteen minutes when Riley suddenly let out a roar and pulling into a lay-by, Andreas said indulgently, "I suppose this is the first toilet stop then!" "No!" Riley roared, ""That thieving bastard Dolores has taken the whisky out of my jacket!" Observing Riley's apoplectic face as he checked in the mirror before pulling back out onto the road, Andreas smirked and headed at pace for Stow-on-the-Wold.

Arriving in Stow three and a half hours later, with no *water of life* having been imbibed, Pa remarked, "The journey seemed quicker this time!" "Yes, Pa!" Andreas agreed, thinking to himself, *that's because I did the bloody map-reading!* Predictably, the senior members of the party headed straight for the bar as soon as they had stamped the stiffness out of their legs. "It's all right. It's like this all the time!" Andreas explained to Reuben and picking up half of the luggage, he nodded in the general direction of the remaining cases. Taking the hint, Reuben struggled on behind and with both managing to negotiate the narrow staircase without tripping over their own feet *or* the cases, they exceeded expectations by depositing the cases into the correct rooms. Returning downstairs to clean out the car, Andreas put the rubbish into a black plastic sack, leaving it beside the litter bin outside the hotel, while the uneaten food was thrown to the ducks, with the poor creatures instantly being invaded by a flock of seagulls, eager to share in the *manna from heaven;* watching the combatants battling for the spoils, Andreas smiled as the smaller birds appeared to have won the altercation.

It came as no huge surprise to Andreas that his fellow travellers were well into their second drink already, accompanied by all the likely suspects in various stages of inebriation. Laughing Lennie, standing alone at the bar, acknowledged Andreas's presence with a nod, while Molly-No-Legs ceased castigating her partner Billy to waddle across and offer her lips. Leaning over, Andreas kissed her cheek, only just managing to avoid the gaping chasm of her mouth. Smiling, she revealed two nicotine-stained fangs and Andreas thought, *Well at least the poor old bugger hasn't lost any more teeth!* Both she and Billy, being lucky if either of them were four feet tall, were struggling to scale their resting places at the bar, with Molly finally having to be lifted onto the bar stool and Billy only just being able to climb aboard his vantage point. Andreas had only *ever* seen Molly waddling around the bar, plying her trade as a prostitute, while Billy circulated, trying to sell items purloined from the local supermarket, so having no idea of how they would dismount from their perches, Andreas humorously thought that *surely* as regular customers, they should have been rewarded by a set of plasterer's steps, at the very least. Purchasing a half of lager, he warned Pa, "Before you think of fixing something up behind my back, I am *definitely* not fighting; this is Reuben's show!" "Okay, son, don't worry and don't you go looking for that piece you picked up the last time we were here; remember you're a married man now!" Andreas thought, *I've scarcely given*

Jan a second thought since we were last here. Jan was the barmaid in a bar he had used for food on his last visit, finding the greasy offerings at the hotel almost inedible and with the ensuing brief affair being before Lu and he had got together, he had hitherto considered the dalliance one small step on the road to *nirvana* but now being on familiar territory once more, he was not so sure of it being such a trifle and being somewhat unsettled by the thought, he hotly muttered with a shake of the head, "No, Pa. I won't go looking for *anyone!*"

With Reuben accompanying him on his stroll into town, an hour was spent in the pointless pursuit of window-shopping closed emporia, until Reuben exclaimed suddenly, "Hey, there's a pub over there that serves food!" Before Andreas could stop him, Reuben had walked through the doorway of the pub where Jan worked and hesitantly following his friend into the familiar darkened room, Andreas looked around the bar nervously; relaxing the moment that he discovered Jan's absence. Joining Reuben at the bar and remembering his promise to Pa, he resisted the temptation to ask Jan's whereabouts, ordering instead, two lasagne and chips, accompanied by a further two halves. Reuben asked, "Are you okay, Andreas? You've gone quiet all of a sudden!" Andreas replied with a wistful smile, "I'm fine, just a little tired from travelling, that's all!" Eating in virtual silence, occasionally sipping their beers, Andreas broached the subject of Reuben's forthcoming foray into the world of Gypsy fighting, warning that his first fight had probably already been arranged. Telling Reuben that he would have to learn how to please the crowd to give them value for their money, he suggested, "If you finish your man too quickly, they won't want to watch you again and no more fights would mean zero opportunity of trying out your new skills!" Reuben asked, "How do I make it last?" "It's not easy and it has to be achieved without making it too obvious or you could both be accused of fight fixing!" Andreas replied, "You have a quick brain and I'm sure you'll get the hang of it, although *I* nearly got caught out early in my career by letting my opponent have a few too many shots at me and got caught with a haymaker; luckily I managed to get up from the floor and beat him but there is no guarantee that you would enjoy the *same* good fortune; you're there to entertain and make money for the punters but do *not* get caught out. Women will also be in attendance, looking for extras and wearing extremely tight John Ls made me as popular with the women as I was with the men for dispatching another opponent!" With Reuben's education now complete, Andreas told him that he was sure he would do well and make a good amount of money for their fellow travellers.

Walking back into the hotel, Riley rushed over in a panic, "Where the hell have you two been, Reuben's got a fight in under an hour, so you'd better get a move on!" Andreas went along with Reuben to his room, to inspect his fighting apparel, which had been arrayed neatly on the bed and delivering his judgement, Andreas recommended, "You need *new* trainers and shorts are too easily ripped off but luckily I took the precaution of bringing along the John Ls that I used the last time I was here!" Looking at his watch, he remarked, "There should just about be time for me go into town and buy new trainers; what size do you take?" Reuben said, "Tens and I think I'll have a shower before I do anything else!" "Good idea!" Andreas conceded, "I used to have a dip in the stream but a shower would certainly be quicker in the circumstances!" Dashing from the hotel, he managed to find a shoe-shop still open and purchasing a pair of suitable trainers, he jogged back to the hotel. Collecting a bag from his suitcase, he made his way to Reuben's room and shouted through the shower door, "I've left the trainers on the bed along with a bag containing oil, a pair of tattered gloves and my long Johns!" Going downstairs to the bar, he assured the waiting quartet that Reuben would be down soon, ready for battle and making his entrance minutes later, with his body shining with oil and wearing Andreas's tight black long Johns, Reuben looked every inch the modern gladiator. Waiting for Pa and Riley to drain their glasses, Andreas noticed several young and indeed, older women who ought to have known better, openly ogling and tossing ribald remarks Reuben's way. He stood like a nonchalant colossus, pretending to ignore the attention but conversely attracting more by continually flexing his muscles. Being proud of the machine that had been created, Andreas was aware that with the end-game of Australia looming ever nearer, this would be a real examination of his expertise. Although confident in his *own* ability to kill a fellow human being, it did concern Andreas from time to time that Reuben might *not* have what it takes to actually take someone's life but observing Reuben's reactions to brutality in Stow, would give Andrea an insight of whether he would be up to the task or not.

With Pa and Riley now being supped up, the entourage repaired to the arena on the hill, eager for blood and anxious to see what the new boy was made of and arriving at the hill a few minutes before his opponent, they found a good-sized crowd had already gathered for the first fight of the fair but with Reuben's opponent also a stranger to Stow, Andreas was unable to offer constructive advice. The fight began and it became obvious after only a few minutes that his opponent was not in the same league as Reuben, with the only problem being in how to prolong the agony. As usual, the rounds were of varying duration, depending on who was winning at the time *and* who the timekeeper had his money on; with no set pattern to proceedings, rules were often made up as they went along and at the end of the third round, Andreas instructed his protege, "Next round, show us some of the moves that your girlfriend taught you, no not *those* moves; the *fighting on*es!" Reuben grinned. "You funny bastard, you're supposed to be helping me win a fight, not make me laugh!" Andreas said, "Finish him off this round and let's get back to the hotel; Mollie-No-Legs is waiting for you!" Reuben ambled over to the centre of the circle to wait for his opponent, noticing that the timekeeper had already given his man a huge dose of time to recover from the punishment already meted out. The unfortunate man staggered to the centre of the circle to receive the coup-de-grâce and threw out a fist, more in desperation than any hope of making any kind of impression on his younger, stronger opponent. However, the impossible happened; Reuben walked onto the punch and after teetering for a moment, an upset became a distinct possibility when the underdog followed up with an enormous right hook that landed flush on Reuben's jaw. After standing stock still for a nano-second, he fell in a heap to the ground and Pa's mouth gaped open as he saw his money disappearing down the drain. Reuben managed to narrowly beat the referee's count, despite the omission of six and seven and was now reeling around the ring, semi-conscious, while Pa and Riley screamed at him like demented dervishes. Guessing that round four would *now be* considerably longer than the previous three, Andreas threw a bucket of cold water over Reuben's head when he was driven back into his own corner by a flurry of punches. Shaking his head, Reuben stood immobilized as his opponent made a grab for him and suddenly becoming less comatose, he grabbed hold of the man's arm and wrist together, throwing him to the floor. Before the timekeeper could ring his hand-held bell to rescue his crony, Reuben ran across and kayoed him with a vicious kick to the chin. The man lay in a heap with his handlers standing over him, splashing water into his face in an attempt to revive him but being totally unconscious, his handlers were forced to throw in the towel. Still in shock at almost losing his money, Pa remarked moodily to Andreas, "It's a bloody good job you threw that water over him!" Reuben interjected, "Oh, I'm pleased you were *impressed* with the acting!" "You were *acting?*" Andreas asked incredulously. "Well, you did tell me to make it look good for the punters!" Reuben answered and still laughing when they arrived back at the hotel, Bill and Jimmy were kept in ignorance of the play-acting, with Andreas not being too sure of the effect it might have on the senior members of the troupe but it was plain from their smacked-arse faces, that Pa and Riley were clearly not amused.

The rest of the stay was spent in a similar vein, with Reuben playing his role to perfection, with each fight being stage-managed to implement the moves he had been taught and every night, despite his good intentions, Andreas found himself scanning the crowd for a glimpse of Jan. Being somewhat disappointed by his lack of success at the end of every evening, he paradoxically felt a deep sense of relief that he had *not* actually seen her. The last day of their sojourn arrived and with Andreas still totally at odds with himself, he had to admit reluctantly that his dalliance with Jan had *not* been purely lust but driving into with Reuben to Cheltenham to buy gifts for the family, provided relief from the constant conjuring up of Jan's beautiful countenance *and* the ensuing guilt thereafter. When shopping was finished, the pair headed back to get ready for Reuben's last fight of the *Fair*.

Thus far Reuben had not lost a fight, so telling him that he wanted his final opponent taken out in the first round, Andreas said that he wanted to leave a lasting impression on Reuben's growing army of fans but catching a glimpse of Reuben's final opponent, he quickly had to revise the game plan. His adversary was a huge Irishman called O'Keefe, *also* unbeaten and with not one ounce of fat occupying his vast frame, he presented a fearsome sight. Andreas said to Reuben, "Go on then Mr Scamp; let's see what you're made of!" The first blow struck was a fearsome left hook to Reuben's cheek and seeing blood seeping down Reuben's face, the Irishman began hurling salvoes of blows to Reuben's head. Having to grasp the huge beast around the waist to gain some respite, Reuben was tossed aside like a rag doll and in attempting to take the offensive, the Irishman's longer reach inflicted more lesions to his face. An adventurous head-butt merely succeeded in giving O'Keefe the opportunity to grasp him round the middle and with Reuben's arms also being trapped, the giant was able to exert a fearsome pressure to his middle section. With a series of short-range head-butts failing to break the hold, the situation was looking dire until the combination of sweat and oil stepped in to lend a hand. Managing to wriggle his arms free of the hold, Reuben aimed a heavy blow to his opponent's temple and feeling the grip loosen, he stamped down on O'Keefe's foot. Now being free from constriction, Reuben was able to execute a textbook spinning kick to the man's head as he lumbered forward, immediately dumping the titan onto his back. Reuben ran across the ring as his foe was attempting to rise, with a well-aimed kick to the head, halting the process but the brave O'Keefe was still not done. Managing to struggle to his knees, he began the long hard task of regaining a standing position, only to be met by a gloved hand suddenly gripping his throat, while the other being poised ominously in the air, ready to dispatch the final blow. The Irish warrior was helpless and with the mob baying for blood, Reuben prolonged the agony by delaying the inevitable; blatantly posing for the howling crowd but finally acceding to demands, he drove his hand downward at lightning speed. The fearsome blow splintered his opponent's nose and as O'Keefe fell back unconscious, there was a collective gasp from the crowd at seeing the exposed bone; his handlers rushed forward to staunch the flow of blood. Smiling, Andreas was satisfied now that Reuben had proved himself ready for Australia; *or* anywhere else in the world and on the way back from the hill, Reuben's ecstatic father said, "Where the hell did you learn to do that kick? I've only ever seen that kind of stuff on the telly!" Andreas observed sarcastically with a grin, "His girlfriend is a six or seventh-dan black belt and he had to learn that move in order to fight her off!" Still being hyperactive from the fight, Reuben did not appreciate the remark and glared at Andreas but fortunately he was back to his usual affable self by the time they all arrived back at the hotel and with news of the win spreading quickly, everyone cheered as he entered the bar but *all* the adulation was not directed Reuben's way. Sidling across to where Andreas stood, Mollie asked, "You not seeing that Jan piece now then?" He replied, "I'm a married man with a family now Molly, so I am off-limits to everyone!" Pulling a face, she waddled over to where Reuben was surrounded by a host of beautiful women and noticing Billy trying unsuccessfully to sell something from a plastic bag, Andreas reflected, *not a very good night for the little people* and going upstairs to the room, he noticed Jimmy already asleep; creeping across the room, he got into bed and surrendered to the night.

11

Deciding that a speedy home journey would only be achieved with an early start, Andreas made sure that each of the motley crew was awake in readiness for the journey, making a point of reminding Pa to pack Ma's present. Receiving assurance that it would be done, Andreas went downstairs for breakfast, where the hotel's acquisition of a new chef saved him from having to seek a decent meal in the pub and the embarrassment of a possible encounter with Jan. Picking up a newspaper from the table in the hallway, he was instantly reminded of his previous visit to Stow, when the assassination of the American president had been splashed across the front pages of every newspaper and he was convinced that the world had not *really* moved on from the tragedy. Appreciating the solitude of an early repast and a catch-up on the news, his breakfast was almost finished before the others began to appear, finding Pa and Riley unsurprisingly bringing up the rear and reminding Pa once more to make sure that Ma's perfume was packed, Andreas left the dining room and leisurely strolled into town.

Taking in the beauty and history of buildings that had once witnessed slaughter on an appalling scale, Andreas visited legendary *Digbeth*, where ducks allegedly swam in the blood of loyalist troops. Sighing deeply, he began to walk back to the hotel, vowing to revisit the town when there was no horse fair; not that *he* had ever seen the sales anyway. Arriving back at the hotel, he judged it providential to check that Pa and Riley were ready for departure and that proved to be a fortuitous decision, with both being stretched out fast asleep on their beds, with empty suitcases still sitting on the floor. He removed his belt and began beating the wardrobe with the buckled end. "For Christ's sake!" Riley roared, "You're worse than my old woman!" Ignoring the denigration, Andreas addressed Pa, "I'm telling you now Mr Bosworth, if you *forget* that perfume, I will tell her how much money you've won!" Rising from the bed, Pa threw the perfume in the case and retorted, "There! Is that better, you snitching bastard?" Walking from the room with a huge smirk on his face, Andreas said, "You'll thank me later!"

The group finally left Stow just before lunchtime, with Pa and Riley's dalliance at the bar being the main cause for tardiness and true to form, the journey was hardly under way before a full hip flask, purchased from the winnings, appeared as if by magic. Andreas remarked to Riley, "She will have your guts for garters if she smells that stuff on your breath!" He growled, "She never comes *close* enough to smell my breath!" A necessary toilet stop proved too good an opportunity for the pair to pass up and using the excuse that the public conveniences were full, the pair disappeared into a pub to avail themselves of their facilities. Allowing them thirty minutes to whet their whistles proved to be a mistake, with the pair having to be forcibly persuaded to rejoin the car. Once that had been accomplished, the homeward journey got under way once more, with Andreas declaring that if another toilet stop was required, it would be in the middle of nowhere, far away from any pubs, *if* that were at all possible! Riley was delivered home first so that no one would miss the second instalment of his grovelling and once Andreas had received his customary kiss from Dolores, the others were transported to their houses. Pa was the last to be dropped off and turning down Ma's offer of stew, he cited the fact that with the Australian journey in the offing, he was desperate to see his family.

Dumping his case on the floor, he grabbed hold of Lulu and kissed her passionately, which proved a great source of amusement to the boys. Having been in love with Lu for as long as he could remember, he was thankful *not* to have bumped into Jan on the trip, not being *entirely* sure what the outcome would have been. Finally releasing Lu, she went to the kitchen to warm up a stew that had been cooked the previous day and ogling her backside as it disappeared through the doorway, he thought, *I'll be doing some warming up later myself with a bit of luck; if the monthly visitor hasn't arrived!* Going to the bedroom to unpack, he put his dirty clothes in a bag and carrying *them* in one hand and presents in the other, he made his way downstairs. All thoughts of fatigue from the stress of having to wet-nurse geriatric children were forgotten as he stood with his arm around his wife, watching his children playing with tin soldiers that had safely travelled in his case all the way from Stow. He remarked fondly, "Those boys are so appreciative!" Looking up at him Lu murmured, "That's because you instinctively know what they like!" Kissing her mouth gently, he replied, "Yes my dear and *you* instinctively know the right things to say!" Bed-time came early that particular night and after claiming his just desserts, languor overtook him and yawning, he whispered, "Sorry my darling, no seconds for you tonight!"

Waking later than usual the following morning, he found the whole family up, dressed and breakfasted and with the Antipodean trip being only two weeks away, he resolved to spend as much time with his family as he could but predictably, his best intentions fell far short of actual fruition. "Viv's been on the phone and wants to see you pronto!" Lu informed him. "I hope you aren't going to be too long; I wanted us all to go shopping!" "Shit!" He remarked. "I suppose I'd better see what he wants but he can wait until I'm good and ready!" Kissing Lu, he left for the office as soon as everything was set fair, albeit a little later than required, "I'll be back as soon as I can!" He called to Lu. Starting up the car, he hit the steering wheel angrily with the heel of his hand, "This had better be bloody important!" He exclaimed. His foul mood gradually dissipated on the drive to the office and being intrigued by the early summons he put his foot down, managing to arrive just before Viv, who had been in court. "Ah, I'm so glad you remembered where Mowll and Mowll is situated. I've arranged for passports *and* inoculations; all *you* have to do is turn up in the appropriate sites at the appointed times and besides swanning off on holidays and playing happy families, have you managed to achieve anything further towards your preparations?" Ignoring the sarcasm, Andreas replied, "Bearing in mind your remarks about Reuben's boyish looks, I purchased plain glass spectacles, a pinstriped suit and an old, beaten-up briefcase to make him appear even younger; a bookish young man would surely *appear* less of a threat!" "Are you absolutely sure about taking him?" Viv asked. "He doesn't look the part, as far as I'm concerned!" Andreas replied hotly, "You wouldn't have said that if you'd seen him fighting in Stow; don't worry, he'll be just fine!" Viv asked, "Has Lu come to terms with the fact that you'll be going away soon?" "No, she hasn't mentioned it so far but being a traditional Roma, she will consider a man's concerns to be sacrosanct. All the same, I wish she *would* actually say something; it might make me feel less guilty!" "Well, best of luck with that one, old chum; have you anything planned for the rest of the day?" "We *were* supposed to be shopping but by the time I get home now, it will be too late!" Viv added, "By the way before I forget, I want to see you and Reuben in the morning; as early as you can make it!" Not being sure whether the last sentence was a snide remark relating to his recent tardy arrival, Andreas ignored the implication, "I'd best set off to face the music, if I'm any later, her face will be like a slapped arse again!" Walking towards the door, he heard Viv's voice, "Don't forget, *early* tomorrow morning!" Knowing that she would not be best pleased at missing a day's shopping, he expected to be hauled over the coals and as soon as he started the car he exclaimed, "Bloody women!"

Dinner was served without a word and desperately needing refreshment, he pushed the half-eaten dinner aside and went to the kitchen for a flagon but finding the cache exhausted, he donned a warm coat and drove angrily to the farm. His ill humour vanished however, the instant Michael informed him of the arrival of the cattle from Argentina, "They are huge buggers!" Michael said, "I've a feeling that big boy might be too much for our heifers!" Andreas remarked with a grin, "Oh, I'm sure they'll manage!" Walking to the field to inspect the new acquisitions, Andreas slightly adjusted his assessment of the situation, "Bloody hell, he *is* a large gentleman. I reckon we'll do well hiring him out for stud duties and I'm damned sure he'd thank us for it!" Strolling back from the field, Andreas asked, "I hope you've got cider ready; I'm cleaned out!" Entering the farmhouse, Andreas kissed his sister and over coffee they discussed the problems he was experiencing with Lu. Michael suggested that perhaps *he* should broach the subject, with Vee adding, "Michael's right. It could be that you have both been waiting for the other to address the problem!" Shaking his head at the simplicity of the *potential* answer to the matter, Andreas commented, "You could be right; I'll give it a try as soon as I get back and thanks for the advice!" "Let us know how you fare!" Michael called out as he walked across the yard carrying a month's supply of cider, "I know you've only got a fortnight to drink that lot but what you don't drink will be perfectly matured by the time you get back!"

Making four trips to the kitchen with flagons, he glanced into the living room in passing and noticed Lu wearing spectacles to read the paper. *That's a new one*, he thought, *when did she start wearing those!* Taking one of the flagons into the room, he removed the stopper and began swallowing the golden liquid but becoming suddenly aware of the disgusted glares, he put down the offending flagon, "Look Lu!" He remarked, "We've already had this out before and I thought it was all sorted. I *have* to go to Australia, whether we're happy with that or not and *if* I go there with this hanging over my head, it could cost me my life. You and the children mean everything to me and all I'm asking is that I go with your blessing; we only have a few days left, so can we *please* try to make those days special!" Lu walked across the room, leaned over and kissed his face softly, "You're right in everything you say and *I* am wrong; I know that this Australian thing has to be attended to *and* that you are the only man for the job but *I* want my husband here with me in one piece; that is my main concern!" Smiling, she added, "Of course you go with my blessing and I'm happy that at least this is one *little* problem that has already been solved!" Deciding to retire early, their conjugal duties were performed with far less vigour than usual, with the more tender sides of their natures assuming the major role. However, making up for the lack of ardour in the early morning and with his wife lying supine and solicitous after the event, he judged the moment to perfection. "Reuben and I have a meeting with Viv this morning but if you like, I'll ring in at nine o'clock to cancel. "No, dear, that's okay!" she said. "I'll see you when you've finished!"

12

Sitting at his desk, looking like the cat that ate the cream, Viv instantly opened proceedings, "I've asked you here because the senior partners have expressed a wish to meet the young men of whom so much is expected and also to apprise you of the travel and accommodation arrangements. Due to prior commitments, they are both unable to attend right now, so we'll begin without them. Your flight leaves on Monday, sixth August, at 10.30 AM, with refuelling stops at Tehran, Bombay and Singapore. On arrival at Sydney, you will be taken by taxi to the Southern Cross Hotel, where you will stay overnight before moving on to the Hotel Windsor in Melbourne. I'll supply you with an itinerary, tickets, money and passports on the day, so don't worry about remembering the whys and wherefores of the journey. Any questions so far?" Andreas asked, "When are you going to reveal the identity of your informant, presuming you do have one?" Viv smiled "Yes, there is one and her name is Jennifer Ellis, one of the girls in the office. I have no photograph for but you will soon get to know who she is and to be doubly sure, she will say that she knew your mother. You must be circumspect in all dealings with her, as she feels that she is already under suspicion of spying, which prompts me to believe that the situation is certainly looking a good deal more precarious than we'd hoped for. I'll see if the brothers are ready for us now!" As soon as Viv had left, Andreas commented, "I'm starting to get that tingly feeling that I get before a fight!" "Yeah, me too!" Reuben agreed, "I can't wait to get out of here!" Viv returned suddenly, beckoning them to follow, "You can come through now!

The brothers were even more frail than Andreas remembered but with Viv not sitting behind the large desk with them in the inner sanctum, they did not seem such a frightening prospect *but* if their bodies were now somewhat in decline, their minds betrayed *no* signs of fragility. Belying their benign demeanour, incisive questions came thick and fast, successfully being parried by the younger men, albeit with Viv's skilful manipulation and with the interview at last coming to an end, the two friends were left mentally exhausted, while the elderly gentlemen's bright blue eyes sparkled with mischievous delight at the discomfort they had just wreaked. Out in the foyer once more, Reuben exclaimed, "I don't want to go through that again!" Viv smiled. "They can be rather a handful but I have to say that you both acquitted yourselves admirably!"

Prudently deciding against going to the gym or accepting Viv's offer of a drink, despite the feeling that he needed and deserved both, Andreas opted to go home to his wife, not in the least swayed by thoughts of the diatribe he would receive if he did not. After dropping Reuben off, he sped homeward, arriving in time to administer a telling-off to Victor for kicking a football against the wall. "For God's sake, watch those bloody windows!" "You're home early, love!" Lu commented, "Just in time for a visit to Ma and Pa's!" "Okay babe but let's have a cuppa first; I'm whacked!" Sitting down to watch the news, he availed himself of a fistful of Vee's newly baked scones, occupying what looked like a new cake tin and after the snack had been consumed, he dutifully rose from his chair when asked to drive to Ma's place.

"What's all this about you and Reuben going to Australia?" Pa demanded. "Why wasn't *I* asked along? You know I've always wanted to go there!" Grinning, Andreas replied, "The truth is that when I said to the photographer that Billy Bosworth might be going on the trip, he told me that he wouldn't snap an ugly old bastard like him, in case he broke the camera!" Ma and the kids screeched with laughter, infuriating Pa even more. Fearing that Andreas would not be satisfied with leaving the conversation there, Lu gave administered the *stare*, an act always reserved for occasions that she deemed inappropriate but ignoring the warning and being emboldened by the laughter, Andreas continued flagrantly, "Tell you what Pa, I'll bring back a koala for you. How's that?" "Cheeky bugger!" Pa retorted. "I can get one of those any day of the week *and* with a double rum in it for good measure. Don't need to go to no Australia for *that* shit!" Not really comprehending the reason for the howls of laughter accompanying his remark, Pa sat down bemusedly in the hundred-year-old chair that had been rescued from the caravan; with even Lu surreptitiously smirking behind her hand at his latest howler. A few drinks later, he calmed down somewhat and thenceforward became for the greater part incomprehensible and could easily have been from the moon or even land Zog.

Managing to wheedle a session in the gym out of Lu by claiming that a final workout before the trip would prevent jet lag, he propped the Blue Flash against the wall and entered the place that even in his darkest times, had always been his sanctuary. Jimmy was nowhere to be seen, so Andreas went below to the changing rooms and opening his locker, he was immediately grateful that he'd had the good sense to have extractors installed, with his gear stinking of stale sweat and damp. After donning the malodorous clothing, he trained intensely for an hour and declaring himself fit, he placed the plastic bag containing his fetid kit over the handlebars and mounting his faithful steed, he cycled to his new bathing site. Finding that even in daylight the spot was much darker than the old one, he decided against tarrying too long and drying himself on the rank towel, he headed home. Arriving just in time to get theboys into their pyjamas, Lulu complained that he was stinking the house out with his evil-smelling gym kit and laughing, he hurled the shorts at Lu's head. Squealing, she ran hell for leather into the kitchen, to the accompaniment of the boys' laughter, until he threw an even more fetid T-shirt in their direction.

Spending an hour watching television with the kids until it was time for bed, he took them upstairs, tucked them in and instructed them to look after Mummy for him while he was away. George asked, "Will you be away long, Daddy?" Andreas fondly kissed his son and replied, "I hope not son and I'll try to make it home for Christmas but even if I don't manage it; you may be sure that I'll be thinking of you every minute!" Putting both arms around his father's neck as he leaned across to kiss him, Victor squeezed him for all he was worth saying, "Please be careful, *daddi!*" Andreas whispered, "Don't worry, son. I'll be back before you know it!" Pausing at the door, he blew them both kisses, turned out the light and closed the door; almost bumping into Lu, who was standing on the landing massaging Rosie's back. Once Rosie's wind had been released, Lu put her gently into her cot and propositioning her waiting spouse, she ordered throatily, "Come on big boy; it's time for bed!

Waking Lu gently in the morning with a kiss to the forehead, Andreas told her that coffee was on the tallboy beside her and innocently sitting up in bed naked, she reached for the cup, scarcely acknowledging his presence. Blatantly ogling and delighting in the sight of her still firm body, he leaned down and began nibbling her neck until his lips finally met hers in a passionate kiss. Replacing the cup to its coaster on the tallboy, Lu pulled him forcefully back into the warm bed and with satisfaction coming quickly, they sank back into the comfort of their soft pillows, where a languorous sleep swiftly claimed them both but wakening suddenly, Andreas realized how little time he had before Viv would be knocking at the door and running to the bathroom to the accompanying sound of Lu's laughter ringing in his ears, he thought, *the bitch; I hope she enjoys her cold coffee.* Carrying his suitcase downstairs after a quick shower and placing it beside the door in readiness, he tiptoed back upstairs to get dressed; with his grey suit hanging on the wardrobe door, ready for him to slip into and knowing that the journey would take all of two days, he opted for the relative comfort of a black sweatshirt and matching leather shoes. Creeping into the children's rooms, he kissed them lightly on the forehead before joining Lu on the landing and laughing he exclaimed, "Give me a kiss, you smelly little mare!" She retorted haughtily, "Whose fault is that, you horny bastard?" Kissing her passionately, he told her not to bother coming downstairs with him and right on cue, Viv began honking the horn of his car. Running downstairs, Andreas opened the door and shouted, "Stop that racket, you stupid bastard; you'll wake the kids!" Standing at the bottom of the stairs, he blew a kiss and silently mouthed the words, "I love you!" Noticing Reuben sitting in the front passenger seat, he stowed his gear in the boot and flopped down onto the back seat. Viv explained the aberration, "I thought I'd pick up Reuben up first to give you extra time with Lu!" Andreas sneered sarcastically, even though the act had proved fortuitous, "You never cease to amaze me with your kindness and consideration!" As they pulled away, Andreas quickly turned round to wave and smiled as he saw Lu returning the gesture from the bedroom window; as naked as the day she was born.

Arriving at Heathrow with more than the mandatory two hours to spare and knowing that Lu would have gone back to bed, he resisted the temptation to phone; wishing all the same that he was lying beside the warmth of her body instead of waiting for a plane ready to take him to the other side of the world. Viv interrupted his reverie. "Come on, Andreas; snap out of it!" Handing over a large white envelope, Viv explained, "Everything you need is contained in this envelope and you should alter your watches to local time wherever you land, so you will have a sense of where you are and how much time you have before arriving at the next port of call. I'm sorry but I have to dash now; I'm in court at one o'clock!" With that, he shook hands, "Good luck, boys!" Turning on his heel, he returned to the car park.

Opening the envelope, Andreas handed Reuben his documents and after sliding his own sheaf into his inside pocket, he deposited the empty sleeve into one of the many litter bins in the concourse. Sitting on a bench to await being called forward for the flight, they were on their second cup of insipid coffee when they heard their flight number being announced and gathering their things together, they headed for the appropriate gate. A thrill coursed through Andreas's body as he climbed the stairs leading to the interior of the plane and having located their seats, they stowed the hand luggage into the overhead rack and settled back, ready for take-off. Reuben said, "I'm really excited now that we're actually on our way!" Andreas smiled and said, "Me too; it's going to be a hard slog for the next couple of days but we might manage a little sightseeing in Sydney!" That's great!" Reuben said. "I wouldn't mind visiting the SCG!" "What the hell is that?" Andreas asked. "It's one of the venues where Australia play international cricket!" Andreas grinned. "You'll be on your bloody own then!" The stewardess asked them to fasten them their seat belts and with the plane's engines bursting into life, they taxied slowly forward to the runway, stopping for a minute, like a bull awaiting the matador and as the craft raced across the runway, they were thrust back in the seat.

Being airborne in seconds, Andreas looked out of the window, watching people below becoming the size of ants, until they burst through the clouds into a beautiful azure sky, believing it to be the most weird, exhilarating experience he had ever known. Being aware that they were now a thousand feet above the earth, Andreas looked across at Reuben, who was surprisingly sitting almost rigid with fear; Andreas commented, "You'd better get used to it, Reuben; we've got a long way to go yet!"

13

Waking with a start, Andreas looked across at Reuben, who was still sitting bolt upright, eyes staring unwaveringly ahead of him. "Why don't you try a brandy!" Andreas suggested, "I've always found it an ideal relaxant and there's still another couple of hours to Tehran!" Reuben replied disconsolately, "I do not drink spirits!" "Well, I suggest you at least give it a try!" Andreas insisted and hailing the stewardess, he ordered two brandy and cokes. Almost choking on the first swallow, Reuben quickly dispatched what was left and putting down the empty glass, he swallowed the second libation with identical haste. "Better?" Andreas asked. Reuben smiled. "Well, the last one wasn't too bad!" Andreas asserted, straight-faced, "Probably because it was mine!" Reuben took to the *elixir of life* like a duck to water, with landings and take-offs at Tehran and Bombay taking place in a blur of alcohol-induced stupors. Taking advantage of a slight hitch at Bombay when one of the passengers was arrested for taking clandestine photographs of Ravi Shastri, the Indian premier, they imbibed a few more brandies. The issue was settled amicably however and the plane was allowed to take off, albeit three hours later than scheduled. On board, they were informed of an unscheduled overnight stop in Singapore as a result of the incident and approaching the island's short runway, Reuben commented, "I'm *really* looking forward to sleeping in a bed, even if it is only for a short while!" Being ferried to the hotel in an airline coach along with their luggage, they arrived at the stop-over, tired but looking forward to a spot of unexpected sightseeing and a short while later, having arrived at the hotel in one piece, Andreas stretched out on a divan bed, remarking, "We'd have been here a damned sight sooner if that plonker hadn't taken a photo of Shastri, after being explicitly told *not* to take our cameras with us when we landed at Bombay but at least it's given us the opportunity of sleeping in a proper bed with sheets and pillows!" Showering, they opted to remain in their travelling clothes rather than unpack, then re-pack early morning and acting on advice from their taxi driver they were taken to *Clementi* Market, where they purchased even more trinkets. Deciding then to visit the world-famous *Bugis* Street, they were treated to an outstanding adventure in eastern cuisine but finding Tiger Beer, the local brew, not to his taste, Andreas conceded that it did actually pack a real punch. Finally tiring of watching the *kai tai's* ply their trade, the pair returned to the hotel, still unsure of what gender the nightbirds had actually been. Being tired from the seemingly endless journey and the vexatious walking around crowded markets, they returned to the stop-over to relax with a couple of brandies, before taking advantage of their comfortable beds.

Arriving at the airport, the following morning, they were informed that a party of six serving infantrymen from the plane had been arrested for creating a near riot in Bugis Street and as a result would not be joining their onward flight to Borneo. Andreas remarked, "Thank God we missed that; the last thing we want is to be involved in an incident like that!" Boarding was acquitted quickly and once they were in the air, safety belts were unstrapped and ordering brandies, Andreas began to explain the implications of the soldiers actions but with Reuben falling asleep before he had finished, Andreas removed the glass from his companion's hand and downed the drink in one, then swiftly dispatching his own, he joined his comrade in the land of Nod within minutes. Waking some time later hearing a message being barked out over the public address system in what seemed to be alien tongues, they instantly assumed that they were approaching Sydney Airport and along with the rest of the passengers, they gathered their paraphernalia ready to disembark. With no complications being experienced, they were checking into the Southern Cross Hotel within an hour, with Reuben signing the register with what looked like a new blue pen from his inside pocket. Borrowing the pen to register, Andreas inspected the CFC emblazoned ballpoint and asked, "Where did you get that little beauty?" "Maria and her new boyfriend went to a football match in London and brought it back as a souvenir!" Adding, as he removed the pen from Andreas's tight grip, "So you can just keep your bloody hands off it!"

After settling into their ground-floor room, Reuben took a taxi to the cricket ground while Andreas opted for a relaxing stroll around Queen Victoria arcade to look for yet more presents; wisely purchasing a large case to carry them all home. Shopping done, Andreas walked slowly back to the hotel and finding Reuben still at what must have been a riveting affair, he lay on the bed, thinking of how best to approach their investigation into the missing money. Lapsing into into a deep sleep, he was annoyingly disturbed by his companion returning with a carrier bag containing Victoria-emblazoned cricket sweaters for the boys and rubbing the sleep from his eyes, Andreas thanked him for the kind gesture, having the feeling that the gift would please Victor rather more than George but at least they would both be warm in the winter months. Andreas addressed his sun-reddened companion, "I've been trying to fathom out how best to approach this investigation and I think it best not to be confrontational but it could mean having to come up with a cover plan to allay suspicion about the real reason we're here!" Reuben answered, "I've been thinking on that subject too and I reckon that if you were to tell the office that we have been sent on a round-the-world learning curve, visiting all of Mowll and Mowll subsidiaries, we could ask questions without arousing too much suspicion!" That's a damn good idea, Reuben!" Andreas said animatedly. "Perhaps we could pretend to pursue a hobby of some sort to give the impression that we're not really bothered whether we learn anything about the business or not!" "How about fishing!" Reuben suggested with more than a hint of excitement, "We're *both* keen on that!" "Yes!" Andreas said excitedly, "That's ideal and hiring a boat would give us an excuse to be out of reach, at the times when we need to be; order a meal for me while I phone the office to organize a boat!" Explaining his need, he was informed that *all* would be ready for their arrival in Melbourne and thanking the young lady, Andreas wondered how long it would be before the boat hire was relayed to whomever was responsible for the misappropriation of the money.

Seeing no sign of Reuben when he reached the dining room, Andreas went through to the bar, where swordfish, that had being caught six hours earlier at Devonport, off the coast of Tasmania, had been ordered for him. Reuben declared, "I couldn't be arsed waiting for food in there!" Automatically turning his head in the direction indicated, Andreas noticed a man in the dining room, watching them, who quickly averted his gaze when he realized that he was under scrutiny himself. Saying nothing of their observer, Andreas suggested a drink before the meal and finally catching the barman's attention, he ordered brandy and cokes; the barman sauntered over, "Any particular preference in your choice of brandy? We have all the popular labels but we also stock Tolley's, a local brew that is stronger *and* much cheaper!" "That will do us fine!" Andreas asserted, with the drink arriving in minutes, he tentatively sipped the amber liquid and gasping with surprise as it hit the back of his throat, he declared, "Now that's what I call a *real* drink!" Seeing off the drinks in time for their meal being placed in front of them, they ordered more of the same and demolishing the swordfish steaks in short time too, they decided that the whole package was *very* much to their liking. Andreas turned to Reuben and perceiving the man still observing them, he suggested loudly to Reuben, "Come on; let's go for a walk!"

Glancing in the wing mirror of a stationary car as they meandered past, Andreas noticed the man from the hotel bar following them and entering a lane a hundred metres from the hotel, they found a likely looking bar, where Andreas immediately ordered Tolley's and Coke. While waiting for their drink, he heard the door opening and casually looking towards the door, he noticed their *shadow* walking to the bar but staying for just half and hour, the man put down his empty glass and left. Informing Reuben of his observations, Andreas added, "I'm probably reading to much into it, as we only arrived today but it might be advisable to be alert just in case!" A few drinks later and not having seen anything remotely suspicious, they returned to the hotel, where alarm bells began to ring the moment they entered the room, noticing instantly that the case Andreas had purchased for the presents was lying half-opened on the bed. Emptying their luggage onto the floor, they first checked that nothing was missing, then being aware that if contraband *were* found, they would not even *reach* Melbourne, let alone discover the identity of the people swindling the firm's investors, they went through their cases with a fine tooth comb. Shrugging in despair at finding nothing Andreas remarked, "They were here for something; we'll have another look in the morning, when our brains are a bit more alert but for now, I'm ready for a good night's sleep!" "Yeah, me too!" Reuben replied. After ten minutes of trying to attain the sleep his body craved, Andreas had a sudden enlightening moment and leaping from the bed, he removed both flight bags from the top of the wardrobe and throwing Reuben's hold-all to him, he emptied his *own* onto the bed. After carefully sifting through the contents and again finding nothing untoward, he carefully began replacing the contents of the bag, with Reuben following suit. Suddenly however, Reuben stopped re-packing and reaching forward, he plucked out a silver pen protruding from the envelope containing his passport and tickets. Unscrewing the top, he removed a small, rolled up sachet containing brown powder and taking the sac to the open window, he shook out the contents, sending the drug to all corners of the city. Disposing of the bag by flushing it down the toilet, Reuben checked that the door catch was in the locked position and returning to their beds, both fell swiftly into a deep, virtually stress-free sleep.

14

Making their way to the airport soon after breakfast, they were called through to the departure lounge shortly after arriving and taking advantage of the time available, they knocked back two quick Tolley's before boarding the craft. Strapping in ready for take-off, Andreas advised, "Be prepared to have your cases and luggage ripped apart by Customs when we arrive!" Reuben looked up in surprise, "Surely you don't believe *Customs* are involved?" Andreas replied calmly, "No but it's highly likely they have been tipped off and incidentally, well done for spotting that pen but for your vigilance, we'd have ended up on our way back home *or* thrown in jail!" Reuben said with a grin, "I'll have to thank Maria, when I see her!" Reuben quaffed a couple of expensive but inferior brandies during the short haul to Melbourne and still feeling distinctly apprehensive, he followed Andreas in the approach to the Custom's shed, having the fear that they *may* have overlooked some small drug-related article in their luggage the previous evening. Entering the *walk of shame,* they perceived officers lining both sides of the large *Nissen* type structure, which did nothing to allay the panic they felt inside and Reuben's fragile facade was instantly torpedoed, the moment that Andreas was detained at the first hurdle. Trying to *appear* nonchalant, Reuben walked past several officers and believing that he would get through without his bags being searched, he was stopped by the last in line. Both sets of luggage were searched thoroughly and with nothing illegal being found, the *rummagers,* reluctantly it seemed, permitted them to leave. Breathing a little more easily after the ordeal, they made their way to the bus stop and within five minutes had boarded a shuttle, bound for the city.

Arriving at the Hotel Windsor around midday, they carried their cases to the lift and were borne swiftly to their spacious and tastefully furnished room on the third floor. Once he had unpacked, Andreas lay on the bed with his feet dangling over the bottom of the bed and for the benefit of a possible bug, he addressed his comrade, "I'm really looking forward to a couple of weeks fishing; work can go to the devil for all I care!" Reuben replied, "Yeah, me too. *I* fancy going out somewhere after we've eaten to see what this city has to offer; there's bound to be a bar somewhere handy!" "Now *that* is a good idea!" Andreas responded and hauling his body from the bed, he walked to the lift, finally making the descent to the ground floor diner after it had passed by them twice. With swordfish being the only dish available on the menu, they decided to renew their acquaintance and between mouthfuls Reuben opined, "I'm guessing you believe the room to be bugged? Perhaps we should have asked for a different room when we registered; they can't possibly have bugged *every* room!" Andreas responded, "I think we have to assume that the room *is* bugged but it could actually work to our advantage, by allowing us to feed them with false information!" One of the waiters walked over to the table to tell Reuben that he was wanted in the foyer. Looking puzzled, Reuben asked if Andreas wanted to accompany him. "No!" He replied, "I'll just hover near the door in case I'm needed!" Moving to a position where he could observe everything that transpired, he noted Reuben talking to a swarthy man whose looks immediately betrayed his lineage and realizing that Reuben would be in no danger from a fellow Roma, Andreas returned to the table to await his friend's reappearance. "My kinsmen want to see us tomorrow morning!" Reuben declared when he returned, "Well you can deal with that!" Andreas retorted. "I'm having a lie-in!"

After a couple of Tolley's in a bar somewhat nearer the hotel, Andreas began to feel more optimistic of pulling off something that had seemed somewhat remote at the outset; being confident now of handling *anything* that came their way. Stringently watchful, they moved on to the next bar, looking at reflections in shop windows on the way, to check that no-one was shadowing them. Moving on to a third bar without having seen anyone suspicious, they relaxed and being aware that there would *not* be too many stress-free sessions on the horizon, they made the most of their freedom by drinking a little more than was advisable in the circumstances.

Returning to the hotel at the end of the evening, Andreas left instructions with reception that he was not to be disturbed in the morning, while Reuben re-acquainted himself with the hotel bar.

Thus Andreas was not best pleased when his sleep was disturbed early the following morning by Reuben shaking him vigorously and dressing quickly, Andreas joined his friend at the bottom of the stairs, immediately demanding to know why his sleep had been disturbed. "It's *you* that my kin want to see!" Walking angrily across the park, Andreas could see two Roma, looking distinctly out of place on the bright green grass and addressing them tersely Andreas growled, "Is it the money?" "The money's fine!" The more senior of the two gents replied, "We just wanted to meet the famous fighting Gadjo. One of our boys was at Stow two years ago and told us of a Gadjo, fighting two or three times a day and despite being floored, bitten and gouged, still managed to finish the week unbeaten!" Andreas's attitude eased somewhat on learning that they had heard of his exploits from so far away and now wanted to meet the famed colossus of the Gypsy fight circuit. "We have a proposition to put to you!" The man said. "In our camp, we have the champion Gypsy fighter of Australia and he wants to fight you for the Empire championship. If you win, you get the weapons for nothing but if our boy wins; you pay double!" Pondering for a moment to see if there was a catch in the arrangement and detecting no hint of a scam, he agreed, "Okay, I'll fight your man, even though our brothers in Canada and New Zealand might dispute our right to fight for the title!" "Right then!" The stranger said. "I'll arrange everything as soon as I can!" "Hold on just a minute!" Andreas asserted. "We have a task to perform here and walking around with cuts and bruises would only attract unwelcome attention. You have my word that the moment the weapons are returned, the fight will take place; on condition that Reuben acts as my second and the rounds are all the same duration!" The man laughed and declared as he walked away, "You won't have to worry about that Gadjo; you won't last that long!" Instantly quizzing Reuben, Andreas asked, "Who is this man I have to fight?" Reuben shrugged his shoulders, " I dunno, this is the first *I've* heard of a fighter being at the camp!" Realizing that he had just arranged to fight some unknown champion on the other side of the globe, he was aware that Lu would disapprove; although she had *not* actually forbidden him to fight before leaving, so taking that to be the green light, he felt a familiar combative thrill course through his body.

Deeming a return to bed now a waste of time and with Reuben having another day of cricket, Andreas showered, changed and visited the perennially open hotel bar for a liquid breakfast of Tolley's. Ringing the office later to acquire the name of the boat-hire company that had been engaged and now being aware of which one to avoid, he hired a taxi to Crib point. Walking along the jetty, weighing up the pros and cons of each craft, he finally found one that was suitable and looking appraisingly at the craft, he received a malevolent glare from its owner in return. Wearing an old straw hat that shielded a bulbous drinker's nose, he possessed one eye wide open, while the other drooped half-closed in a palsied attitude. "Is this boat for hire?" Andreas asked the odd looking cove. Screwing up his wizened face, the old man replied, "That's what I'm here for, son!" "Can I hire by the week?" Andreas enquired. "By the bloody year if you want!" The man answered, "As long as you pay me up front!" "That's fair enough! I'll come down tomorrow with the cash and if I get a decent discount, I'll give you a fortnight's money up front, *irrespective* of whether or not we use it for the second week and any time we don't need the boat, you can make a few bucks by rehiring it but if you tell anyone of our arrangement, I'll feed you to the sharks!" "Done!" the old man replied, "I'll knock ten dollars off the price and don't worry, I ain't likely to go telling anyone about the deal; they'd think I'd gone soft in the head!" Andreas turned to walk off the way he had come and heard the old man mutter, "Bloody Poms!"

Finding that Reuben had still not returned from what must have been another thrilling affair, Andreas opted for an early lunch of more swordfish and when lunch was over, he borrowed the local phone directory from reception to peruse the ad-section for a hotel nearer to the jetty, finally settling on the Sebel Hotel, which possessed the fillip of having a gym and swimming pool. A further ten minutes would elapse before Reuben showed face and after enduring five minutes of Reuben's synopsis of the day's play, Andreas finally interrupted him mid-sentence, "I've managed to book us into a hotel nearer the wharf and we will be moving more or less straight away!" Looking decidedly underwhelmed at the decision, having been deprived of a catnap, Reuben remarked, "I'd better have lunch then, knowing how impatient you are; the move will probably be in the next hour!"

Settling the bill, Andreas picked up his luggage and with caution having becoming second nature to them, they nonchalantly walked down the road until they had turned the corner, then hailing a passing cab, they were swiftly taken to their new quarters on the west side of the city. Entering the second floor suite, they were greeted by the glorious sight of a blue, shimmering seascape, appearing to be so close, it was easy to believe that you could just dive into it's silver ripples from the balcony. Opening the glass windbreak, Andreas could see boats at anchor, gently bobbling against the marina wall and with a puff of sea air wafting close-by, he was incapable of resisting the urge to inhale the invigorating ozone. Much freshened, he set about stowing his clothes and when that task had been acquitted, he confessed, "I purposely chose a hotel with a gym, so we can keep fit for what or whomever we may face, never dreaming how picturesque it would be!" Reuben answered, "It's certainly a beautiful view and we can have a *shufti* at the gym later but I'm afraid I didn't bring any gear!" "Me neither but there's bound to be a sports-shop in the city!" Andreas averred, "We'll pick up something suitable tomorrow!"

Ordering what had become their usual on entering the bar, Andreas warned his companion, "Make the most of this; it won't take long for them to discover our new location!" Watching an Australian Rules football match on a huge screen from the bar, Andreas noticed that the display was balanced precariously, or so it seemed, on a well-worn bracket attached to the wall and as soon as the whistle blew to announce the end of the match, he got to his feet and suggested a stroll, being surprised to perceive the television still attached to the wall. Sauntering along the promenade, with the gentle breeze blowing into their faces, Reuben was tempted by a van selling shark-meat and chips, declaring, "I think I'll try some of that on the way back!" Walking to the end of the walkway, they visited several bars lining the main road, all selling *tinnies* from the bar, prompting Andreas to speculate that a flagon of farmhouse had it beaten all ends up but Reuben drank them like there was no tomorrow. Meandering back to the hotel, Reuben *purchased* his portion of shark meat, tearing off a piece for his friend to try and finding it over-tough, Andreas was convinced that the shark would not have found *him* so indigestible. Arriving back at the hotel,

Andreas decided to go straight to bed, leaving his companion watching re-runs of the day's cricket.

Being rudely wakened in the morning by the sound of refuse-collectors noisily throwing emptied bins onto the pavements, Andreas grumbled at Reuben's apparent inability to close doors and quit his bed to close the French windows. Going to the bathroom, he turned on the shower managing after several unsuccessful attempts to get the temperature to his liking and stepping into the shower, he was immediately shocked into wakefulness by a fierce cataract that almost ripped the skin from his body. Soon becoming inured to the fierce flow however, he decided that it had been the most invigorating shower he had ever had and recounting the episode later to Reuben, he was informed that it was a power shower, apparently all the rage in America. Resolving that it would be the first item on his shopping list when they got home, he smiled broadly at the mental image of Lu screaming in fear as the fierce stream of water struck her body and was still beaming when he accompanied Reuben to the dining room. After a fish-free breakfast of scrambled egg on toast with insipid coffee, they returned to the room, donned their suits and left for the office.

15

The small doorway of the Melbourne branch of Mowll and Mowll was positioned between an estate agent's and a sports shop; thereby eliminating a lengthy search for training gear and climbing the narrow stairway, they came across three doors, none of which bore name plates but hearing the chattering of typewriters from one of the doors, they tentatively opened the portal. The cacophony suddenly ceased as if their entry had been a signal to stop work and one of the typists, appearing to be the more senior both in age and status, walked over to greet them, hand outstretched. "You must be the visitors from England!" "Yes!" Andreas replied with a smile, "We are the Poms!" Instantly becoming the subject of a mild ripple of amusement, the euphemism succeeded in breaking the ice but the click-clack of the typewriters began again, as the manager entered the room. Signalling the newcomers to enter his office, he introduced himself, "I am Steven Van der Wahl, the manager of the Melbourne branch of Mowll and Mowll!" Thrusting forward his hand, he added, "We were informed of your imminent arrival two days ago but alas, *not* the reason for your visit!" Ignoring the statement, Andreas shook his hand, finding that spite of his size, Van der Wahl's grip was limp and his hand clammy, evoking memories of McAvoy the Scotsman, from whose clutches he had been saved by Ma and Pa's timely intervention. Playing the silent partner role to perfection, Reuben left the talking to Andreas but with eyes that were constantly on the move, he transferred mental images to his brain for future reference. Apart from an overturned rubbish bin, the contents of which were strewn across a small section of the room, there was little in the way of clues for either of them to form an idea of his character. The room was virtually devoid of fittings, with a filing cabinet, two chairs and a desk being the only items of furniture. The mandatory phone and complimentary paraphernalia from a Sydney haulage company called Dexter, adorned the desk but pointedly there were *no* family photographs anywhere. Finally replying to the manager's heavily weighted question, Andreas informed him that they were there on a learning curve but having been informed of the leviathan swimming around in the Bass Strait, they hoped that a fair sized chunk of their time in *Oz* would be spent fishing. Van der Wahl's body language signalled relief on hearing of their plans and being more relaxed and self-assured, he smiled, "Feel free to ask about *anything* you don't understand; my staff will assist you in any way that they can, as long you do not distract them from their work!" Promising that they would try not to be too much trouble, Andreas added, "We *would* however like to learn how you attain the high level of efficiency that this branch is reputed to possess!" Van der Wahl smiled obsequiously, "*I* claim the credit for that; I have certain rules and standards that I make sure are *strictly* adhered to!" Moving towards the door, he mentioned that he had been informed of their change of hotel, "Was it not up to your expectations?" "It was fine!" Andreas replied, "We just wanted somewhere nearer the dock!" With the short interview apparently at an end, Van der Wahl ushered them ino the outer office, "I'd be obliged if you could give my secretary details of where you are now staying!" "Of course!" Andreas responded. "I'll do that before we leave today!"

Rejoining the fray in time for the mid-morning break, Reuben was made aware of the route to the toilet, while Andreas accepted an offer of coffee from one of the young typists and returning with refreshments, she said, "I knew your mother!" Andreas said, "Perhaps we could meet and discuss that fact over a drink?" Answering with a smile, she replied, "I am Jennifer Ellis; Jen to my friends and discussing issues in a more relaxed setting, is an ideal way to get acquainted. I know a bar that is loud but discreet and only a stone's throw from here!" Andreas answered, "I am Andreas, my associate is Reuben and we'd like to get started on this matter as soon as possible, so if it's convenient, could we meet this evening?" "That would be fine!" She asserted and arranging to meet them in the Shakespeare Bars between four thirty and five, she returned to her typewriter. Hearing only the last few seconds of the conversation, Reuben remarked, "It doesn't take *you* long to get fixed up!" Andreas smiled, "I'll explain later!"

Lunchtime arrived and having learned nothing of any use to their cause, Andreas suggested adjourning to the sports shop to purchase training gear, "We *must* keep up our fitness levels, in the end it could give us an edge over God only knows whom or what we may encounter!" Reuben added with a grin, "There is also your fight for the Empire championship to be taken into account!" Andreas scowled and waiting to be served, he asked, "Did you see anything of any interest in his office?" Reuben answered, "No family pictures but there was stuff from a haulage firm in Sydney on the desk but more importantly he somehow knows of the hotel change!" "Bearing out my early impression that he is not to be trusted!" Andreas replied, "The girl we are meeting later is the one that alerted the brothers to the missing money and I'll leave it to you to see if she can shed some light on the haulage firm. I want to know *who* is running the business and their history with the firm; if it's *kosher*, they can be eliminated from the investigation!" Placing his basket on the counter, Andreas remarked, "Why can't Britain have this method of purchasing goods? We're always ten years behind the rest of the world!" Reuben replied, "Never mind Andreas; we'll soon be in the eighties; maybe things will change *then!*" Purchasing sandwiches from a newspaper kiosk they sat on a park bench to eat, noticing the sign for the Shakespeare Bars just across the way.

With the *afternoon* proving equally as unproductive as the morning, they ambled along the road towards the Shakespeare Bars, employing the method of taking turns at looking in shop windows, to make certain, by way of mirrored images, that they were not being followed. Entering the bar, Andreas, ordered two Tolley's and cokes with ice, being miffed at being charged for the cubes of frozen water. Noticing Jen sitting alone at a table against the wall, they walked across and getting down to brass tacks right away, she advanced the theory that the manager and at *least* one other were possibly involved, "His secretary is the likely *other one* as they are romantically involved, with almost anyone of the others being the possible third culprit!" Getting to his feet, Andreas said, "While I'm re-charging our glasses, Reuben has a few questions that he thinks may hopefully give us a clue to what has been going on!"

Reuben leaned in closer, "I noticed the complimentary items from a haulage company called Dexter on his desk; do you have any information on the company?" Shaking her head Jen replied, "I've seen their stuff about the place but I know nothing about the company?" "If you can turn up *anything* about the company and in particular, its connection to the firm, it *could* help our mission!" He commented, "I couldn't help noticing that there were no family photographs in his office; does he *have* family?" "There used to be a wedding photograph on his desk but it disappeared when he started knocking around with his secretary Laura. I don't *think* he has children but it should be simple enough to find out!" Overhearing the last sentence as he walked back to the table with drinks, Andreas asserted, "You've already done enough by alerting us to the problem of the missing money and Mr Bailey instructed me that I was *not* to jeopardise your position!" Jen smiled, "Mowll and Mowll pay me well for what I do!" Andreas replied, "Admirable sentiments but you will *not* take unnecessary risks and *that* is an order!" Promising to be careful, she suggested, "The only *possible* cause for concern is the rumours about girls disappearing in the past and never being heard of again but whether there is any truth to the stories; who knows!" "Right, that's it then!" Andreas ordered, "I absolutely forbid you to participate further in this matter; you will leave *everything* to us!" Seeking to mediate in the issue, Reuben interrupted, "Is there somewhere handy we can get a decent meal, I'm starving?" "There's a nice restaurant a hundred yards from here that we can try!" Jen answered and having one more drink before leaving, they walked the short distance to her choice of eatery. The food was tasty and well prepared but with fish once more the basis of the main course; the meal contributed little to the genial bonhomie enjoyed by the new friendship but Tolley's, added to the earlier libation, brought an instant animated sparkle to Jen's dark brown eyes, with her ready smile completely eradicating all thoughts of the precarious mission they were about. Both boys were disappointed when she decided to call it a day and escorting her to the waiting cab, they were rewarded with a kiss that left a trace of her perfume on both their cheeks and as they returned her wave from the taxi, Andreas declared, "I've never before met a woman, to whom I took to quite so readily!" Agreeing with his friend's approbation, Reuben remarked light-heartedly, "I think we'll take her back with us!" With the pavement being less busy, they decided to visit the wharf to see the old man and feeling the need for caution, they hired a cab from the rank furthest away from the office.

The wind was a little fresher along the jetty and buttoning up their flimsy cheesecloth shirts in a vain effort to keep the breeze at bay, they reached the hoarding declaring the location to be Old Ned's Boats and with Ned standing on his boat arms akimbo, he looked Reuben up and down and asserted, "Huh, more bloody *didicoi* Poms!" Andreas muttered impatiently, "We've come to tell you that we will using the boat early tomorrow morning!" Climbing up the iron ladder, Ned stepped onto the wharf and handing over the keys, he remarked, "If you think I'm getting out of my bed, to ferry you out there and watch you wasting a day catching bugger all, you've got another think coming!" Massaging his arms to coax warmth into his body, Andreas told Ned, "After today the boat will only be used by us, as we will be using it at odd times during the day and night and *have* to know that it will be there when we need it; I'll be here on Sunday to let you know definitely if we will need it for the second week!" Watching the young men walk away, old Ned took off his hat, scratched his head and remarked, "Bloody Poms!" On the way back to the hotel, Andreas forewarned Reuben not to talk openly in the room, "I had to allay suspicion by giving our new address, so we may have had a visitor already!" Reuben suggested, "Perhaps it might be a good idea to be careful what we say in taxis too!" Nodding in agreement, Andreas remarked, "We should maybe think about getting a car; it would certainly be more convenient!" Reuben agreed, "This organization are so deeply entrenched, it's unlikely our task will be resolved any time soon and a car *would* be ideal for running back and forth to the camp!" With another problem added to the list of things to resolve, they walked back to the Sebel to ready themselves for the task ahead.

Walking to the wharf in the wee hours, the lads were looking forward to a few hours fishing and starting up the motor, they headed out into Prince Philip Bay, with the powerful Chaparral 300 cutting through the waves like a hot knife through butter. "Did you notice the echo *sounder* we have on board?" Reuben asked. "No!" Andreas replied, "Does it tell you where the biggest fish are?" Smiling patronisingly Reuben replied, "Kind of I suppose; it locates wrecked ships by bouncing sound waves and where there are wrecks, there are fish; there are also nets in the cabin if you get tired of casting your rod!" Dropping anchor when the sounder had located a fair sized wreck, they set up the hired, heavy-duty rods and Reuben pointed out a chart that had been pinned to the cabin wall, depicting all the different species of fish, making it easy to identify anything they were fortunate enough to catch. With the wind thankfully having abated, the craft bobbled gently on the calm sea and with the gentle rhythmic motion making Andreas nauseous, he pulled out a hip flask from his pocket and took a long, hard slug of Tolley's. Sensing his friend's discomfort, Reuben grinned and shouted, "First time in a boat then?" Andreas could not answer, being afraid of splattering the deck with the contents of his insides but after a short while, being unable contain it any longer, he hung his head over the side of the boat. Hearing Reuben's raucous laughter throughout the ordeal did not help the situation but when the bell at the end of Andreas's rod began to ring, his delicate stomach was forgotten as he reeled in his first of many fish.

Deciding that they had caught more than enough after three hours, they packed away the rods and weighed anchor, with Andreas informing his comrade, "We won't go back just yet; we've got *plenty* of time and I want to go to Bass Strait to see the sharks!" A mile further on, they anchored once more and picking up handfuls of the smaller fish, Andreas hurled them in an arc across a wide area of the briny; within minutes the sea was alive with a moderate-sized shoal of writhing great white sharks. "Is there a point to all this?" Reuben asked timorously. Andreas asserted grimly, "They may come in handy for something I have in mind!" With no further explanation forthcoming or deemed necessary, Reuben's face paled at the thought of something or *someone* being fed to the beasts. Andreas laughed and shouted, "Hey, you lot. This is the bastard that ate your brother last night!" The shouting appeared to incite the denizens of the deep even more and it became Andreas's turn to laugh as Reuben's face completely drained of colour. Weighing anchor for the second time that morning, they headed homeward and with Andreas still mocking Reuben's pallor, they pulled up at pier 35 to fill up with a hundred gallons of eighty-seven octane gas. When the task had been completed, they coasted across to where they had picked up the *Bonnie Prince* and Andreas declared, "I don't know about you but I could do with a shower before we do anything else!" Carrying the catch to the grateful hotel chef, they returned to the room and showered until the stench of fish had been expunged completely. Within half an hour they were waiting outside for a cab to take them to the office; Andreas remarked as the taxi pulled up, "Come on; let's see what Jen's been up to!"

16

Taking a cab to the city, they began discussing their new companion, "I'm really looking forward to seeing her again!" Reuben announced, "I feel as if I've known her all my life!" "Easy on the eyes too!" Andreas suggested with a wink and reaching the outskirts of the city, the cab had to stop to let an ambulance and police car overtake. "That doesn't look good!" The cabbie remarked, "If there's a crash ahead, there's sure to be delays!" That statement turned out to be an accurate assessment, with whatever the incident had been, shaving a precious hour of investigative time from their quest. Van der Wahl's secretary, Laura, greeted them at the top of the stairs when they finally arrived, "How did the fishing go?" "It went very well thanks!" Andreas replied. "We caught loads of trevally, for which the kitchen staff were extremely grateful and now we know exactly what we will be having for dinner this evening!" Pulling a face, she shuddered, "Ugh, I can't stand the things, slimy creatures with expressionless eyes!" *hmm a bit like your bloody boyfriend* Andreas thought.

Walking into the main office, Andreas peered over Jen's shoulder, catching the faintest smell of her delicate perfume and a glimpse of an expansive cleavage, that under different circumstances he would have welcomed, discretion gained the upper hand, guiding him to Van der Wahl's office. Entering the office, he asked, "Do any of our customers ever call here in person?" The manager looked puzzled, "Why do you ask?" "It's nothing important!" Andreas remarked, "I'm just intrigued by the haulage firm Dexter; all the stationery and calendars in the office advertise their wares, yet nobody seems to know anything about them and you *did* tell me to ask if there was anything you could help with!" Panic was plainly written all over his face but recovering his equilibrium, he covered up quickly, "Our business is conducted solely by phone, so there is no *need* for customers to call here and I'm sure that if you look more carefully, you would find stationery from other firms somewhere around. Now if there's nothing else, I have important work to attend to!" Being summarily dismissed, Andreas knew that his arrow had hit the mark and even if it was not *Dexter* responsible for the appropriation of funds, it was plain that at least one of the firms was involved and that Van der Wahl was in it up to his neck.

Andreas told Reuben and Jen later in the day, "We now have a possible suspect for being the head of the organization; are there any grounds for putting anyone else in the frame, other than Laura?" "Not really!" Jen replied "It's just a feeling I have that the scheme would need three to make it work!" Reuben suggested, "It should be a simple matter to confront the pair, have them arrested and get back home pronto!" "You're forgetting one important thing!" Andreas replied, "We have to nab the whole bunch and like Jen, I refuse to believe that there are just two involved and at least one of the firms is culpable too. On the surface it would appear that some kind of laundering has been taking place and if that is so, we still have to retrieve what we can of the stolen money; so you see Reuben, there is *still* plenty to keep us occupied!"

At the end of another working day, they decided to give a second try to the restaurant where they had dined the previous evening; hoping to get something other than fish. Discovering however that they had arrived a little too late for meat and with only trevally being left on the menu, the irony of the situation was not lost on them. The fish and chips merely sufficed but washed down once more with an ocean of finest Tolley's brandy, the offering was despatched with relish. At evening's end, she asked if they wanted to share the taxi to save them having to queue for another cab and jumping into the rear of the car, the pair took advantage of the offer. Dropping Jen off at her apartment block in Charles Street, Andreas noticed that the door had been jammed open with a brick and deciding that the act was probably a regular custom, he cast it from his mind. Arriving back at the Sebel, they changed their clothes and after a brisk walk, they were once more aboard the *Bonny Prince*, relieved to discover that the neap tide had heralded a substantial drop in the wind. Their craft was a powerful machine but in gale force winds it was as likely as any other small vessel to flip over; an experience they would rather forego, with monster fish lurking beneath the waves waiting for a ready meal. With the aid of the sounder, they dropped anchor in the same area as they had fished the previous morning, with the subject of Jen inevitably cropping up as soon as they had dropped anchor. Andreas remarked, "It's a bloody good job I'm married, or I would definitely be trying my luck!" "I have to say that if it weren't for Claire!" Reuben suggested, "I would also be sorely tempted; she certainly ticks all *my* boxes!" Andreas laughed, "Claire would put you in bloody hospital if she caught you two-timing!"

One hour later, after reeling in yet another *trace* full of trevally, Andreas declared, "This is hardly what you would call sport; it's too bloody easy; come on let's share the spoils with my pets!" Weighing anchor, they headed for Bass Strait and Reuben complained, "I'm really not comfortable about keep coming out here!" "I want to see them looking for food every time they hear our engine!" Andreas answered ominously. Within minutes of Andreas throwing handfuls of trevally across the water, the beasts were dining and weighing anchor after witnessing the banquet, they headed for pier 35, with one or two great whites following in expectation. Andreas looked at his watch, "We'll have to make haste Reuben, we're running a little late!" Tying up to the bollard, the remaining fish were once more thrown into a sack and carried swiftly to the kitchen, ready for consumption later in the day. Showering and making ready for the office, they checked that every door in the apartment was closed, before going downstairs to await a taxi. Standing at the hotel door, they sheltered from the sun until the arrival of the cab and ten minutes into the journey, Andreas remarked that unlike the previous day, the road appeared to be hazard-free, "Who knows; we could actually be on time!"

Arriving early, they noticed Jen's absence right away and Andreas mentioned her non-appearance to Pauline the senior typist; nodding philosophically she rsponded, "Steve caught Jen going through files in his office and sacked her on the spot; even though a suspension would have been the more appropriate option; so now we have to work one short until he gets someone new!" Continuing her harangue, she dropped a bombshell, "This isn't the first time this kind of incident has arisen and it causes havoc in the office!" Remembering Jen's tale of missing girls, Andreas was all ears, "Oh, you've had to work short-handed before?" She replied, "Well, thankfully it doesn't happen too often but yes, it *has* happened in the past!" Andreas frowned, "What happens to the girls he fires? Do they get employment elsewhere, or does he block their re-employment?" "I never really thought about it, to tell the truth!" She replied, "We've certainly never heard of them again but then Melbourne *is* a big city!" Andreas did not like the sound of the news and walking across to Van der Wahl's office, he was just about to enter, when Pauline called out, "Nobody's allowed in his office when he's out!" Andreas smiled, "I left my rather expensive pen in there yesterday, I'm sure he won't mind me retrieving it!" Before she could protest further, he walked into the shuttered office, closed the door and moving quickly to the filing cabinet, he opened the drawer labelled "D–H". Quickly rifling through the drawer, he found no file for Dexter but still believing that they *were* connected to the firm somehow, he took his pen from his inside pocket and waved it as he re-entered the room, "It was underneath his desk!" He lied with a smile.

Spending the remainder of the morning odd-jobbing for the girls, he tried to prise information about the fate of other girls who had been dismissed but being frustrated by his failure to discover *anything*, he left the building with Reuben and headed for the Shakespeare Bars to see if Jen had uncovered anything before getting caught. An hours wait later and fearing the worst, Reuben remarked, "I don't want to be alarmist but I think we're wasting our time here!" Andreas concurred, "You could be right; we'll try again later and if she's not here, we'll try the restaurant but sadly it's not looking good. I'll look in the directory to see if I can find her telephone number!" Noticing the bathroom door lying wide open when they returned to the hotel, alerted Andreas to the fact that they'd had a visitor; silently checking luggage and clothes, they found nothing untoward and suspecting that a bug had been planted, their quick search of the room also proved fruitless.

Finding Jen's number and ominously getting no reply from his call, Andreas recommended immediate action, "Come on Reuben, food can wait; we'd better get to her apartment right away. If she *isn't* there, we'll assume the worst and search the place to see if anything can be learned!" Walking down the road, they hailed a cab and arriving at Charles Street, they found the communal door still jammed open, enabling them to gain access to the second-floor flat. Banging on the door and getting no response, Reuben turned the handle, "It's locked!" He declared inserting his metal comb into the locking mechanism and putting his shoulder to the door, he felt the lever begin to move; gradually applying more pressure, the door suddenly gave way, propelling him and a few slivers of paint into the room. Andreas began the search immediately, while Reuben scooped up the debris from the break-in onto a sheet of paper and flushed the small package down the toilet. There were no visible signs of the flat having been previously ransacked, so they were able to search the apartment methodically and Reuben came up trumps almost straight away, finding a dossier containing the personal details of every member of staff. Caching the file into his inside pocket, Andreas was about to give up searching for further items of interest, when he came across a diary in her underwear drawer and scanning the journal quickly, he noted entries with dates and times by the sides of them. Motioning to Reuben with a nod towards the door that it was time to leave, they checked that no tell-tale signs of their presence remained and hastily quit the building.

Having to wait five minutes longer for a cab than it had taken to locate and search the flat, Andreas remarked tetchily, "It really *would* have been better to have hired a car!" Finally managing to wave down a cab, he added as he climbed in the rear seat, "In view of what we suspect has happened to Jen and the other girls, this mission is certain to involve more violence! We'll try to learn a little more from the girls; especially the older one, who appears to have been there the longest; I don't *think* she's involved although we can't be sure of *anything* at the moment. Maybe your family can turn up something about Dexter; if we'd thought to ask them in the first place, Jen might still be around!" Reuben asked, "Do you believe the Dexter outfit *are* the culprits?" "We have nobody else in the frame at this point!" Andreas replied, "I have to say that sadly it looks as if Jen has gone the way of the other girls!" Grim faced, Andreas, added, "If it did turn out to be the worst scenario, this affair's aim would not just be about retrieving stolen money; it would be a mission of revenge, not *just* for Jen, of whom we had grown very fond but the other poor wretches too. Viv *told* me not to compromise Jen's position here and I will have failed both her and him if she *has* lost her life and someone will pay dearly for *that*. From this moment on there will be no more pussy-footing around and being sure that Van der Wahl is at least a part of the gang, I'll see what I can drag out of him *and* his lady friend!"

* * *

At that same moment the two young friends were part of a subject, under discussion between Steve and Laura. "What do you make of our visitors?" Steve asked. "They seem harmless enough!" Laura answered, "All they seem to do is go fishing and the questions they ask are all work-related, so I don't see that we have anything to worry about!" After pausing for a moment, she added, "Cannon is going to ruin everything with his fetish for slaughtering young women. Somewhere along the line, a friend or relative is going to start asking questions!" Steve sighed wearily. "We should never have got involved in this thing in the first place but it's too late to back out now and I fear for *our* safety if we *don't* pass on information; the best thing to do is just keep our mouths shut and after all, we get well paid for very little participation!"

* * *

Not being privy to that conversation however, Andreas and Reuben were on the point of finishing off yet another helping of trevally and pushing his empty plate to one side, Reuben suggested as he awaited for a cab to take him to the gypsy camp, "I'll see that the staff list gets to the camp, in case there are any names they recognize!" Deciding to return to the room, Andreas stepped from the lift and noticing a maid at the end of the corridor, putting laundered sheets into a cupboard, he had a sudden brainwave. Taking a twenty-dollar note from his wallet, he walked along the corridor and approached the girl, "Have any new staff been taken on in the last two days?" She replied, "I'm afraid that giving information of hotel business is strictly forbidden and I don't want to lose my job!" Andreas persisted, "Something valuable has been taken from my room, which I will have to report for insurance purposes and although I'm convinced of your honesty, you *would* naturally be one of the main suspects but if I were able to handle the matter myself, no one else would have to get involved *and* you would have a twenty in your purse!" Hesitating for a moment, she replied, "I saw a man come out of your room and run hell for leather round the corner!" As Andreas handed over the note he promised, "There'll be another twenty if you can tell me of staff changes!" With fear being etched on her expansive face, she eyed the note and nervously stuttering she gave him favourable news, "The housekeeper was replaced yesterday but that's all sir!" Handing over the note, Andreas asked, "Do you know why he or she was replaced?" "No-one's got a clue!" She replied, "I arrived for work this morning and found that we had a new housekeeper!" Andreas probed further, "Is he a good housekeeper?" "If you'll excuse me saying so sir, he doesn't seem to know his arse from his elbow and he's *not* a nice feller at all!" She responded animatedly, "All the girls are frightened witless of him, including me!" "A bit of a bully eh? Will you let me know if there are more changes or if you see anyone hanging around outside my room? There would be more money in it for useful information!" Her face lit up, "Don't worry sir; I'll keep my eye out!" Andreas smiled, "Don't worry about getting into trouble; this is *strictly* between you and I!" Smiling, she returned to her chores and Andreas went to his room to get ready for his first session in the gymnasium.

Walking towards the gym, he was looking forward to a spot of light training, he stopped briefly to ask the receptionist the whereabouts of the housekeeper's office and deciding to visit the man later, he continued on his way to the gym. With his work-out becoming a punishing hour's slog, the refreshing cold shower after, soon revived his aching body and walking back to the room, he found Reuben lying on his bed reading the local newspaper. Motioning Reuben into the corridor, Andreas asked, "Did they agree to help?" "Yeah, they're only too willing to help in any way they can and will contact me as soon as they have anything for us!" Reuben replied, "Here's a copy of the file I made before handing over the original!" Remembering his conversation with the maid, he asked, "Did you see the maid in the corridor when you went out earlier?" "No; has she disappeared too?" "No!" Andreas said impatiently. "I've put her on the payroll and she informed me that she saw a man coming out of our room, so taking you out of the equation, we've had another visitor!" Re-entering the room, Reuben threw the rolled-up newspaper onto his bed saying, "I'm going to have a quick shower and get changed; are we fishing tomorrow morning?" Andreas replied, "Yes and if we leave early enough, we can catch the girls before they start work!" Picking up the newspaper and managing with a huge effort, to tear his eyes from the semi-naked young woman on page three, he spotted a four-line snippet at the bottom of the page, the report telling of an unidentified female with an estimated age of mid to late twenties being found floating face down in the Yarra the previous day. Reuben emerged from the bathroom with a towel wrapped around his middle and showing him the article, Andreas shrugged resignedly and went downstairs to see the new housekeeper.

Finding him seated behind his desk, Andreas reported the fake theft of a gold chain, "Going back to my quarters from the gym, I saw someone coming out of my room and run down the corridor; it all happened so quickly that I was unable to give chase and when I searched my things, I found a gold necklace missing!" The housekeeper replied, "It must have been one of the maids changing towels!" Andreas persisted. "When I entered the room, a door was lying open that I know for certain was closed before going out and the person I saw was a man; definitely not a maid changing towels!" The housekeeper replied tetchily, "I'll investigate the matter tomorrow when all the staff are here!" Turning to leave, Andreas noticed a hi-fi receiver system behind the door and smiling, he thought, *now that could prove useful for relaying false information.* Going directly to the bar, he ordered two Tolley's and sat back to await Reuben's arrival. Showing up ten minutes later, Reuben complained that the ice in the drink had almost melted but ignoring the whinge, Andreas immediately addressed the probability of Jen being the young woman in the newspaper article, "I think we have to face facts Reuben, our Jen is almost certainly dead!" Adding menacingly, "We'd better start making things happen before someone else disappears!"

17

The alarm clock rang out stridently the following morning and staggering to the bathroom, he stood under the fierce, chilling spray, in an effort to de-clutter his mind, ready for the task ahead. Managing to waken Reuben at the third attempt and with his friend opting not to shower or shave, they arrived at the quay in good time. The early-morning silence was shattered by the raucous engine of the Bonny Prince and conducting a thorough search of the boat to determine that everything was *kushti*, Andreas declared, "I feel totally relaxed when I'm down here; nothing to worry about but catching fish and feeding my pets!" Reuben pulled a face and guiding the craft into Prince Philip Bay, he remarked, "Do we *have* to visit Bass Strait again, they give me the creeps!" Andreas laughed at his friend's aversion to the rapacious fish, "We *will* be feeding the buggers but I promise we won't stay long, I wanna go to Mowll and Mowll to see if we can stir something up; this is all going too slow for me?" "Hallelujah to that!" Reuben replied, turning on the echo-sounder, "I'll organise a suitable car while we're there, so I can visit the camp to see if they've turned up trumps on the staff list!" "Good idea!" Andreas affirmed and looking grimly at his friend, he asked, "I hope you're aware of what we will almost certainly have to do?" "I was aware of that from the outset!" Reuben answered, "Don't worry, I'll be ready when the time comes!" "I'm sure you will!" Andreas responded, "That's why you were asked along!"

Andreas was looking forward to working a spot near the place they had been the previous two mornings and finding the site teeming with trevally as well as a few good-sized Oz salmon, they were sure of more free meals. At Andreas's insistence and despite Reuben's unwillingness to visit the sharks, the good-sized haul enabled them to reach Bass Strait ahead of schedule. "God knows *why* you have to keep coming out here!" Reuben griped, "There are two reasons!" Andreas replied, "These much-maligned creatures are natural disposal units *and* I don't want fuel consumption being called into question should someone happen to disappear!" Being somewhat disturbed at learning what he suspected anyway, Reuben said no more on the subject for the remainder of the trip and once the now semi-domesticated animals had gorged on what appeared to be half of the catch, Andreas guided the boat to pier 35. Calling to the boys as they filled the craft with high octane, he asked, "Don't you blokes ever get bored?" "Hell no, we've loads to do!" Came the reply, "We've got a dartboard, oven *and* a television, so with filling up boats between chores too; we're kept too busy to get bored!" Returning to the wharf, they made their way back to the hotel kitchen with a gunny full of fish and after a shower and a change of clothes, they went to the door to wait for the taxi. Andreas said, "I'm going to ruffle Van der Wahl's feathers by searching through his files and if you can sort out a hire car in the meantime, this will be the last time we have to stand outside waiting for cabs. It'll be lunchtime by the time we get to the office, so there *shouldn't* be anyone around to see what I'm doing; if I get the information I'm after, I'll assume command of the place and send them all home for the day!"

Van der Wahl and Laura were alone in their offices when Andreas arrived and walking boldly into Steve's office, he found the manager sitting at his desk reading a newspaper. Looking startled Steve growled, "Isn't it usual to wait until you are invited before entering; that's the way we do things here!" Ignoring the remark, Andreas walked over to the filing cabinet and began removing files, "I'm going to go through the files!" "The hell you will!" Steve retorted, rising from his chair, "Get your Pom arse out of here and piss off back to wherever it is you came from!" Feeling that enough time had been wasted, Andreas decided that a more direct approach was called for and placing the files on the desk top, he felled Steve with a totally unexpected blow to the solar plexus. Using the desk as a crutch to lift himself from the floor, Steve drew himself to his full height, "Just who the *hell* do you think you are?" Andreas replied, "Actually I'm your boss and here to investigate the theft of money from customers' accounts, so sit on that chair and keep your mouth shut!" Steve suddenly launched an attack but a roundhouse kick to the chin sent him flying into the corner beside the filing cabinet and standing menacingly over him, Andreas snarled, "I've a few more tricks up my sleeve that I am only too willing to implement!" Steve meekly picked himself up and slumped down onto the chair and noticing Laura's alarmed face at the adjoining window, Andreas shuttered all the windows, yanked the phone from the socket, locked the office door and strode purposefully to her office, "Do *not* make a fuss or your boyfriend will suffer!" Returning to her partner, he worked his way methodically through the files; managing to reach the last dossier fairly quickly, he found nothing connected the firm to Dexter. Throwing the file angrily across the desk, he demanded, "Dexter have a connection to this office and I want to know why there is no file for them here?" "We have no customers called Dexter!" Steve answered blandly. Andreas smiled, "We've had this conversation before but this time I want the truth!" Noticing a shadow on the blind, he opened the door, finding Reuben about to enter the office and ushering him back into the main office, Andreas told him that with the girls returning soon, the interrogation would have to be conducted away from prying eyes a*nd I know just the place*, he thought, "I hope you managed to get a car; I want to interrogate these two at the encampment and being convinced there is at least one other office member concerned in this affair, *that person's* identity will have to be learned, to prevent them spilling the beans!" Reuben commented, "It's a bloody good job I did get a car then!" Andreas remarked, "Laura is the weak link, so I'll concentrate on her and if I get what I'm after, I'll be able to tell the girls that we are in charge and send them home for the remainder of the day!" Adding with a grin, "Thus eliminating the problem of getting this pair into the car!" Entering Laura's door he sat on her desk and demanded the name of the other staff member involved in the scam, "Before you answer, it's only fair to tell you that if you do not give me the name of the person directly above you *and* that of the other person involved in all this; I will kill both of you without a second thought. However, give me the information I seek and you both walk out of here unharmed!" Looking down at the floor, she began to cry and softening the tone of his voice, he entreated, "The name of the office member involved will suffice for starters!" Still looking at the floor, she declared, "They'd kill me if I tell you *anything*!" Feeling that he was at least getting *somewhere*, Andreas pushed her further, "*One* name will be enough!" Her pleading eyes looked up and for a second he almost weakened; until Jen and the other unfortunates' fate came to mind and deeming it vital that the identity of other member of the circle was learned, he resolutely stuck to his guns, until finally, after a half hour, she conceded defeat, revealing the name that he had sought. The girls had already gathered in the middle of the outer office, aware that *something* was afoot, so Andreas entered the main office to address the assembled girls. "Steve and Laura have both been dismissed for a major misdemeanour!" He announced, "Reuben and I are now in charge but don't worry, *nothing* will change dramatically as a result of this and I've decided that as a goodwill gesture, you can all have the rest of the day off; *with pay!*" Looking puzzled but happy, the girls began to troop out of the office but stopping Christina, who was walking in the middle of a cluster of chattering typists, Andreas took her aside "Excuse me, Miss Beacham, can I have a word in the office before you leave?"

Asking the startled young typist to be seated, Andreas looked her stonily in the eye, "The three of you have been rumbled!" He snarled, "I will give you the same options I gave the other two; I can put it in the hands of the police, or release you and let it be known that you gave me information. You can make the situation a whole lot easier on yourself but giving me information will enable you to walk away scot-free; the choice is yours!" Looking at her sternly, he asked, "I want the identity of the person directly above the three of you *and* where the money is being laundered to; just two snippets of information and you walk out of here unharmed. However if the name you give me is different from the one given by your accomplices, I will throw you to the dogs!" Answering tearfully, she replied, "I don't know anything; I just do as I am told!" Pausing for effect, Andreas snapped back in reply, "There will be no more chances if you continue to lie!" She looked from the floor to his face and finding no pity, she tearfully admitted, "I pass on orders and information, as well as paying out money to Steve and Laura!" Having a feeling that something was not ringing true about her role in the organization, Andreas quizzed her further, "If that's so, from whom do *you* receive orders and to where the money has been spirited away!" Crying even more loudly, she blurted out, "The money has been invested in a drugs racket!" Andreas snapped, "The identity of your immediate superior?" She looked up at him with pleading eyes, "I can't tell you; he will kill me!" "I need that name before I can let you go!" Andreas averred and muttering between sobs, she revealed, "His name is Johnny Cannon and that's *all* I know!" Andreas reassured her, "For the time being, you will remain with the others!"

Calling in Reuben to babysit Christina, he returned to the office to confront her two cohorts and standing menacingly in front of the pair, he commented, "I have the name of the man directly above you but I need you to confirm his identity. If you give me a name other than that given to me by Miss Beacham, I will let you go and let it be known that you gave me information; I'm sure the housekeeper at our hotel would be only too happy to pass on a message!" A look of stark fear reaffirmed Andreas's suspicion of the housekeeper's involvement and their apparent dread of the housekeeper could prove useful in the future. Van der Wahl blurted out, "Seeing that you appear to know his name already, it will serve no purpose to lie; it's Johnny Cannon!" With the name being corroborated, Andreas believed that this discovery would open up other avenues in their pursuit of what they now knew to be a drugs cartel and still being unconvinced of Christina's apparently minor role, he realized that taking her to the camp too, would give him the opportunity of uncovering her *real* position in the organization. *A humble typist seems such an odd choice for the roles she performs,* he thought, *she has to be more important.*

Continuing his interrogation of Van der Wahl, he asked, "How did you become involved with this organization?" Steve answered, "You'll learn nothing more from us that you don't already know!" Andreas smiled, "I will throw both of you to the housekeeper if you don't tell me *everything* about your involvement!" They both visibly paled once more but noticing that Laura was the more frightened of the two, Andreas immediately focussed his attention on her. "I want to know everything; I'm sure that you're aware of the consequences if you don't comply!" Laura looked at her partner with something akin to scorn as she began the narrative, "Steve went to jail for embezzlement in Sydney and as soon as he was released, he came to Melbourne and thanks to forged references, was appointed manager here!" She paused to throw another withering glare in his direction, "Quite by chance, he bumped into Johnny Cannon, who was a former cellmate and after a few drinks, this idiot couldn't resist the temptation of boasting about his ingenuity in obtaining his present post with forged references and that he was once again, helping himself to clients' money. Cannon saw the opportunity for making use of what he had learned and informed his bosses of everything that was going on. One evening when we were relaxing at home, we received an unexpected visit from Cannon with one of his equally odious friends and by the end of the visit, we'd been blackmailed into stealing even larger amounts, only discovering too late that the embezzled cash was being used to finance drug smuggling!" Because the admission had come from Laura, he was more prepared to believe the tale and some of it did actually tally with what he'd learned from Christina but Laura let slip another possible lead, "Please don't let it be known about the information I've given to you; Cannon is a really nasty piece of work, especially where women are concerned!" Andreas thought bleakly, *I think we may have stumbled on the identity of the women' assassin and the reason why Laura was so scared.*

18

With the captives having been trussed up safely in the rear of the car, Reuben dropped his friend at the hotel and headed for the gypsy camp; leaving Andreas to shower and change into more suitable clothing. Closing the room door, he crept down-stairs and managing to sneak past the receptionist without being seen, he walked quickly to the housekeeper's office; resolving to employ the same direct methods that had reaped such rich rewards with Van der Wahl. With that thought in mind, he strode single-mindedly into the room and delivering a savage punch to the housekeeper's mid-section, he rendered him incapable of crying out for help. Ripping out the cable from the hi-fi system, he tethered the man's hands behind him, then making himself comfortable in the vacant chair, Andreas idly picked up an industrial staple gun lying on the desktop and drawled, "I'm going to ask you a couple of questions that require truthful answers; if you lie or refuse to give information, I will use the long, thick staples in this gun to pin you to the desk!" Ignoring his protestations of innocence, Andreas demanded, "Where I can find Johnny Cannon and what is the name of your immediate superior?" Reacting at the mention of the name, the housekeeper covered the slip quickly, "I don't *know* anyone of that name and even if I did, I still wouldn't tell you anything!" Picking him up, Andreas dragged him over to the desk by his hair and grabbing a few sheets of A4 paper, he crammed them tightly into the housekeeper's mouth, "That will stop you from screaming but feel free to nod your head whenever you feel ready to talk!" Realizing after a pause that the man was not going to talk without coercion, Andreas laid the man's head on the desk and picking up the stapler, he snarled, "If you are pinned to the desk, you will be *unable* to nod and taking that as a signal that you are still disinclined to talk, I will shoot staples into more intimate parts of your anatomy!" Flattening the man's head against the desk, Andreas pressed the stapler against the man's ear and asserted, "You have one last chance!" When no nod of the head was forthcoming, Andreas fired a staple into his ear, swiftly followed by three more strategically placed fasteners and being confident that his ear would be ripped to shreds if he struggled, Andreas walked towards the door, "I'll leave you for a while to evaluate your position and I hope for your sake that you will be in a more communicative mood when I return!" Turning out the light, he locked the door, pocketed the key and making his way to the restaurant to order lunch, again courtesy of the hotel, he decided that fishing would definitely be taking place later.

Returning to the apartment after lunch, he decided to search for where a bug could have been hidden and after searching almost every place he could think of, he was on the verge of giving up the ghost but with his gaze falling upon the air-conditioning unit on his last scan from the centre of the room, a light came on in his head. Unplugging the unit, he unscrewed the cover and finding the bug immediately when the back of his hand brushed against the gadget, he detached the object, crushed it with the heel of his foot and threw it into the waste bin. Reuben soon arrived from the camp with news, "Ronaldo, the head of the tribe, informed me that Cannon is back in Melbourne somewhere, suggesting that a man of his high profile, should not be too hard to find!" Andreas said, "Before we cross that bridge, I've got the housekeeper tied up in his office and being pretty sure he's involved somehow, he can join his friends at the camp. We'll go downstairs to check on him and see if he has anything to tell us!" With the receptionist being absent from her post, there was no need for stealth but they scurried along the corridor, just in case she should return suddenly. Opening the door and turning on the light, Andreas saw the captive lying in the same position but having his eyes closed, it was difficult to discern whether he was asleep or had simply passed out, so he called out, "Oy, you!" The staples held fast and with the A4 muzzle proving effective, agony was reflected in his face; Andreas growled, "We'll leave you here a while longer, then we're all going for a nice ride and I'm sure you will soon be more than ready to talk!" Leaving him in the dark once more, the two friends made their way to the bar, where Tolley's was once again on the menu but after just one drink and noting that the hotel was now as quiet as a grave, they deemed it time for action. Andreas returned to the housekeeper, while Reuben drove the car to the rear of the building, to facilitate the removal of the housekeeper.

How the hell am I going to separate him from that desk? Andreas thought as he began searching for something to prise the staples free but coming across a pair of stout scissors in the top drawer of the desk, he inserted them under each staple in turn and levering the ear from the desk, Andreas had the thought that if the man's mouth hadn't been stuffed full of A4, everyone within a mile's radius would have been alerted to his plight. Cutting the flex binding his feet, he stuffed the scissors into his jacket pocket for possible future use and frog-marched his prisoner to the door. Moving quietly and quickly along the corridor wall, his heart missed a beat, as an elderly couple were negotiating the last few steps of the staircase and holding his breath as they passed by, he realized that they could be seen from the desk. Grabbing the housekeeper by the throat, he walked him back out of sight and looking around the concourse, he decided that the kitchen would provide the safest escape route. It was simply a matter of waiting for an opportunity to present itself and luckily that moment arrived sooner than anticipated, with the receptionist emerging from behind her desk to walk to the entrance to give directions to the elderly couple. Taking advantage of her absence from the desk, Andreas headed for the kitchen, half-dragging his prisoner and was half-way across the chosen route, when he heard the lift whirring. Realizing that there was a chance of being caught before they could reach the kitchen, he propelled the prisoner in front of him and crashing through the swing-doors at speed, he narrowly avoided being seen. Frog-marching the heavily bleeding housekeeper through the back door, he forcefully thrust him into the car and as Andreas joined his prisoner in the rear of the car, Reuben remarked sarcastically, "You took your bloody time?" Andreas said nothing while Reuben continued his harangue, "Look at all that blood on the seat; *somebody* will have to clean that up in the morning!" Andreas still kept his silence but when his friend persisted, "It'll take a load of rags to wash that bloody lot off!" Andreas leaned forward in his seat and growled viciously, "Just shut your bloody mouth and drive!"

Arriving at the camp without further incident, Andreas demanded, "Fetch the others over; I want them kept together!" Pushing the housekeeper to a clearing on the edge of camp and checking that they were close enough to the glow from the fire to see what they were doing, Andreas waited for Reuben to bring the other three captives. Ensuring that their hands were bound securely in front of them, Andreas addressed the miserable-looking quartet, "If I get the information I need to close this affair, you will all be released unharmed immediately but if I get nothing useful from you, I will kill each of you; one after another; it's your choice!" Walking along the line, he paused in front of each of them, "Does anyone want to tell me anything?" Remaining silent, they looked down at the ground until they heard Andreas saying, "Right, Reuben, strip them!" Taking the scissors from his friend, Reuben quickly cut the clothing from their bodies and when the task had been acquitted, Andreas asked the same question and with no one uttering a word, he snatched up the rags from the ground and threw them onto the fire, "You will have no dignity until you talk!" Leaving only Van der Wahl capable of walking, Andreas tied the housekeeper and the two women to a thick overhanging branch; pushing Van der Wahl towards the car, Andreas looked pointedly at Laura and remarked, "*You're* next!" With the half-light of the fire failing to conceal her terror, Andreas and Reuben turned from the scene, walking off into the night, dragging a naked, struggling Van der Wahl behind them.

Choosing the early hours of the morning had been a wise move, lessening the chances of being stopped; driving in the early hours with a naked man trussed up in the rear of a car, would have definitely meant a swift return to Britain without changing the situation one iota. Arriving at their destination, Reuben walked along the wharf to make sure there were no prying eyes and receiving the thumbs-up, Andreas marched Van der Wahl along the cold, cobbled slab ground, consigning him quickly into the hold. Setting off immediately, they soon reached an area of the vast sea that had become familiar to them and demanding information, he asked for the name of his immediate superior and that of Jen's killer but still receiving the same response, Andreas picked up the nets from the cabin floor and cast them out over the waves. Reuben restarted the motor to begin trawling the area and after three circuits of the boat, they headed for the deeper waters of Bass Strait with a full hold. Reuben cut the engine as soon as they arrived at the spot and pulling the captive from the seething mass of fish, Andreas pushed him to the port side of the boat. Throwing handfuls of the smaller fish into the water, five dorsal fins were seen heading for the boat in minutes and Andreas uttered grimly, "If you do not give me names, I will throw you to those creatures and fortunately you will not suffer *too* long!" Van der Wahl tried to wrench himself away from the edge but Andreas's vice-like grip on the back of his neck prevented him from moving, "Talk, you bastard, or I swear I'll throw you overboard!" Van Der Wahl screamed, "It was Cannon who did the killing! I begged him not to kill the last one but he said that Hendy *always* let him have a kill, *especially* if women were the intended victims!" Andreas snarled, "You consigned those women to death when you gave him the information he needed to satisfy his craving, which makes you as guilty as him. I want to know where I can find this Johnny Cannon *and* who else is in the mix!" Van der Wahl laughed nervously and shouted, "You already have him! He's back at your camp, tied up to that bloody tree!" Andreas's face showed surprise and anger on learning that the man he sought was already his captive, "Who else should I be looking for?" Getting no reply, Andreas said, "I want names *and* how the operation is run; your life will be spared if you tell me now!" Van der Wahl looked down at the fish circling the boat and knowing that whatever he did, his life *could* be forfeit but opting to gamble that Andreas would *not* actually throw him to the sharks, he replied, "Cannon can tell you more than me; he's the one that killed your friend Jen and took great pleasure doing it!" Not noticing the rage in Andreas's eyes, he continued wildly, "He told me that she was the best of them all because she screamed more and died slower than the others!" Andreas shouted to Reuben to start up the engine and as the craft roared into life, Van der Wahl's body was thrown off balance and using the impetus of his unsteady body, Andreas lifted him up over the edge and with his screams lost in the wind blowing stiffly from the north, they headed for pier 35.

19

Heading for the camp, Andreas finally broke the uneasy silence, "Well, at least we got *some* useful information!" Without taking his eyes from the road, Reuben replied, "You mean before you tossed him to those hell-fish!" Andreas retorted sharply, "I thought you were aware that it might come down to this and don't waste sympathy on Van der Wahl; he got exactly what he deserved. He virtually signed Jen and the other girls' death warrants, which makes him as culpable as the executioner who casually dispatched them for kicks. I'll make sure *all* the bastards pay for their deaths and if it means feeding them to *hell* fish; so be it!" "I suppose so!" Reuben replied, "I'm just deeply troubled, knowing that we've been responsible for someone being torn to shreds and devoured!" Andreas asserted, "It really wasn't that easy for me either but in the end, it may serve as a warning to the others and the sooner this affair is finished, the better it will be for all of us!"

Dawn was breaking when they finally reached camp and the unhappy trio, naked and suspended by their wrists from a branch were sleeping, with the stench from their bodily functions permeating every nook and cranny within twenty yards of the site. Holding his nose, Andreas admitted, "That's something I overlooked but maybe if they are left that way, the lack of dignity will dispel any lingering notions that their lives are *not* in jeopardy!" With the camp beginning to stir, Andreas kicked Cannon awake, noticing that a few of the tribe had congregated, idly staring at the naked strangers and not wishing to keep them waiting longer, Andreas tethered the women to a separate branch to hose them down, leaving Cannon to endure the foulness from his body. "My next undertaking is to

110

learn all you know of Hendy, particularly *where* he can be found. As soon as I get answers, you will have your freedom and dignity returned but a painful death will be your reward for silence!" Andreas turned impatiently to Reuben, "You can run me to the office; there are a few things that I want to look into and I'll question the *rest* of the staff to see if I can turn up anything of interest!" Casting his gaze on the three suspended from the sturdy branches, he commented, "They can stay like that until it is their turn to take a nocturnal ride with us!" Cannon protested, "You can't leave me like this; it's inhuman!" Andreas retorted viciously, "So was what you put those poor girls through; the sooner you give us the information we need, the quicker you will be cut down and released!" Pausing for a minute to see if anything was forthcoming, the two comrades-in-arms turned on their heels and walked away.

During the journey back to Melbourne Andreas declared, "They're obviously more afraid of their superiors than they are of us; perhaps we should up the ante!" Reuben responded, "I'm glad I'm not your enemy Andreas; you are one callous bastard!" Getting no response, he shrugged his shoulders and asked, "What is it you hope to learn at the office?" Andreas answered moodily, "It's just possible that there is something there that may connect this Hendy to the affair *and* I want to find out Christina Beacham's true role in all of this. On the face of it, an ordinary typist's value to such an organization would seem to be negligible and it *could* help our cause if we discover her *real* function!" Reuben suggested, "A typist would be *ideal* cover for someone higher in the organization!" "You may be right and if I *don't* find answers at the office, it may involve having to return to Sydney, so I'll spend a day or so in the office and deputize someone to take charge, just in case we have to leave for a few days!" Leaving Andreas at the office, Reuben returned to the hotel to catch up on lost sleep; *if* he could cast the horror he had witnessed just a few hours earlier, from his mind.

Work ceased as soon as he entered the office, and with everyone looking up expectantly, he took advantage of the silence by addressing the staff, "Three employees, have been dismissed for misconduct but *your* jobs are safe for the time being!" Addressing Pauline, "I want *you* to take over the running of the office in my absence and you'd better see about hiring a new typist but do *not* use the same agency that Miss Beacham was engaged from. If you'll step into the office we'll discuss terms and I'd be obliged if the rest of you would continue your work in the usual way. Ushering his new manageress into the office he informed her, "I will sanction managerial pay for you on a temporary basis until things get sorted out and I would like to know a bit more about Miss Beacham. Any snippet of information, however small and innocuous it may seem, might help to form a profile of her; was she married or engaged, did she have children and what are her roots? Anything she may have let slip to the other girls could very well prove important, so I'd like to know who her friends were in the office!" "Of course, Mr Bosworth, I'll do everything I can to help!" Smiling, he told her, "Call me Andreas; in fact you may as well call me by my real name now; I am Andrew Jenkins!" Knowing that the disclosure of his identity would carry prodigious weight, he asserted, "Have you someone trustworthy that could be spared for a while; I need someone to help me go through the files again?" "I can spare Angela and incidentally she was the only one who seemed to be in any way friendly with Christina; you could possibly learn something from her if you're working together!" Andreas smiled, "Thank you, Pauline; you have been a great help already!" A few moments later, Angela tapped lightly on the door and walked in, "Excuse me sir; Pauline asked me to help you go through the files!" "Ah yes!" He replied and looking up, he saw a very attractive young woman before him, *keep your mind on the task ahead Andreas*, he thought. "Money has been embezzled from accounts, so I need you to help me go through every file in the cabinet, to establish which accounts have been compromised. I want to know how much has been taken *and* who handled the accounts; if we can do that, it's possible that we'll be able to piece together enough information to eventually lead us to to the people responsible for these thefts. There's also a chance that some accounts may have been transferred here for laundering purposes but we'll start by going through the accounts that were established after mine, with special interest in anything concerning a firm called Dexter and a person called Hendy. Have you ever heard those names mentioned in relation to dealings with this firm?" "I've never had to type anything containing those names but I know that a firm called Dexter supply stationery and I *have* heard the name Hendy, although I'm not too sure if it's in connection with the firm or something totally unrelated!" "Don't worry, I'm sure you'll remember!" Andreas suggested, "We'll get started immediately on files A to D!" Walking over to the filing cabinet, she reached up into the top drawer and having to avert his eyes from the spectacle of a large expanse of leg, he thought, *the sooner I get home the better.* With the files now placed on the desk, they began the time consuming task of scrutinizing seemingly endless material and stopping for a mid-morning coffee break, Andreas asked, "How well did you know Christina?" Angela smiled, "We went for a drink once or twice after work but no more than that, why do you ask?" "I'm trying to form a profile in my mind of the three dismissed members of staff and knowing that women like to confide in their best friend, I thought it likely that she may have let her guard down by discussing her past with you!" "She was hardly my best friend!" Angela replied, "I can't think of anything offhand that she may have said but if I do, I'll tell you right away!" Andreas smiled, "The dust from these files is making my throat dry. Do you think you could rustle up more coffee, stronger this time, with plenty of sugar and no milk?" Returning with two cups, she placed them on the desk and told him, "I don't know if it will help at all but I asked her once how she had learned the business so quickly and she told me that she'd been brought up in a business environment!" "Hmm that could be something and if you think of anything else at all, no matter how insignificant it may seem, it could help form a profile, so do let me know immediately!" One hour later, there was a large pile of files on the floor that had yielded nothing of any interest and with Angela leaving to make more coffee, Andreas lounged back in his chair, stretched his body and thought, *I'm sure the answer is in those files.*

With a further hour of scanning files still not producing a result, Andreas suggested lunch and acting on her advice, they walked past the astonished gaze of her fellow typists, to what she described as a nice little place, not two minutes from the office. Situated close to the bar that he and Reuben had been using, he discovered that nice little place that it was, he was still charged for ice. He asked, "Why do they charge extra for ice? Is it an Oz thing?" She smiled and answered coquettishly, lifting an eyebrow, "Probably a Melbourne thing. I used to live in Sydney and cannot remember it *ever* being done there!" With the ice now broken, so to speak, they relaxed in each other's company and in a very short time, Andreas had learned more about the workforce than he ever would have by poring over staff profiles. Letting her talk animatedly without interruption he tried to concentrate but being more than a little preoccupied with the shape of her mouth and facial expressions when she phrased certain words, he had to force himself to heed what she was *actually* saying. However, his full attention was aroused when she let slip that Christina had once been a boarder at an all-girls' school in Sydney. She did not elaborate on the matter and not wishing to halt the flow of words, he committed the fact to his memory bank for future reference. On her third Tolley's special, she began to stir the drink with a straw, while moving her body provocatively in time to music that was spewing forth from a jukebox. Smiling, he commented patronizingly, "Perhaps we ought to return to our chores!"

Resuming the onerous work, several clients warranted a closer inspection but with nothing *conspicuous* leaping out from the reams of paper, he asked Angela if she had any ideas. She laughingly replied, "I have but they're nothing to do with work!" Deliberately ignoring her words, he declared, "I'm convinced the answer to all this is in those files somewhere but we've been through them with a fine-tooth comb and still found nothing!" She answered, "If I knew exactly what it was you were looking for, maybe I could help!" "I don't really know myself!" He replied and asking her to bring more coffee, he joked, "Better make yours black!" While she was away, he reviewed the mystery in more depth, *Hendy and Dexter both have a connection to the firm, with neither apparently being a client but what if they were clients, filed under another name and what could be the connection to Christina Beacham? What if they were both in the same file; it wouldn't be D and H or H and D, I'd have noticed that but B for Beacham could be in the mix.* Walking briskly to the cabinet, he pulled out the first drawer of files, striking the cabinet with his open hand when that too, drew a blank but looking in the drawer below for H and B, he hit pay-dirt right away and opening the file, he began to read. "Got the bastards!" He cried out loud, "Philip Hendy and Christopher Beacham; the typist is his bloody daughter!" Grinning when Angela returned, he told her, "Forget the coffee; I've found *just* what I was looking for; look here!" Showing her the file, a smile came to her face as she read the names, "*Now* I remember where I heard the name Hendy. He came in here about eighteen months ago; a huge bald-headed man that Steve addressed as Pip!" Andreas replied,

"*That* could be useful; your assistance has been invaluable but for now I will have to shoot off and tell Reuben of the discovery!"

Walking from the office in a more buoyant frame of mind, Andreas hailed a cab and arriving at the hotel minutes before Reuben set out for the camp, he told him of his discovery, "I'll come with you to the camp to see if I can use this knowledge to loosen their tongues!" Andreas had butterflies in his tummy at the prospect of learning more about his enemies and arriving at the camp, Reuben pointed out youngsters pelting the hapless trio with tomatoes and after he had chased away the tormentors, Andreas hosed down the women, "Well now, you are in a fine old mess but you could end *all* of this distress *and* walk away with your lives by giving me information!" Walking back and forward in front of them, staring them in the face, he stopped in front of Laura and said, "Let me run through what we have learned so far; being aware for some time that clients' accounts were being embezzled, we subsequently discovered that you and Van der Wahl were the culprits!" Walking over to Cannon, he sneered, "*You* informed your bosses what was going on and blackmailed the pair of fraudsters into stealing even more money to fund a drug-smuggling operation; dispatching anyone along the way that appeared to show interest in what was going on, especially if they were women!" Walking back to where the women were hanging, he remarked over his shoulder to Cannon, "Your ear is still bleeding and the flies seem to be causing you distress but don't worry they're only laying eggs!" Christina was hanging naked and defenceless but she was still hostile, Andreas remarked, "I know that you attended business school but what I couldn't understand was why a humble typist would be considered worthy of a role in such an organization!" Looking into her eyes, he muttered, "Shall I explain, or will you tell me yourself?" Glaring at her adversary, she replied, "You tell me; I wouldn't want to spoil your fun!" "You were the liaison officer in the affair; the pay-mistress and the organizer!" Pausing, he murmured, "Answerable only to...*your father;* I *will* discover who else is involved but you can make it easier for all of us by telling me anything else I should know!" "Why should I tell you anything!" She snarled. "My father will find you and have you slaughtered for what you've done already!" Walking away from the scene, Andreas and Reuben left the prisoners to mull over his words, with Andreas adding, "We may not have to go to Sydney after all; it's just possible they might come to us!" Pausing for a moment, he remarked that he could do with something to eat, "Is there any chance of a snack in this place?"

The snack was stew, with God alone knowing the identity of the beast that had been used in the making but with second helpings having been requested and consumed, they walked slowly back to the prisoners, noticing that the stench from Cannon had obviously worsened. Reuben remarked that complaints had been made about the smell, to which Andreas replied, "I can understand that and we'll move them when we return and clear up the site at the same time!" Reuben said, "Can't you just hose him down? It would be a lot simpler?" "You're right but I want him to suffer a little longer and in his present state, he might be a little more inclined to cough up information!" Singling out Laura, Andreas stuffed his handkerchief into her mouth, saying softly, "If you want to tell me anything at all, just nod your head!" She began to struggle violently and checking that the knots were tight but slack enough to allow her to stagger to the car, she was bundled into the rear of the car. Andreas climbed in beside her and with Reuben observing speed restrictions and directives, they reached the wharf in good time and with the jetty being deserted once more, she was dumped unceremoniously into the hold. Setting off for their fishing spot Reuben was filled with trepidation, knowing the fate that awaited the former secretary but speeding to the site, he removed the net from the cabin, ready for the task; trawling the area, they soon had enough fish to supply the hotel kitchen and provide a lure for the sharks. Heading for the Strait, Reuben glanced at the naked form lying among the wriggling fish; noting the abject terror in her face, he turned his head away sharply and dropped anchor. Pulling the captive out of the hold, Andreas marched her over to the side of the boat, while Reuben threw a bucketful of fish into the sea. With the leviathan responding promptly, the water quickly became a maelstrom of savagery and when the hors d'oeuvre had been consumed, Andreas's pets circled the boats, eagerly, awaiting the main course. "Now you know the fate of your lover, perhaps your sealed lips will tell me everything I need to know!" Andreas declared, "You can save your own and possibly your partners-in-crime's lives too; it's up to you!" She began sobbing uncontrollably, "Please don't do this to me; I know nothing!" "You knew enough to sign those girls' death warrants by passing on their names to Cannon!" Andreas averred, "At least I'm giving you a chance of saving your neck, which is something those young girls did not have. I want to know who else is involved besides Hendy and Beacham and where and when the exchanges take place!" Still sobbing, she admitted, "I know what I have been involved in and there hasn't been a day when I haven't regretted it; the only thing I know is that it takes place every fourth Friday and I believe that the bosses are from Sydney!" Reuben interjected gently, "Think back to the time when they first visited you, can you remember exactly what was said; it may gives us a clue to unlocking this affair?" Ceasing her sobbing momentarily, she replied, "Cannon told us that he was representing a Sydney triumvirate that wanted to take over the milking of accounts and turn it into a world-wide affair, promising that we would be well paid for our co-operation. That is all I know; I was never told *anything* specific!" A shiver ran through her body and rubbing her arms rigorously she began to weep once more; Andreas turned to look for his jacket to drape over her shivering body but deciding to spare his friend the trauma of having to kill a second time, Reuben took matters into his own hands; sweeping Laura up into his arms, he dropped her struggling body into the sea. Frenzied splashing was the only sound heard as she was swiftly dragged beneath the waves, to share the same grim fate as her lover. Andreas, mouth agape was still standing with both hands holding the jacket open but finally donning the garment, he fired up the motor and headed for pier 35. He told his friend, who was sitting on the deck with his back against the side of the boat, "Don't beat yourself up Reuben; it had to be done. We cannot afford to leave *any* of these vermin alive. Directly or indirectly, each of them played a part in the killing of innocent girls and the theft of clients' accounts; all to fund an evil trade responsible for the death and suffering of millions of people all over the world!" "I know, I know!" Reuben replied. "I just wish we could get the hell out of here and go home!"

20

Having managed only two hours of sleep, Andreas showered, dressed and drove to the office, where he found Pauline and Angela almost unable to contain themselves. They hastily trailed after him into the office and closing the door, Angela said, "I had an idea that you would still need my help, so I decided to enlist the help of my ex-boyfriend who is a detective in the Sydney police force!" "You never cease to amaze me!" Andreas commented. "What did he have to say?" "Both Hendy *and* Beacham have been under surveillance at various times during the year, with both managing to avoid arrest!" "Any known associates?" Andreas asked. She replied with a smile, "Yes and here's the tie-in. Four years ago they were involved in stealing antiques for the foreign market with a crook called Henry Wright, who is a haulage contractor. Wright was responsible for cartage and export but there was never any proof; each time trucks were stopped, the items on board were legitimate freight and without evidence nothing could be proved!" "Forgive me but I can't see the tie-in!" Andreas exclaimed. Angela explained, "Dexter is *Wright's* company, with the name being some kind of pun of his surname; *he* is the third member of the triumvirate and has a file in the cabinet under his own name and is probably still responsible for carrying goods!" Andreas grinned broadly, "I have all the names now, thanks to you and your ex; I really can't thank you enough!"

Driving back to the hotel as quickly as the mid-morning crush would allow, he ran into the room and roused Reuben, "Wake up, wake up!" Being woken from a dream, where he was the opening batsman in the England cricket team, Reuben roared, "What the hell is going on? Is the hotel on fire?" When Andreas relayed Angela's news, he received a somewhat subdued response, "That's great but we still don't know where or when the exchange will take place!" Andreas replied, "Hopefully we can either get something from the remaining two captives *or* the diary but the key to it all, is where the shipment is being delivered *to*. I have to go to the wharf today to book the boat for another week, so maybe I can tap into Old Ned's local knowledge on that subject. Hurriedly getting dressed, Reuben drove off to the wharf and Andreas remarked during the journey, "I think it would be better all round if we took both prisoners fishing tonight; we have just about everything we need but under duress, there is always a chance that one of them may let slip something we've overlooked!" Walking quickly to the berth with an envelope full of money, Andreas handed over a further week's boat rental and asked, "If I had to arrange a rendezvous with a boat, where would be the best place along the coast?" The old man answered smartly, "Young man, you're standing on it!" Andreas smiled, "There will be extra money in this if you *can* help me; have you ever heard of any such meetings along the wharf occurring regularly every four weeks?" The old man thought for a moment and replied, "Can't say that I have and the berths here are tenanted by boat owners, so there are never vacancies!" Andreas asked, "Would it be possible for a boat to be vacated from its berth for a certain length of time to allow another boat to land for a meeting?" "It's possible but highly unlikely!" The old man informed him, "Nothing can ever be done on the wharf without everybody else knowing about it the next day!" Disappointed, Andreas turned to leave but putting the envelope into his dungarees pocket, the old sea-dog added, "I think the place you're looking for would be pier 35. Boats call in there to refuel at all hours and such a meeting could easily be arranged without causing too much interest; is that what you're looking for?" Andreas's face lit up, "That's *exactly* what I was after!" Handing a further hundred dollars to the oldster, Andreas warned, "Forget this conversation ever happened!" "What never happened?" Ned replied with a toothless grin. Andreas smiled and as he stepped onto the wharf, he heard the old man say, "Bloody Poms!"

Reuben suggested, "Your idea for taking out both of the prisoners tonight seems to have been a wise choice then; the delivery could very well be this Friday and it's Wednesday now!" "Yeah, we'll see about that later but now I want to organize a thank-you meal for all the staff and we owe at least two of them a whole lot more than that!" Returning to the hotel, they organised a party for the Mowll and Mowll Australian branch and drove to the city

Entering the office, Andreas told the staff that they could finish work for the day "You're all going to a booze-up!" Covering their typewriters, the workers hastily packed away their equipment and entered two waiting taxis, bound for the Sebel and arriving at the hotel a short while before the cabs, enabled Andreas to be on hand to *greet* his staff and usher them into the function room. "There is a tab behind the bar!" He proclaimed, "So let's have a good time!" "Did you get any other snippets from your ex?" He asked Angela during a lull in proceedings. "No!" She replied, "Although I did ask him to put a tail on Wright and let me know the moment that he disappeared off the radar again!" "Angela, you are proving to be a valuable asset; your initiative is worthy of better things and I will have to think of a suitable reward!" The way she looked at Andreas made him realize that he had better leave that particular conversation hanging in the air, even if the attention *was* flattering. Having heard of the staff party through the grape-vine, the chef had laid on a large gratuitous spread, with fish of course being the main constituent. When the food had been eaten and the tab exhausted, the two friends began finalizing their plans for the night ahead, "I'll give Cannon a shower before we leave!" Andreas decided, "He smells like a cesspit and Ned would not be happy with a stench like that wafting around in the boat!" Reuben said, "We only need the date of the delivery, are you absolutely sure that it will be pier 35?" "It's the logical place but I have to confess that I would *never* have thought of the place if the old man hadn't suggested it. Come on, let's get going; the sooner it's done, the better!"

Ronaldo greeted them, "I can't see you getting too much out of your captives; one of the children overheard them talking and they are both aware that in all likelihood, they are going to be killed!" Andreas said, "I don't suppose the child overheard anything else; something that could be of use to us?" "I wouldn't think so; he didn't go too near because of the smell but ask him yourself, I'll call him over!" The boy walked over sullenly when summoned, and something of his dour demeanour reminded Andreas of Walthaar, except that the boy smiled, even if it was in response

120

to being promised money for remembering anything else that the prisoners had said. "The woman told the man that he wasn't to say *anything* about the delivery because you were going to kill them anyway and *he* said that maybe the others had just been hidden away somewhere or even freed. Then she told him not to be so stupid!" Mimicking Stephanie, the boy repeated in a falsetto voice, "My father will be in the area soon and when he finds out I'm missing, he will keep looking until I'm found; the longer we can hang it out, the better chance we have of surviving!" Laughing at the boy's pale imitation of a woman's voice, Andreas handed the lad a twenty dollar note, "Thank you, son you've earned that!" Running to his mother waving the note, the boy began to howl when she snatched it from his hand and thrust it into her apron pocket. Andreas laughed, "Some things do not change, no matter where you are. I just hope he gets a few sweets out of it!" Reuben proffered the suggestion, "The boy's information backs up the theory that if Beacham is expected, there must be a delivery due soon; so it all hangs on Old Ned's knowledge of the area being sound!" Ignoring Reuben's doubts of Ned's accuracy, Andreas answered, "I think we will have to assume that the men working on the pier are on the payroll, although it's possible they have just been paid to be absent from their post for a while. If we have to kill them too, it could mean dealing with a dozen or maybe even more. I suggest picking them off one by one rather than spraying bullets all over the place; there's always a danger of a stray bullet hitting the fuel tanks!" "We could really do with another man Reuben advised, "Should we take one of the men from the camp along with us?" Andreas agreed, "It would certainly make things a lot easier; go and have a word with Ronaldo?" Strolling to where the two prisoners sat on the ground, Andreas ordered them to stand and dragging a gushing water pipe across, he hosed down both prisoners, until all the grime had been removed from their bodies. Walking over to Cannon, he asked, "Do you have information for me?" Pausing for a moment, he continued, "I already have most of the information I need; it only remains for me to learn where the drugs are being delivered to and when!" Realizing that he was wasting his time by repeatedly asking the same questions, he resignedly tethered their feet together with another of Gunnar's tried and tested knots and pushed them roughly towards the car. There was difficulty in cramming two hands-and-feet-bound prisoners into the rear of the car but finally managing the task, Andreas climbed onto the back seat and was still stuffing rags into the prisoners' mouths as Reuben started up the motor and pulled slowly out of camp. Arriving at the wharf without having been stopped, his fears of a debacle when getting the prisoners *out* of the car, proved to be well founded, with both captives tumbling from the car in a heap. Unfortunately, four drunken youths passed by, taking a shortcut to town, "Do you need a hand!" One of them offered as Reuben was attempting to pull the captives to their feet. "No, mate, I'm fine; they've just had too much to drink but I can handle things. Thanks for the offer though!" "No problem!" the youth replied and as soon as the quartet had staggered out of sight, the two friends began to stow the captives on the boat. Starting the engine, Reuben eased the boat from the berth, saying, "That was close; it's a bloody good job you can tie knots!" Andreas laughed, "It's also a bloody good job they were too drunk to notice that they were both naked!" Dropping the anchor into the sea when their destination had been reached, Andreas cast the net in an arc over the water. Within an hour, they had caught enough fish to warrant another free meal and weighing anchor, Andreas remarked sarcastically to the prisoners, "Feel free to help yourselves if you are hungry!" Steering the craft towards their deep-water destination, Reuben immediately dropped the anchor into the calm water and hauling the pair out of their resting place among the fish, Andreas dragged them to the side of the boat. Throwing another bucket-load of fish into the water, Reuben shouted, "Watch this you pair of bastards!" The hungry carnivores arrived on cue and Andreas smiled, "Now you know what happened to the others and the same fate awaits you if we don't get the delivery date from you; it won't be a pleasant end but fortunately for you, it will not last long. You can gain nothing by taking your secret to the grave but you *can* save lives, including your own, by telling us what we need to know now!" Cannon screeched to Christina, "Tell him, for Christ's sake!" Turning to Andreas, he pleaded for his life. "You have to believe me; if I knew, I would tell you!" Turning once more to Christina, "Tell him! I'm begging you; please tell him. He's going to feed us to those creatures!" She looked scornfully at Cannon, "You coward, don't you realize that they are going to kill us anyway and at least by keeping quiet, we can save my father's life?" Cannon screamed loudly, "Bugger your bloody father! It was him that got us all into this drugs racket!" He turned to Andreas again. "I don't know when it is but I can tell you where!" Christina had other plans however and before Cannon could utter another word, she suddenly launched herself into the sea. With the combined weight of the girl and the great beast that had seized her, a screeching Cannon was swiftly pulled in to meet his maker. With the sea quickly becoming a bloody maelstrom, Cannon screamed in agony and terror, while Christina simply disappeared from sight, silently accepting her fate. Within two minutes, the sea had calmed and the fish began to circle the boat, looking for seconds. Believing it churlish to deny them, Andreas threw a few large trevally their way and sped off to Pier 35.

21

Andreas called cheerily to the boiler-suited man at the pump, "Usual, please, if you have enough!" He replied, "Don't worry about that we *never* run out!" Andreas asked, "I suppose with all the boats filling up here, you must have quite a few deliveries?" Extracting the nozzle, the man remarked, "We have deliveries every night except Fridays, when it's done on Saturday morning instead!" Leaving with a smile on his face, Andreas headed for the wharf and as he was mooring the craft, he remarked, "Thanks to the young boy at the camp and Laura, we know for sure that a delivery is imminent, added to the information we managed to squeeze out of the fuel attendant and Ned, we just about have everything we need but I *would* have liked confirmation from the prisoners!" "Will that mean keeping watch *every* bloody Friday?" Reuben queried. "Not necessarily!" Andreas replied. "I'll have another look at Jen's diary; I've an idea, it will be this Friday but I'll see what Ronaldo thinks!" Reuben wearily suggested, "Come on, let's take the fish back to the hotel and grab a couple of hours shut-eye!" Andreas agreed without a word of protest, being too tired for further discussion.

The following morning, Reuben remarked, "I have good news; Ronaldo is to be the man accompanying us!" Andreas commented with a smile, "I promised the boys I'd try to be home for Christmas and *that* is looking far more likely, now that the head man is with us!" Putting the diary into his inside pocket, the two friends went to the car and set off for the camp, where they found Ronaldo, arms akimbo, standing in the middle of the camp. Nodding knowingly, Ronaldo asked calmly, "The time has come then?" "Yes!" Andreas replied, "If you give me your weapon before we leave, I'll stash it with ours back at the hotel!" Removing the diary from his pocket, he handed over the journal to Ronaldo, "I have an idea of when the delivery will be made but I'd appreciate your opinion!" While leafing through the small diary, Ronaldo reminded Andreas solemnly, "Don't forget your obligation!" Andreas shook his head and asked, "Who is this man I am to fight? I've seen no one around the camp that looks anything like a Gypsy fighter?" Ronaldo smiled, "You will see soon enough!" Closing the diary he handed it back to Andreas, "As far as I can tell, it will be this Friday!" Andreas turned to Reuben, "I *was* right but *if* they don't turn up, we *will* have to check every Friday!" Ronaldo returned with his weapon and Andreas informed him, "We'll pick you up at three o'clock tomorrow afternoon, with traffic being at it's heaviest then, there'll be less likelihood of us being stopped!" Placing the weapon carefully in the boot, he noticed with satisfaction that the weapon was identical to their own, which would enable them to fire from the same distance. Andreas confided to Reuben, "I don't think we could have a better companion!" Adding with a grin, "I just hope it's not him that I have to fight at the end of this affair!" Reuben commented with conviction, "Yeah, in truth we Scamps *are* a tough bunch !" Keeping that thought in mind, Andreas decided to spend an hour in the gym in preparation and on completion of the allotted work-out, he strolled to the wharf to settle up with the old boatman. The crafty old salt remarked, "I knew from the start you were up to something no good and now I know it's got something to do with pier 35, I reckon five hundred smackeroos would make me forget I ever saw you!" Andreas handed over the extra notes saying, "Oz bastard!" The old man reacted, with a sly grin, "Pom bastard!"

Returning to the hotel, he joined his companion in the dining room and discussing plans for the future of the company, he told Reuben that he intended promoting Pauline to manageress and making Angela her secretary. Looking puzzled, Reuben asked, "Just *what* is your role in the firm?" Realizing that he had slipped up, Andreas sighed and explaining the whole story, he summarised the situation, "So you see, it's basically my money that's been embezzled and the knock-on effect is that our people could be made homeless if my business crashes. It's only right that you should know exactly what is involved and if you do not wish to continue with your part in the affair, I would be sorry to see you go but I would fully understand!" Reuben replied, "Do not worry Andreas, I will not let you down. Part of why I agreed in the first place was that I could not live with myself if I let you take on this task alone and of course the money's pretty good too!" Andreas smiled, "Thank you for that; now let's go to the office and tell the girls of my decision!"

Smiling as he halted their work to deliver news of the promotions and taking satisfaction from the reception, Andreas told the crew, "I'll put money over the bar, so you can all celebrate later but unfortunately Reuben and I will not be there; we have important work to do!" Ushering the two newly promoted members of staff into the manager's office, he told them that their new wage structure would be back-dated to when Steve and Laura were fired. Noting the pile of papers waiting to be signed, he said, "You may as well get used to *that* task now; I won't always be around and while you're at it, you had better get three extra typists to cover the two of you and Christina!" Leaving after a cup of Angela's coffee, he deposited money behind the bar for the girls' celebration and returned to the hotel bar for a glass of refreshing Tolley's but calling it a day after three drinks, he left Reuben propping up the bar.

The following morning, taking care not to waken Reuben, Andreas donned his training gear and jogged to the wharf to clear away the cobwebs from his mind and help prepare him for a fight that he had no real enthusiasm to participate in. Running along the wharf, he saw the old man waving and walking towards him with a sly grin on his face. Stopping, Andreas said, "I hope you're not going to try and screw more money out of me, you old bastard!" "Not today son!" Ned replied with a dismissive flourish of his hand, "I'll wait until you've finished at pier 35!" Andreas ran off laughing along the wharf turning into a street, where vendors were already setting up their stalls at the kerb edge and running down the already bustling thoroughfare, he headed for the hotel. Finding Reuben tucking into a large breakfast in the dining-room, Andreas attempted to steal a slice of fried bread from Reuben's plate, narrowly missing having his hand pinned to the table, "You'll have to be a bit quicker than that!" Andreas asserted. Reuben replied, "I wasn't really trying; I want you capable of shooting straight for a change!"

"You're early!" Ronaldo remarked when they arrived. "We made an early start to avoid the risk of traffic snarl-ups!" Andreas replied, "We can't afford to have anything go wrong at *this* late stage!" Driving back slowly to the hotel, Reuben dropped Andreas at the door, then left immediately to acquaint Ronaldo with the terrain overlooking pier 35. Andreas lay on the bed and slipping into a trance-like state as Jimmy, had trained him, he prepared himself for the task ahead and rising from the bed after fifteen minutes of total relaxation, he realized that the kitchen staff would be returning in under half an hour, to prepare for the next meal. So taking the lift down to the cellar, he dragged the arsenal from it's hiding place to the foot of the stairs, then quickly and silently, transferred everything to the boot of the car. Returning to the room, he had just settled down to watch the local news, when Reuben burst into the room and declared, "We've found the perfect spot that gives us a clear view in all directions!" Rising from his seat Andreas responded, "The guns and ammunition are in the boot, so everything is set to go and as it's almost dusk, we may as well leave now; there's no advantage in waiting for nightfall!"

As soon as they reached the hill overlooking the pier, they strapped the hand guns to their waist, removed the high-powered rifles from the boot and set them in place on tripods. Ronaldo suggested fanning out to cover a wider area and as soon as they lay down in an arc overlooking the pier, they could see that the move enabled them to cover the whole pier. Their vigil had now begun in earnest and Andreas submitted, "If the greasers remain on the pier, they will have to be killed too; we can't afford to leave witnesses and it's always possible that they are on the payroll anyway!" The group took turns at keeping watch and halfway into Reuben's second watch, he woke the other two, "I think they're here!" Peering over the edge, they could see a vessel approaching the pier at speed and within minutes a car had driven onto the pier from a copse at the side of the road. Reuben commented, "Christ, I hope they didn't *see* us!" Ronaldo murmured quietly, "There would have been an almighty fuss by now if they had!" The greasers shook hands with the men as they got out of the car and as soon as the ship had berthed, the crew joined their companions on the pier. The ship's captain placed a parcel on the ground while his counterpart did likewise with a satchel containing what Andreas presumed was money and facing the ship, they sank to their knees to begin checking the contents. Andreas whispered, "Are you ready?" Receiving the thumbs up, he checked that the safety catch was off and taking aim, his first shot bowled over the man who had just finished tying the ship to a bollard. Andreas's companions began firing and one by one, the gang crashed to the ground, with the exception of the men executing the exchange, who were oblivious to the havoc being wreaked behind them. Finally realizing what had happened, they drew their weapons and got to their feet, unwittingly presenting a better target and joined their fellows in hell as the next fusillade hit them; the whole gang had been wiped out in little over in a minute.

Loading the weaponry into the boot, they drove down to the pier, with Reuben commenting, "Well *that* was painless; for us!" Withdrawing their handguns, they walked towards the bodies, while Andreas grabbed the two holdalls and stashed them into the boot. Joining the others, he scanned the road for unwelcome visitors and detecting a movement out the corner of his eye, he whirled round and pumped two rounds into one of the gang who had somehow survived the holocaust and had his weapon raised, ready to shoot Reuben in the back. Andreas said, "We'd better make sure they are *all* dead before we continue!" Every inert figure had a bullet fired into his head before the search could resume and rolling over Reuben's would-be assassin, Andreas searched the man's pockets and pulled out his wallet, "Eureka, I've found Beacham!" After a few minutes, Ronaldo shouted, "I've got Henry Wright over here!" The search continued until at last, being aware that only two of the *main* protagonists had been present, Ronaldo calmly suggested torching the pier, "That way there will be no evidence of what has happened here and the ship and what's left of the crew will also go up!" Andreas remarked, "That's a good idea but how will we do it? We wouldn't get as far as the main road before the heat made toast of us?" Ronaldo had the answer. "We set light to their car, then get the hell out of here and by the time the car explodes and ignites the tanks, we should be well clear!" With Ronaldo volunteering to torch the car, Andreas opened the rear door to facillitate the escape, while Reuben who had exchanged his handgun for a high-powered rifle, blasted the remainder of the crew, who were running for their lives down the ramp. Lighting an oily rag, Ronaldo threw the firebrand into the back of the gang's car, before sprinting the short distance to the waiting car and racing up the hill, they turned onto the road leading to the camp, only slowing when they considered themselves clear of danger. Travelling for a further ten minutes, they heard a huge explosion and being hit by shock waves seconds later, they were forced onto the grass verge. Reuben cut the engine and they clambered out of the car to watch the glow from the inferno, lighting the night sky. Reuben remarked, "Jesus Christ, I hope no one has been hurt!" Andreas asserted, "There will be a few broken windows but I think the pier is too far away from built-up areas to cause any real damage!"

Continuing to the camp in silence, they were greatly relieved to reach their goal in one piece and Ronaldo immediately began caching the drugs, money and weapons into his caravan, while Andreas and Reuben headed straight back for Melbourne, hoping that their non-attendance at the hotel had not aroused suspicion. They had removed one tentacle of the gang but realizing that Hendy's absence from the scene would almost certainly involve a journey to Sydney, celebrations were somewhat muted, with the knowledge that the journey home had become even further away.

22

Reaching the outskirts of town, they could see that chaos reigned supreme, with the blaze still burning brightly against the backdrop of the dark sky, showing no signs of abatement; fire engines, racing to extinguish grass fires caused by the explosion and traffic lights working only occasionally, all added to the general confusion. The car's progress was predictably slow but in spite of the mayhem, they still managed to reach the hotel by mid-morning. Parking the car in its usual place at the rear of the hotel, he could see that no other car had been damaged but the front doorway however, was a different kettle of fish; hanging precariously by a few shards of wood on what remained of a hinge. Shaking his head, he muttered, "I definitely did not think that the blast would reach *this* far!" Entering the crowded candle-lit bar, they ordered their usual tipple with the barman asking, "Was there much damage to your room?" Andreas answered quickly, "No, we were lucky, the front seems to have taken the full force of the explosion. Was anybody hurt?" He asked, "Only minor cuts from flying glass but it's a *miracle* no one was killed!" Andreas enquired, "Do they know what caused it?" The barman responded grimly, "One of the coppers told me that pier 35 had gone up. Apparently a car went on to the pier, somehow caught fire and blew everything apart, including a ship that was in there for refuelling. No-one knows what the car was doing there but there's been a lot of bodies found, although I wouldn't think there's much left to identify them by; or anything else if it comes to that. The fire service have got it under some kind of control now, so I suppose they'll just let it burn until all the fuel is exhausted; there's no point in risking more lives!" "Yeah you're probably right!" Andreas replied and walking over to a vacant table, taking care not to tread on the broken glass littering the floor, he asked Reuben, "What do you make of that?" "It sounds as if we'll have to lay low for a while!" he replied, "We don't want to arouse suspicion by sodding off too soon!" "I agree but we'll have to go to *Sydney* fairly soon!" Andreas conjectured, "I want to be home for Christmas and that's only six weeks away!" "Maybe we can get something from your friend's ex-boyfriend?" Reuben suggested. Andreas glared at him, "She's no more my friend than she is yours but yes, that *could* prove beneficial and assuming that he's heard of the blaze, he will no doubt have cottoned on to the fact that *we* were responsible but hopefully any evidence we may have left will have gone up in smoke. We'll go to the office this afternoon and see how the land lies there but for now; I'll see if they can rustle up some food for us here; I'm famished!" Coming as no *great* surprise, they were told that none of the kitchen appliances would be operable until the electricity had been switched back on again, so deciding against waiting for the afternoon to visit the office, they headed for the city in the hope of picking up a meal there. Surprisingly, the city centre appeared to be functioning as if nothing untoward had occurred, with traffic still crawling along the main drag and street vendors inexorably advertising their wares from the side-walks. Unfortunately, normality did not extend as far as Mowll and Mowll, with only a few having made it to the city, leaving a fair amount to be dealt with by what was essentially a skeleton staff. Pauline and Angela were overjoyed at having two more hands to the pump and with Andreas directing proceedings from the office, Pauline and Angela returned to the typists pool. Reuben spent the time skivvying for the girls and with everyone forgoing lunch, the IN tray was finally emptied towards the end of the day and deciding that such sterling efforts on the firm's behalf warranted a reward, Andreas treated the hungry troops to a well-earned drink and a very late lunch at a blast damaged restaurant. Making one glass of Melbourne's finest last for over an hour, he asked Angela if there had been any news from Sydney. "Not so far!" She replied with a wry smile, "I'll give him a call later and let you know if he's heard of your escapade!" Andreas feigned surprise, "What escapade would that be?" He replied, heading for the door.

Returning to the hotel, Reuben parked the car while Andreas strolled to the wharf to see if any damage had been incurred *and* to explore the possibility of hiring a boat to Sydney. He could see the moment he walked onto the jetty that the wharf had borne the full impact of the explosion, with detritus from the sea flooding every berth, while boat owners were busily engaged in bailing out their semi-submerged craft, albeit with the moorings miraculously still intact. The old man glared at Andreas and said, "Bloody Poms! I had a feeling it would turn out something like this!" Andreas replied solemnly, "They had to be stopped Ned and it was the only way that we could completely cover our tracks. For what it's worth, I'm truly sorry and when I return home, I promise that I will make it up to you all!" Ned shook his head, "I know but that doesn't help us *now!*" Andreas conceded the fact and suggested, "Look Ned, I have money at the camp which I'll deposit with my firm and part of that cash will be used to reconstruct this wharf; it'll be twice as good as what it was before!" Andreas paused for a moment, then asked, "I want to hire a boat capable of reaching Sydney; would that still be possible from here?" The old man replied, "Not with all this mess and it would take you two or three days to get there anyway; your best bet is to go by car. It'll take ten to twelve hours and that's allowing for refuelling at Albury and Gundagai but don't go trying to get there quicker; there's a heap of patrol cars on that road, who have nothing better to do than wait for people like you who are always in a tearing hurry!" "That would do us fine, I'll drive there and my mate can drive back!" "If you want my advice!" Ned suggested, "It's six hundred and twenty-eight miles of the most boring, desolate scenery you will ever have seen, so you'd be better taking turns at the wheel as often as you can!" "You've been a great help Ned and I won't forget that!" "Don't bother yourself; I suspected all along what was going on down there and I don't hold with bastards like that trading on other people's misery. Now is there anything else I can help you with?" "You've already done well by us and like I said; I will not forget!"

"We'll need a different car!" Reuben suggested when Andreas informed him of the change of plans, "The one we have is certainly not built for a long haul to Sydney!" "You're right!" Andreas replied, "Will you organize that? Nothing *too* flashy mind; we don't want to draw attention to ourselves!" "I suppose *you're* off to see your lady friend?" Andreas replied to the barb, "I *am* going to the office while you're sorting out the car and make sure you get a good trade-in!" Walking through the reception area of the hotel to the car, Andreas noticed that the entranceway had already been restored; a sure sign that things would gradually return to normal. With traffic crawling along just as slowly as it had before the explosion, Andreas cursed their luck at having left the hotel a half hour too late. After an interminable and frustrating drive, they finally entered the office, throats burning from the dust and more than ready for the coffee that Angela hastily brought into the office. She told him that her ex-boyfriend had rung and guessing that they were responsible for the explosion, he passed on his congratulations; unofficially of course. Neither admitting nor denying the plaudit, Andreas asked, "Will you ring him later to say that Reuben and I are going to Sydney to finish the job and would appreciate a little assistance from him? Nothing that would involve his participation; just a little local information!" "*I'll* go too!" She asserted, "You would be less likely to be stopped if you have a woman in the car!" Andreas declared firmly, "Absolutely not; it will be too dangerous!" Shaking his head, Reuben suggested, "She is right Andreas; don't forget we will be carrying arms and with a woman in the car, we will be less likely to be pulled over!" Realizing that they were both actually right, Andreas finally relented, "Okay but you will stay at your ex-boyfriend's place until we are ready to return!"

Finishing his coffee, Reuben left to organize a more suitable vehicle, while Andreas was forced to vacate the office, as Pauline was conducting interviews for new typists and it had been decided that his presence would *not* be required. When he entered the bar that they had frequented since their arrival, Andreas strolled to the bar and without a word passing between them, the barman poured his usual and placing two cubes of ice into the glass, the barman smiled, "No charge for the ice mate; that's for strangers!" Returning to the office after a couple of hours, considerably more cheerful and slightly worse for wear, he found his friend, sitting on a chair with a mug of coffee, "Looks like I'll be driving again then!" Reuben commented and arranging to pick up Angela the following morning, he deposited Andreas into the rear of the new car. Waking when the slamming of the car door announced their arrival at the hotel, Andreas staggered *into* the newly repaired door on his way to the room and laying on the bed fully clothed, he fell once more into a deep alcohol-induced sleep.

Stepping into a cold shower the following morning, brought an immediate state of wakefulness and donning his training gear, Andreas walked down the stairs to find the gym miraculously still in pristine condition. Applying himself to a strenuous programme for an hour and with his body caked in sweat, he walked into his second cold shower, returning his mind and body to something approaching normal. Walking briskly into the dining-room, he met Reuben who was on the way out, "Have you packed your case?" Reuben asked, "We're running late; I've got to pick up Angela and go to the camp for the weapons!" Adding with a grin, "You're getting as bad as Pa and Riley!" Andreas replied, "Do what you have to do; I'll be waiting at the door by the time you get back!" After a large breakfast, he returned to the room, packed his case and went down to reception only just in time to meet his travelling companions.

23

Setting off on the next stage of the venture and with trepidation playing a major role, the three companions were for the most part taciturn and appreciating that the old man's assessment of the terrain had been correct, when they reached the halfway point to Albany, Andreas offered to take over the wheel. Gratefully accepting the offer, Reuben climbed into the rear of the car without disturbing Angela, who had slept for the duration of the journey, including the changeover, not actually wakening until halfway through refuelling at Albany. Strolling across to the station's small cafeteria, they ordered food that when it arrived at the table, was almost void of taste, causing Reuben to grumble, "We should have asked the hotel to make up sandwiches before we left!" A walk around a small store by the side of the garage helped relieve their aching bones *and* loosen Andreas's purse strings, by purchasing expensive boomerangs for his sons and once toilet needs had been attended to, they were ready to embark on the next leg of the journey. Complaining that the relentless sun had given him a headache, Andreas asked Reuben to stop, so he could sit in the back and taking up the small space left by Angela's once more comatose, spread-eagled body, he was the recipient of a kick to the groin area, as she attempted to return to her berth in the land of Nod. Looking at the monotonous scenery for a further twenty minutes, Andreas also fell under the spell of Hypnos, being woken some time later however, when his breathing was significantly restricted by Angela's black tresses. Then managing to manoeuvre himself into a more favourable position, he was further disconcerted by a whiff of shampoo, along with dust, blown in through the open window by a gust of humid air and with Angela's perspiring body being like a second skin, he wished that he had chosen to remain in the front. His wish came sooner than expected, when the car suddenly came to a halt and stretching as he got out of the car, Reuben asserted, "Right, your turn!" Wearily disentangling himself from Angela's unconscious embrace, he joined Reuben in stamping and stretching by the side of the road. Reuben remarked, "Christ, I could do with a Tolley's!" *"I'd* settle for water!" Andreas whinged, "We'll see what they've got to offer at Gundagai!"

With their exercise regime having had the required effect, the two companions got back into the car, with Reuben having to take the passenger seat, as Angela had now taken possession of the whole of the back seat. Easing out onto the road once more, Andreas headed for Gundagai, noting that after only five minutes, Reuben was fast asleep and with only a few more miles on the clock, he almost succumbed to sleep himself but easing across to the side of the road, he got out of the car, walked around the barren spot until his head had cleared and reinvigorated, he set off once again, noting that his fellow travellers had slept through the whole episode. Refuelling at Gundagai, Andreas wakened Rip Van Winkle, leaving Sleeping Beauty to finish off her siesta, then accompanied by sleeping-on-his-feet Reuben, he headed for the shop. The two friends returned to the car in minutes, with containers of water and lemonade, stowing half in the boot, with the rest being placed on the floor in the rear of the car, with Angela once more sleeping through a needful operation. Being finally wakened when Reuben slammed the car-door, she rubbed her eyes, swung her legs around to where the floor was once visible, sustaining a small scratch when she caught the back of her leg on a carrying handle. Muttering to herself and without a word to her travelling companions, she disappeared into the toilet for half an hour, leaving the men to order food for her and once her ablutions had been attended to, she joined them in the cafe; just in time for another tasteless repast. With Andreas declining another visit to the shop, in case it involved parting with more money, they were back on the road within fifteen minutes. Finally arriving at their destination after two further changeovers, they were tired, more than a little grumpy but thankfully not thirsty and Angela, who headed straight for her room, was not seen again until the following morning. Reuben and Andreas, needing sustenance of a different kind before retiring for the night, unpacked quickly and strolled into the bar for a well-earned decent meal, being washed down with their usual tipple. Once their bellies had been filled, they sat at the bar, until on the borders of sleep and with half-empty glasses in their hands, they finally decided that enough was enough, when the glasses were in danger of slipping from their grasp.

As dawn broke, the smell of food being prepared downstairs seeped through the air conditioner, renewing the hunger pangs denied by insipid food and the onerous, energy-sapping journey. Taking care not to waken Reuben, he dressed and carefully closing the door, he made his way to the dining room and had almost demolished a decent-sized breakfast when he was joined first by Reuben, being closely followed by Angela, who informed the pair, "My ex-boyfriend Bruce rang earlier to arrange a post-lunch meeting in the hotel and agreeing on your behalf, I thought it would give us the whole morning to recover from that awful drive!" Reuben thought, *how the hell would she know it was awful?* Suggesting a guided tour of the city, she began to regale them of the wonderful history of the city but pulling a face, Reuben opted instead for another visit to the cricket ground, leaving his friend to endure the dreaded sight-seeing tour. Walking out of the air-conditioned hotel into the heat was akin to being thrust into an oven and inwardly cursing, Andreas consoled himself with the fact that it would only be for a couple of hours. The morning however turned out *not* to be the disaster that Andreas had feared and being surprisingly impressed with the beauty of the city, he was *disappointed* at leaving the opera house and harbour bridge to return to the hotel for the meeting with Angela's ex.

Bruce strode confidently into the bar, with Andreas being immediately struck by his size and being built along the lines of a brick outhouse, he was a huge specimen even by police standards but as he walked towards the table, Andreas noticed that he had a pronounced effeminate gait and the reason for their break-up became instantly apparent the moment he spoke. After the introduction and niceties had been observed, they got down to brass tacks right away, with Bruce informing them that Hendy had been under close observation for some time but had disappeared off the radar just a few days ago, "I will help you all I can but in my position, I cannot be *seen* to have helped you. If you get caught, you're on your own!" Handing over a large brown envelope containing photographs of six men, he informed Andreas, "These are the main protagonists and every one of them is a potential danger!" Removing three of the stills, Andreas tossed two of them onto the table, remarking, "We won't be needing those!" Glancing at the photographs, Bruce remarked, "Just Hendy and his crew left then. Tread carefully where he is concerned; he is the most dangerous of them all!" Andreas asked, "Have you any ideas on where he may be? The sooner we get started on this thing, the better!" "Not yet, I will notify you when he's on the move!" Looking at the likeness of Hendy in his hand, Andreas pensively suggested, "How about if he were to be made aware that we are here? Would that draw him out into the open?" Bruce frowned, "It would almost certainly bring things to a head more quickly but would be extremely dangerous; are you sure you want to go down that road?" Andreas replied impatiently, "Yes, I want things over and done with as quickly as possible!" Looking up from the likeness in his hand, he asked, "Do you think you could you put Angela up until this matter is all settled?" Putting up his hand to silence her protestations, Andreas said, "We have enough on our plate without worrying about the possibility of you being kidnapped and used as a lever against us!" Bruce agreed, "It makes sense Angela and if information of their presence here were leaked the day after tomorrow, that would give you until Wednesday to move in your things!" Turning to Andreas, Bruce advised, "I have no wish to interfere in your plans but it might be advisable to have separate rooms; it could fool them into believing there is only one person to deal with *and* make it easier for Reuben to watch your back. Hendy is devious and utterly ruthless, so you will both have to be on your guard twenty-four hours a day and try to second-guess what he is thinking every step of the way. Angela will give you my number and as nothing can be seen to implicate me, you will have to memorize it!" With business concluded for the time being, they shook hands and Bruce *minced* to the door. Watching his departure, Angela explained, "In case you were wondering; yes he is!" Andreas replied, "That's got nothing to do with anything, he seems like a good bloke and his sexual preferences are his own business. Come on, let's go to reception and book another room for Reuben!" The receptionist lifted her eyebrows when informed of the change but both girls collapsed with laughter when Andreas explained, "Everything is fine; it's just that my room-mate passes wind and snores all night!" Reuben began packing the instant he was informed of the room change, "I hope it's a room with a view!" "Oh it is!" Andreas replied, "I made sure that you can watch everyone who comes in and goes out!" Reuben's smile disappeared, "I was thinking of one that looks over the girls on the beach but then I suppose; *someone's* got to look after you!"

Having moved Reuben's gear into the new room, they walked down to the bar to re-acquaint their association with Australia's finest, with Angela's appearance heralding a lengthy session on the tipple. After a few drinks, Reuben remarked, "Seeing that I'm babysitting, I'll pop in later to make sure that you've closed your door!" Andreas replied, laughing, "I always close the bedroom door; once bitten twice shy!" Reuben laughed, "Yeah, I heard all about that from Gunnar; it's a wonder that poor dog didn't die from something!" Guessing correctly what had taken place, Angela said, "I *do* hope it didn't distract you *too* much?" Not wishing to dwell too long on an amusing, unfortunate and painful incident, Andreas swiftly changed the subject, "Whose round is it?" Rising resignedly, Reuben went to the bar and Angela used the hiatus to inform Andreas, "I'm going to call it a day after this one; I'm not a big drinker like you two and I'm feeling a bit woozy!" "Yeah, I won't be too long myself!" Andreas replied, "I'm still tired from that bloody journey!" When her glass had been emptied, Angela kissed Reuben on the cheek and teetering towards Andreas, who had offered up his cheek, she took hold of his chin, turned his face towards her and gently pressed her lips to his, leaving him in a state of shock as she closed the door behind her. Laughing, Reuben remarked, "That's been on the cards for quite a while!" Andreas finished his drink and got to his feet, with Reuben advising perfidiously, "Don't be tempted into going to the wrong room!" Realizing that he would have to pass her room en route to his own and noticing that her door was ajar as he walked along the corridor, he *was* tempted. Looking into her room, he saw that she was sitting upright reading a book; noting his presence, she put the book onto the tallboy and slowly removed the sheet from her naked body, "Make sure that bloody door is closed!" She commanded with a sultry smile, knowing that the inner struggle for his fidelity had just been irrevocably lost. Sometime in the night, he left her side, carrying the clothes that he had so hastily discarded a few hours earlier and making his way to his room, he slept for a couple of hours on top of an empty bed.

With Andreas once again employing his tried and tested remedy for alcohol-induced torpor, his second cold shower of the day preceded his dressing by mere minutes and joining Reuben halfway through breakfast, Andreas remarked to his companion, "Christ, she's having a bloody good lay-in!" Reuben answered, "You're joking; she left with Bruce an hour ago!" Being slightly peeved that she had not waited to say goodbye, yet relieved in a way at not having to face her, he declared breezily, "Bruce will be spreading the word that I'm here tomorrow, so I'd rather you did *not* bugger off to the cricket!" "That's okay; the game finished yesterday, so you'll have the pleasure of my company for the whole day!" Andreas said, "This will be the last day that we can be seen together and assuming that an attack would not take place during the day, we can use your room at night and spend the days up here!" Walking around the city later in the morning, they idly window-shopped, while deciding to spend the afternoon re-visiting the sights that Andreas had visited the previous day. Sydney was certainly a beautiful city, in spite of the two- legged vermin that walked its streets and during a protracted hour at the bridge and opera house, Andreas remarked, "When all this is over and done with, I'd like to come back here one day with my family and trace my mother's path in Australia!" By the time they returned to the hotel, they were both in a better frame of mind and although Andreas was not looking forward to another period of incarceration, he knew that it was a necessary step in their quest to defeat a formidable and resourceful foe.

24

With lunch over, Reuben went to the bar, leaving Andreas to catch up on lost sleep but with the worries of the situation in which they found themselves and the previous night's Herculean efforts in Angela's bed, Andreas slipped easily into a deep recuperative sleep. However the protective, subconscious part of the brain brought him instantly alert, as soon as he heard the door handle being rattled and leaping out of bed, he flattened himself against the wall, ready to launch himself from behind the door but to his relief, he heard Reuben's voice, "Andreas, will you wake up; I've been hammering on the door for the last five minutes!" Opening the door, Andreas apologised, "Sorry mate, I must have fallen into a really deep sleep but realizing now that being totally unarmed up here, could easily have provided an opportunity for Hendy to polish us off, I'll leave you to transfer everything from the car, while I take a quick shower!" Reuben was just bringing up the last of the arsenal from the car as his friend was dressing and strapping on a shoulder holster, Andreas commented, "From now on we'll carry these at all times, we'll be far less vulnerable and it might also be a good idea to sit at either end of the dining room, to enable us to catch any would-be assassin in a cross-fire!" Agreeing to the suggestion, Reuben proposed that they go down to the bar to unwind and making sure that the safety catches on the weapons were turned to the on position, they made their way downstairs separately, with Reuben using the lift and Andreas the stairs. Taking their usual berth at the bar, Reuben asked, "Have you phoned Bruce to see if there's any news?" "I'll do that now!" Andreas decided, rising from his chair, "A little more information would not go amiss!"

Answering the call, Angela told him, "Bruce said to tell you that Hendy has been seen drinking in his usual nightclub!" "Did he mention the name of the club?" Andreas asked. "It was the El Matador!" She said, "In the Darling Harbour area!" Andreas's brain began to work overtime, "I don't suppose you'd fancy a night out in a Spanish club in Darling Harbour?" "That would be great!" She replied, "Give me half an hour to get ready!" Returning to the bar, Andreas related the gist of what had been said and smiling at his friend, he added, *"Your* presence will not be required Reuben; I would be less likely to attract attention accompanied by a woman!" "What can you possibly gain by going *there!*" He asked, "Or perhaps you just want an opportunity to be alone with Angela!" Ignoring the remark, Andreas replied, "I want to build up a profile of the man in my mind to see if I can discover anything about him that might give us an edge and I'd be more likely to spot something if he was in a relaxed atmosphere!"

Arriving at the brightly-lit cellar club, Andreas found the subdued lighting in the downstairs room a stark contrast to the garish entrance and recognizing Hendy instantly, he propelled Angela to a table some ten feet from his quarry. Observing the man holding court with his cronies for a full hour and having gleaned a fair impression of his make-up, Andreas decided it was time to leave and putting his hand in the small of Angela's back, he guided her to the stairway; with the intimate gesture betraying the fact that he was beginning to feel a little more than friendly towards the young woman, whose bed he had shared the previous night. Dropping her at Bruce's flat, he chastely kissed her cheek and denying himself the chance to hold her in his arms, he returned to the cab. Reuben was still sitting in the same position at the bar when he returned to the hotel, albeit in a more advanced stage of inebriation but under Andreas's steadying hand, he was guided to his room.

Having an early breakfast at separate tables and with no-one else being around, he was able to relate the events of the previous evening's date, "We sat near enough to hear what Hendy was saying but *not* close enough to attract attention and I reckon Bruce was spot on about him being intelligent and resourceful; enough to give us cause for concern anyway. I've a feeling that our best plan at this point would be to just sit back and wait for *them* to come to *us!*" Reuben agreed with his assessment and when both had finished eating, Andreas suggested, "I'll wait here to check if any of the guests are among the mugshots!" With Reuben returning to his room, Andreas sat drinking coffee until *all* the guests had put in an appearance and not seeing any familiar faces, he returned to his room. Turning on the television, in readiness for Reuben's first sentry duty of the day, he realized that the routine of alternating sleep and acting as watchman, allowed them to at least get *some* rest; with vigilance becoming second nature to them, recharging the batteries was vital.

At the end of their first week's incarceration, Andreas was sleeping fully clothed and armed, when Reuben suddenly shook him awake, saying, "Wake up, there's something strange going on outside!" Going to the window, Andreas peeped through the side of the net curtains and could plainly see a car parked opposite with a driver and three passengers, all gazing up at the windows of the upper floors and being sure that this was the moment they had been waiting for, Andreas remarked, "It looks as if the showdown is about to begin; as soon as you see them getting out of the car, go down to your room and keep a weather eye on the lift and stairwell, then when you are sure they are on *this* floor, follow them up and we'll take them front and rear!" Twenty minutes later, three passengers got out of the car and seeing them walk towards the hotel, Andreas declared, "This is it, Reuben; you'd better go downstairs now!" Attaching silencers to their weapons, they quickly went to their posts, with Andreas awaiting the head-on confrontation, patiently sitting in a chair facing the door, albeit feeling slightly apprehensive. Opening fire the moment the door imploded, Andreas hit both men silhouetted in the doorway; with his weapon still raised, he peeked around the broken door jamb and noting that the corridor was empty, he tiptoed along to the stairwell door. Easing the portal open, he was instantly relieved to see Reuben standing over the body of the remaining would-be attacker. Andreas suggested, "I think the driver should be handled by both of us; we don't want any slip-ups or injuries!" Making his way to the front of the hotel, Reuben watched Andreas exit the back door and slowly begin walking towards the rear of the car with his weapon raised but noticing Andreas's resolute advance in his wing mirror, the driver noisily set the vehicle in motion, only noticing Reuben's presence at the last minute. Standing in the middle of the road, Reuben swiftly took aim and put a bullet through the windscreen; with the car slewing to the left, it finally came to a stop, level with where Reuben was standing. One bullet had proved sufficient and Reuben declared as he blew the smoke from his gun, "Christ there's some poke in these little bastards!" Quickly searching the attacker's pockets, they kept back anything that might prove useful, throwing the rest in the back seat of the car with the body and without pausing, the other three were treated with the same irreverence. Closing the car's windows, they drove slowly to the harbour and picking a spot where a passenger-ship was lying as still as a grave at anchor, they rolled the car to the water's edge and with one huge heave, four members of the gang were despatched to a watery grave. Watching bubbles rising to the surface, Andreas remarked, "There'll be nothing left of them once that boat's engines start up; it's just a pity Hendy wasn't there too and unfortunately that'll mean having to move hotels again!" Returning to the room, Andreas consulted his watch and commented, "It's three thirty and the hotel staff will soon be stirring, so we haven't much time to clean up the blood and debris; I'll sort out the room, while you clean up the stairwell!" With the task being acquitted quickly and incurring the minimum of noise and fuss, they were left with enough time for a couple of hours sleep.

Booking out and settling the account a few hours later, Andreas allayed suspicion of any wrong-doing by saying that their room had been broken into, with several uninsured items of jewellery having been stolen. Seeing no visible reaction to his words but being aware that the would-be assassins *had* known which room to go to, he consigned the receptionist's face to his ever-increasing memory bank and responding to the reported theft, she commiserated with them, "That sort of crime unfortunately is prevalent in city hotels and there's not a lot can be done about it; especially if the items are not insured but I trust everything else has been to your liking?" "Everything else was perfect, thank you!" Andreas replied, then asking with a smile, "Can you recommend a hotel a little nearer to the harbour? We would like do a spot of fishing while we are here and it's such a long way from this hotel!" "Certainly, sir!" She said with a smile. "The Excelsior would be an ideal choice!" Andreas said, "Thank you, you've been very helpful!" Walking through the door with their luggage, they made for the nearest bar for a liquid breakfast.

25

S itting at the only vacant table in the bar, Andreas remarked, "We've got two options; we can look for a different hotel, which would probably buy us a couple of days to plan our next move *or* book into the Excelsior and set ourselves up as targets straight away!" Opting for expedience, Reuben suggested, "I'd rather go to the Excelsior; one way or another, it would *all* be over quickly!" "I'm with you on that!" Andreas replied, "They will be aware now that there are two of us, so it's pointless having separate tables and rooms!" Finishing their drinks, they drove to the Excelsior and with impressions of the interior several notches higher in quality than the facade, they asked to see a plan of the rooms, finally opting for a suite on the top floor. Being impressed by the panoramic views from both windows, the choice was deemed to have been a wise one and after unpacking, they began transferring the weapons to the suite, effectively turning their hidey-hole into a mini-fortress. Being fairly sure that they would receive no intruders on their first day in the retreat, they nonetheless secreted handguns beneath the folds of their jackets before going down to the dining room and managing to get a table where they could observe the hotel entrance, they relaxed with their meal; until Andreas realized that in their haste for food, the weapons had been left unhidden in the room. Pointing out that fact, he asserted, "We don't wanna be taken by surprise with our own weaponry!" Reuben suggested that the flat roof above the room would be an ideal spot, "We could also camp up there at night, *and* be able to hear anyone entering the suite!" Andreas's face lit up, "That's a damned good idea and if I can get Bruce to drop off a couple of pairs of high-powered police binoculars; we'd be able to see all over this part of this city!"

As soon as the weapons were taken to the roof, the bulk of which was cached in the covered lean-to that housed the lift-winding gear, Andreas rang Bruce for binoculars and within the hour, the receptionist had rung to say that someone was downstairs asking to see him. Putting the confiscated wallets in his jacket pocket, he walked down the stairs and handing over the bill-folds, he commented, "*They* won't be bothering you again!" Examining the ID's, Bruce remarked, "They're Hendy's lot all right and as he hasn't been seen anywhere for the last three days, another attack *could* well be on the cards!" Desperate to try out the glasses, he thanked Bruce for the information and with the intention of returning to the suite to help Reuben taking the last of the guns and ammunition to the roof, he walked across reception. In his absence however, Reuben had been busy spiriting the remainder of the arsenal onto the roof and was now also in reception, purchasing sandwiches and cans of lager from the small foyer in reception.

Using the lift, they returned to the suite together and immediately climbed the interior fold-away ladder to the roof to try out the binoculars. Securing the safety catch, they began scrutinizing the buildings across the road and watching the traffic below and seeing nothing suspicious, Andreas picked up one of the sandwiches. Having eaten almost half of the snack, he noticed a movement and the glint of the sun on metal from a darkened room, below and to the right of their own. Putting aside the sandwich, he trained the glasses on the spot and watched as the occupant withdrew into the darkness, returning seconds later carrying a chair. "It's probably nothing!" He remarked, "I'll keep my eyes peeled however, just in case; we cannot be *too* careful where Hendy is concerned!" Watching intently while finishing the sandwich, he saw the man return and pick up the shiny object from the table beside him; Reuben who had also been observing the apartment asked, "Do you want me to take him out?" "It could be totally innocent, so hold your horses for a while; I want to see if anyone else is in the room, so if you concentrate on watching what's happening at ground level, *I'll* keep an eye on the room!" Seeing no signs of movement from within the room, Andreas stated, "I don't *think* there's anyone else over there but he's just picked up the object he'd put on the table and it *did* look remarkably like a weapon of some kind; anything happening your side?" "There's a car outside the hotel in a taxi parking space and although it's difficult to tell from this angle, it doesn't look like a cab to me!" Andreas advocated, "*I'm* ninety-nine point nine percent convinced that the man opposite has some kind of rifle and with that car being outside, I think it's safe to assume that they are *all* part of the gang; I'll keep my eyes on the man opposite while you go downstairs and check out the car!"

Easing the fire-door open, Reuben could plainly see four people inside the car and deciding that it was *not* a taxi waiting for a fare, he returned to the roof with his findings, "They've gotta be gang members!" Andreas paused for a moment, then asked, "Can you kill that bloke over the road at this range?" Without a word, Reuben took a high-powered rifle from the lean-to and assured Andreas, "I'll kill him okay; distance is no object with this little beauty but do we really need the fuss *if* it *is* all innocent?" Andreas said, "I think we have to take the chance; with him out of the way, we'd be able to safely deal with the car's occupants!" Taking aim once more, Reuben gently applied pressure to the trigger and seeing his target's head flop forward onto his chest; he was confident that his accuracy had been consummate once more. Keeping a close watch on the car below, they noted that at different times its occupants left the car to stretch their legs and with its apparent permanent occupancy of the space proving beyond doubt that it was not a taxi, Andreas nodded, "Right, let's get them!" Descending the fire stairs, they crept out of the door with their weapons ready and quickly taking up their positions, Andreas edged along the wall, using parked cars as cover, while Reuben stood motionless in the doorway. Receiving the thumbs-up from his colleague, Andreas ran to the rear window and thrusting his gun through the open window, he fired four shots into the occupants of the two rear seats. The panicking driver hastily started the car but with Reuben already in the road taking aim, he was a few seconds too late; two deadly accurate shots fired in quick succession shattered the windscreen, leaving the driver and passenger slumped over the dashboard. Going over to the car, Andreas smiled grimly as he saw a pinpoint-accurate hole in the centre of each forehead, "Without a doubt Reuben, you are the best shot I've *ever* seen!" "What are we going to do about the sniper over the road?" Reuben asked. "*I'll* sort him out!" Andreas replied, "I want to see if he had an accomplice!" Andreas told him,

"Drive this lot to the harbour and wait for me to arrive!" With all items of identification having been removed from the bodies, Reuben set off with his cargo, meanwhile Andreas was looking upwards, trying to gauge where the sniper's room was situated. Having made his decision, he climbed the stairs to the third floor and locating the room, he crashed through the door, gun at the ready. Perceiving the man with his head bowed in death, he pulled him upright by his hair, noticing with satisfaction that he too had a bullet hole in the centre of his forehead. Scanning the room for evidence of an assistant, he noticed two mugs of partially consumed coffee on the table and deciding to wait for the accomplice, he sat on a stair opposite the lift. A half hour or so later, he was on the verge of giving up the mini-vigil when he heard the lift whirring into action; darting to the end of the corridor and leaving the fire door ajar, he saw a man emerge from the lift. Looking left and right and seeing no-one, the man strode confidently towards the room but double-taking when he saw the broken door, he reached for the gun hanging from a shoulder holster; Andreas's bullet struck struck just as his hand closed around the pistol grip, shattering the weapon *and* the chest cavity below. Both bodies were crammed, one after the other into the rear of the car and heading for the harbour, he found vexatiously, that he had to stop every couple of minutes for lights to change in his favour. Arriving at the harbour he was faced by an irate Reuben, "Took your bloody time, didn't you!" Ignoring the remark, Andreas removed wallets and driving licences from his passengers and told Reuben, "Give me a hand to stuff these two in there with their mates and wind the windows up, we don't want anything floating to the surface!" Once the bodies had been consigned to the deep, they returned to the hotel, satisfied with their night's work.

Going over the previous day's events at breakfast, Andreas remarked, "Predictably, Hendy was not there but two of the men from Bruce's photographs *were* and now that most of his main men are accounted for, he must be running short of fire-power!" Reuben suggested, "He might have to send for out-of-town reinforcements and that would not be done overnight, so we *could* be safe for now!" "That's true but we cannot *assume* anything! We've had it relatively easy so far because we had the element of surprise on our side but they will be better prepared for the next time and there's always the chance that he'll send one or two men, hoping to catch us off guard!" "You're right!" Reuben conjectured, "He could even have someone planted in the hotel?" "I think that's almost a certainty!" Andreas answered, "In fact I'll make discreet enquiries at reception when we've finished here!"

Taking a fifty dollar note from his wallet, Andreas made his *discreet* enquiry, receiving the news that there had been no staff changes but three gentlemen with no reservations had checked in that same day, expressly asking to be housed on the same floor and for an extra fifty bucks, Andreas was given the number of their rooms. Ordering room service from the desk he re-entered the lift, pressed the button for the fourth floor and walking along the corridor, he listened at the doors of the new guests. Hearing muffled sounds coming from the last room tried, he put his ear against the door but hearing the voices getting louder as they approached the door, he was forced to make a dash for the stairwell and leaving the door ajar once more, he saw three men emerging from the room; noting sadly that the ever-elusive Hendy was *not* among them,

Returning to the suite, he noticed that Reuben had laid the weapons out neatly on one of the beds, having fallen asleep on the other and loading the weapons, Andreas put them into the back room, believing it wise to be prepared. Being satisfied that all was now in place, he relaxed by watching the television, until he heard a knock at the door and realizing that it was too early for room service, he picked up his gun. Opening the door, he was surprised however and very much relieved to see Ronaldo standing in the doorway. Greeting him warmly, Andreas asked, "How the hell did you know where to find us?" Tapping his nose with his finger, he answered, "I was born and raised in Sydney; very little escapes the network of my large family!" Andreas brought him up to date on all that had happened and laughing, Ronaldo remarked, "I only came because I thought you could use an extra hand but by the sounds of it, you don't need me!" Hearing his kinsman's voice, Reuben woke and staggered into the room still half-asleep. Returning to full wakefulness as soon as he heard a knock on the door, Reuben snatched up his gun from the table and opening the door, Andreas came face-to-face with one of the men from the room below, now wearing a hall porter's uniform and carrying a tray of sandwiches. Trying to push his way into the room, the man found Andreas an immovable obstacle and giving it up as a bad job, he tetchily thrust the tray into Andreas's hands. Turning to the others, Andreas quipped, "It seems that guests are now being employed delivering meals; they must really be short-handed!" Ronaldo suggested, "I'll go down to order room service for myself and discover who is *really* responsible for delivery from reception!" Handing him a fifty Andreas grinned, "You may need this!"

After ordering room service and handing over fifty bucks at reception, Ronaldo learned that the name of the porter in charge of room service was Pete Johnstone, who could always be found in the kitchen when he wasn't delivering meals to the rooms. Walking along the corridor, Ronaldo informed Pete Johnstone that he would be requiring room service but that he could finish his break first and smiling at the receptionist in passing, Ronaldo returned to his room. Admitting the porter a short while later, Ronaldo watched closely as the tray was placed on the table and as soon as the man had left, Ronaldo waited until he heard the lift doors closing. Then covering the short distance to the lift, he was in time to see that the lift had stopped on the fourth floor and sprinting up the flight of stairs, he watched the man walk along the corridor and enter one of the rooms. Returning to his room, Ronaldo quickly ate his meal, then walked up the stairs to report what he had learned; Andreas remarked, "That's four we have to take out of the equation and I reckon that we'd be better doing it while we still have surprise on our side!" "That's true!" Ronaldo conceded, "However, I think you *really* should be making plans to go for Hendy himself; without *his* leadership, the rest of the crew will be easy meat!" Andreas responded, "You're probably right but the men below need taking out *before* we start planning anything else!"

Playing cards in the afternoon, they were disturbed by a gentle knock on the door and stuffing his gun into the waistband of his trousers, Andreas walked to the door to allow the fake porter into the room. Noticing the extra person in the room, the fake porter spun round; just in time to see Andreas kicking the door shut. Drawing his pistol, Andreas told the man to put the tray on the table and frisking him, Andreas found a handgun hidden in a holster beneath his borrowed porter's waistcoat, "Now there's an unusual accessory for a porter!" Andreas remarked as he tossed the gun to Reuben, "Keep him covered while I tie him up!" "Aren't you going to kill him?" Reuben asked. "Not yet, we might be able to squeeze Hendy's whereabouts out of him!" Andreas replied and cramming a flannel into the unfortunate man's mouth, he added, "Hendy seems to have a new strategy for defeating our waiting game, so we'll change our tactics too but first we'll pay a visit downstairs?" Ronaldo rose from his chair but Reuben stopped him, "No need for you to come, Ronaldo; there's only three of them now. Put the kettle on; we'll be back shortly!" Going silently down the stairs, Andreas stayed by the stairwell door, while Reuben walked along the corridor to listen at the crooks' doors and indicating that the second door that he tried was the target, he drew his gun. With Andreas joining him, they stood either side of the doorway and charging into the room, they killed the surprised pair before they had time to draw their weapons. Andreas suggested, "There's one still knocking about somewhere, so I'll check the other room while you take the weapons to the suite; we may *need* a bit of extra firepower later on!" Gathering the guns in his arms, Reuben walked back along the corridor, while Andreas walked resolutely to the room furthest away from the stairs but before he could reach the door, he heard the handle being turned. Flattening his body against the wall, he raised the handgun, lining it up on the doorway and as soon as the porter's head appeared, he fired. As soon as he saw splinters flying through the air, he realized that he should have waited until he had him completely in his sights and as Johnstone darted back into the room, Andreas shouted, "Shit; if I'd left this to Reuben, Johnstone would now be dead!" As Andreas related what had happened, Ronaldo asked, "Do you think it would be possible to climb down from this room?" Reuben suggested, *"I'd* do it but I think the best option would be to smash in the door and rush him, even though it *is* potentially more dangerous!" "I think Reuben's right!" Andreas proposed, "People will be coming back from lunch soon and the sooner this thing is sorted, the better!"

Standing in the centre of the doorway, with his gun raised and with the two Englishmen taking the flanks, Ronaldo awaited the signal and as soon as Andreas nodded, the flankers kicked in the door. Diving instantly into the room, Ronaldo hit the deck, with Andreas and Reuben following closely behind but the bird had flown. Johnstone had escaped and noting the air-conditioner cover on the floor, Andreas smiled wryly, "Of course; working here, he *would* have known escape routes!" Returning to the suite, Reuben grimaced, "God knows how many *more* men Hendy has but with the weapons we seized added to our own, we should be okay for firepower!" Ronaldo disagreed, "Their weapons will have to be ditched in the harbour along with the bodies; we will not be able to cart both lots of weaponry around with us and with Hendy now being aware of what has happened here, you will have to change hotels pronto, "It will be dark in an hour and that will provide ideal cover for what has to be done!" Pointing to the trussed-up captive, he asserted, *"He* will have to be disposed of with the others; we can't leave any loose ends!" "This has forced our hand!" Andreas stated, "We will *have* to take the offensive now but where do we go from here? He is bound to discover what hotel we move to?" Ronaldo smiled, "Maybe not; I have a plan in mind which we'll discuss after we've disposed of these vermin; don't bother checking out; just pack everything in the car and go. Nobody knows of my connection to you, so I am good to stay here for now and I'll meet up with you later in the Boat Inn, which is just across from the harbour entrance; don't worry, I will sort everything. Now go, the light is fading already!"

Arriving at the harbour, Andreas tied the prisoner securely to the back seat, rendering him incapable of floating to the surface and committing the car to the deep, they waited until no more air bubbles rose to the surface. Andrea muttered sombrely, "Wouldn't it be kind of poetic, if this is where they fished our Jen out; this one is for you and the girls Jen!" Driving the short distance to the Boat Inn they sat at a table with a much-needed Tolley's and Coke to await Ronaldo's arrival and attempting to alleviate Andreas's guilt in allowing Johnstone to escape, Reuben advanced the theory, "I know it was an inconvenience having the porter escape but in a way I'm glad; it's given us the chance to give Hendy a dose of his own medicine a lot *sooner* than planned. I never did like the idea of setting ourselves up, even though it *was* the correct method at the time and who knows, maybe this has tipped the scales in our favour!" Andreas smiled, "Thanks for that Reuben but really I should have let you shoot him; you are a far better shot than me!" "It just kind of comes natural!" Reuben replied, "Something in the genes, I suppose!" Arriving at that moment with a huge smile lighting up his face, Ronaldo declared, "I've been really busy but before I explain the plan, Hendy has been seen uptown trying to organize outside help, which means that with his numbers being *that* low, we could have the ideal opportunity of getting rid him!" Andreas asked, "I don't suppose Bruce mentioned where he had been seen?" "He said it was the El Matador, one of his old haunts; it's a below-ground-level nightclub that I had the pleasure of acquainting myself with the last time I was here. It's like a sort of upper-class dive but I wouldn't recommend you visiting the place just now, there's every chance of a price having been put on your head!" Andreas smiled, "I know exactly where it is; I took Angela there a short while ago, in order to have a look at Hendy and see what he was all about!" Ronaldo continued, "The hotel I stayed at while I was here is directly opposite the club and I've booked a suite for us on the top floor; Hendy would never guess in a million years that you would be so close and he *will* turn up there sooner or later; that's a certainty!" "That's terrific!" Andreas exclaimed, "When can we move in?" "As soon as you like, there is no demand for rooms until just before Christmas, so I was able to book until the end of the week, with an option to book *another* week if needed!"

Booking into the new hotel the following lunch time, they climbed the stairs to find Ronaldo already outside the door waiting for them, cradling high-powered rifles in his arms. Knowing that he hadn't passed them on the stairs, or that he would not be stupid enough to use the lift being armed, Andreas asked, "Is there a secret walkway up here?" Ronaldo laughed, "There's a fire door that doesn't lock properly just along from the main door, which I found by chance when I left my key in the room the last time I stayed here!" "Now *that* could prove very useful!" Andreas asserted. Noting that the windows overlooking the club, gave a perfect view of the whole street, he suggested, "Being here will be a whole lot better proposition than waiting around like sitting ducks *and* we'll be able to get some shut-eye for a change!" Ronaldo suggested, "I'll park your car on the other side of the city, as Hendy will certainly know the number by now and I'll also bring booze back with me!" "Be sure to get Tolley's!" Reuben joked, "I haven't had any for ages!"

26

Waking at three o'clock on the third morning of their vigil with a raging thirst, Andreas rose from bed and staggered around the pitch-black room completely disorientated, taking several minutes for him to realize that he was in yet another unfamiliar hotel and eventually locating the kitchen, he filled a glass with cold water. Idly watching a crowd of people emerging from the club, he noticed someone standing aside from the people waiting for taxis and almost choking on his drink, he realized that the person was Hendy, or someone remarkably like him. Rushing blindly into the sitting room for his binoculars, he tripped over a carelessly discarded shoe but quickly recovering his equilibrium, he returned to the window, binoculars in hand but the man had disappeared into the night. Finishing his drink he returned to bed, hoping to grab another couple of hours before dawn but with the possible sighting of Hendy making sleep difficult, he was brought back to reality with a bump a few restless hours later, with the clamour of dustbins being emptied and thrown back noisily onto the pavement. Leisurely showering and dressing, he walked around the hotel looking for likely pitfalls and strategic vantage points, finding on his return that his friends were already wide awake, in various stages of undress. Telling them of the possible sighting of their foe, he suggested taking it in turns to watch the club in the early hours, "That way we could all get at least *some* rest!"

With three further nights elapsing without a glimpse of Hendy, they were beginning to believe that he had gone underground once more but on his second stint of the day, Reuben spotted Hendy coming out of the club just before closing time and get into a large white Buick with darkened windows. Andreas remarked, "That'll make it easier for us then, we just watch for the car, instead of the man!" Friday evening arrived and because it was the start of the weekend, there were even more folk queueing up to enter the club and with Reuben showering and Andreas eating a microwave pizza, it seemed like another uneventful night but Ronaldo broke the tedium by suddenly declaring, "The Buick has just pulled up!" Andreas rushed over to the window and saw Hendy entering the club alone, so with only Hendy and the driver to deal with, Andreas declared, "This is the moment we've been waiting for but we'll still have to be cautious; he knows we're around somewhere and will be taking precautions just as we are. As soon as Reuben has finished in the bathroom, we'll check the area, while he covers us!" Once the search had been conducted and with nothing untoward having been encountered, they returned to the suite, where Andreas finished off the cold pizza, while his companions opted for sandwiches brought back a few hours earlier by Ronaldo.

Looking at his watch later in the evening, Andreas rose from his chair and feeling those familiar butterflies in his stomach, he declared, "It's midnight Ronaldo are you ready?" Strapping on their weapons, they slipped quietly out of the fire-door, to begin patrolling the surrounding area and after declaring the surrounds clear, Andreas stood in a doorway on the opposite side of the club with Ronaldo taking up *his* vigil on the same side as the club. Shivering, Andreas consulted his watch and noting that it was now one thirty, he walked along the deserted street, silent apart from the muffled sound of the club's disco. On the stroke of two o'clock, Andreas was watching Ronaldo patrol his beat along the hotel side of the road, when he saw him suddenly dart across the road and looking towards the club entrance, Andreas could now see Hendy waiting patiently outside for his limo. Believing that they had everything covered, they walked purposefully from either end of the road with their guns raised. Stopping by a parked car, Andreas lined up the sights on Hendy's unmoving frame but as his finger left the trigger guard, he heard the muffled sound of a gun being fired and feeling the wind of a bullet passing close to his face, he instinctively ducked behind the car. In trying to discern where the shot had come from, he almost had his head blown apart once more and sitting on the floor with his back against the car, he could see the sniper on the roof being reflected in a shop window. Noticing that the man was firing in both directions, Andreas realized that the man was using the same shop window to detect when he and Ronaldo were about to make a move. The limo drove by so close that Andreas could almost have put out a hand and touched it but being pinned down by relentless covering fire, the car passed by unscathed. Hearing more shooting, Andreas watched the reflection in the window and saw the gunman's arms flailing as he fell back and with the weapon clattering into the street, he declared loudly, "Reuben to the rescue, even if it is a bit too late!" Picking up the rifle from the road Ronaldo remarked, "That bastard's got a charmed life; there goes our best chance of surprise and things will only get tougher now!" "Aye and it'll probably mean moving again!" Andreas declared woefully. Walking quickly back to the fire door, they trudged disconsolately up the stairs but entering the room, they found Reuben standing with arms folded across his chest, grinning, "Well that's it then!" He said, "We can pack up and go home now!" "What are you talking about, you idiot?" Andreas retorted, "He got away in the car; that was the sniper you shot!" "No!" He insisted, "I shot Hendy *and* his driver as the car turned the corner, just before I shot the one on the roof; you were right about all that clay-pigeon shooting coming in handy!" Andreas was stunned. "Are you sure?" He asked. Reuben looked offended, "Of course I'm bloody sure; two shots, two hits; bang bang, just like that; the car swerve, then I heard the crash and that was just before I got the sniper!" Andreas demanded angrily, "Why the hell didn't you shoot the sniper first; he could have killed us!" Reuben explained, "If I'd shot the sniper first, Hendy would have gotten away!" Adding with a grin, "Besides, I knew that you slippery pair of bastards wouldn't allow yourselves to get nailed!" Shaking his head in disbelief, Andreas exclaimed, "I'll go down and take a look, just to make sure they're not just injured but with *your* prowess, there's fat chance of that!" Going back down the stairs, he walked briskly along the street, joining the crowd that had already gathered and elbowing his way into middle of the throng, he saw two bodies, covered with sheets from head to toe, being carried away on stretchers, while the white limo was lying at rest against the wall, being hosed down. Finding it hard to believe that the affair was finally all over, the initial feelings of relief and elation were soon supplanted by the fear of being caught, so walking as unobtrusively as he could from the scene, he made his way back to the room. Addressing Ronaldo, he said, "He's dead okay; so tomorrow morning you'd better get rid of the weapons and make yourself scarce!" Ronaldo replied with a grin, "Ours is a large family and the arms will be back in Melbourne long before we will!" "Right!" Andreas declared, "*I'll* have a word with Bruce to see if he can smuggle us out of here!"

Ringing Bruce after breakfast, Andreas pronounced, "Our work here is finished; Reuben shot Hendy and his driver in the early hours of this morning, so we'll be out of your hair in a couple of days' time!" Bruce replied, "I did hear the news and may I be the first to congratulate you *but* I have to inform that you will not be able to leave straight away. The local force are aware from the angle the bullet entered both bodies that the shot was fired from above and although you are here ostensibly on a sightseeing trip, it would look very suspicious if you were to return to Blighty straight away and the last thing you want is to be dragged back here for questioning; I'll give you the word when it's safe for you to leave!" With Andreas's euphoric bubble being instantly burst, he thought philosophically that perhaps it could prove to be a blessing in disguise; having lived on a knife edge for so long, a few weeks relaxation *may* help them to unwind before returning home. After delivering the bad news to his companions, Andreas suggested, "Come on, let's all have a few in the El Matador to celebrate!" With the *few* drinks becoming an all-day binge, Andreas bought a bottle of Tolley's at stop-tap, along with several large bottles of Coke. A couple of hours later, with the two Roma slumping into a drunken sleep on the two armchairs, Andreas sprawled wide-awake on the settee, turning over the night's events in his mind, wondering if he would *ever* recover from the feeling of having to be alert twenty-four hours a day but sometime during the night, he finally surrendered to the sleep his body craved

Intrusive and insistent hammering brought Andreas immediately to a state of wakefulness and with his hand reaching instinctively for his handgun, he discovered that it had disappeared and so had Ronaldo. Accompanied by more hammering, a voice called out loudly, "Come on in there; wake up, it's the police!" Opening the door, Andreas came face-to-face with two large members of the Sydney constabulary, "We'll be back in five minutes!" The larger of the two informed them, "So get yourselves sorted!" Recovering from the excesses of a few hours earlier,

Reuben asked, "What's the story?" "The truth!" Andreas replied, "We've been in Melbourne investigating discrepancies in the firm's accounts and now that everything has been sorted out, we are holidaying in Sydney for a couple of weeks before returning home! We've been extremely fortunate; Ronaldo disappeared, taking the weapons with him!" The police returned and asked if they had heard a commotion during the night; Andreas answered, "I didn't see what happened but I heard a car crash and ran down to see if I could be of any help but when I got there, it was all over and two bodies were being taken away on stretchers!" The officer told them, "Those two people were shot and killed late last night and it's possible that the shots were fired from this hotel; would you mind if we look round in order to eliminate you from our enquiries?" Andreas replied, "Of course, officer; go ahead! Would you like a cup of tea? I'm just making one?" His fellow officer shook his head remarking, "You bloody Poms and your tea!" Having searched the apartment thoroughly and found nothing, the two cops walked to the door, "You're in the clear for now but I'm afraid you will have to wait before returning home; nobody will be leaving this hotel until we have discovered exactly what took place! You are not under suspicion at this juncture and are free to explore the city; so enjoy your stay, gentlemen!" "Okay, officer, I'm sure we'll find something to do!" Andreas said, waving the empty Tolley's bottle.

Andreas rang Bruce the moment they had left and with Angela answering the call, he told her, "Tell Bruce we've *had* a visit from the police!" She responded excitedly, "I can't really believe it's finally all over but Bruce says that you have to wait a while before going back, so maybe we can all have a meal somewhere to celebrate?" "That would be great and seeing that you know your way round the city better than us, you can choose the *where!*" "I've got a place in mind!" She replied, "A quiet little place called the Metropole Bars, where the drinks are good and the meals even better. I'll see you both there at eight o'clock and you will need a taxi; it's on this side of town!" "Fine, we'll see you later then!" Hearing the last statement, Reuben remarked, "I don't care what it is you're arranging, you can count me out. I've seen enough of your ugly face to last me a lifetime and if *you're* going to make yourself halfway presentable, you'd better start getting ready now!"

27

Arriving shortly before the allotted time, Andreas waited in the foyer and after a few minutes, Angela arrived alone. "Where's Bruce?" He asked. "He's night shift and couldn't get anyone to exchange!" She replied. "Oh well!" He responded with a shrug, "Let's eat!" Finding a vacant table, he ordered a bottle of rosé and after a ten-minute hiatus, the waiter walked across and asked, "Would sir and madam like to order now?" "Whatever you choose!" Andreas suggested, "Will be fine by me too!" Turning to the waiter she ordered, prawn cocktail starters, two medium-rare chateaubriand steaks, with chocolate cabbage and cream to follow and noticing that the wine bottle was almost empty Andreas asked for more wine, "You seem to know your way around!" He commented as the waiter walked away. "Enjoyment is guaranteed!" She assured him. Noticing that there were few fellow diners, he feared that there may be a reason for the lack of customers but taking his first bite of the steak, he declared loudly, "*This* is absolutely the best slice of meat I've ever tasted!" With the last morsel disappearing, the empty dishes and wine bottle were speedily removed, making way for an impressive piece de resistance. A cabbage, perfect in every detail but made entirely of chocolate was wheeled in for their delectation and cutting into the spectacular *bonne bouche*, the garcon placed a slice onto each dish, before discreetly retreating out of sight. After second and third helpings, Andreas sat back with linked hands against his stomach, declaring, "I could not possibly eat another thing; Oz has to be the gastronomic centre of the universe!"

Taking what was left of the wine, they walked through to the bar, where several patrons were placing their bets, while four poker-playing patrons were studiously perusing their cards and Andreas wondered idly if gaming tables might be worth exploring for Jimmy's club back home. Snapping out of his reverie when the bill was presented on a silver platter, he suddenly realizing that he had not brought enough cash along. Turning to Angela, he asked,"What do I do now? I haven't brought enough money with me!" She replied, "Just sign your name on the bill and come in to settle the bill tomorrow; that's the way things are done in here!" Ordering more wine when they returned to the table, Andreas found that halfway into the bottle, he almost fell asleep and apologizing, he muttered shamefacedly, "I'm so sorry; I'm not usually so rude!" Slurring her words even more than her companion, she told him, "Don't worry; we'll get a taxi!" The cab arrived and Andreas slid in next to his dinner-date, not really sure of where he was being taken but when he perceived her unlocking an imposing oak door, he knew instantly to where he had been transported.

Being woken in the morning by Bruce moving about the apartment, Andreas returned to reality quickly and with Angela lying naked beside him, he guiltily recalled the passionate sex they had shared on the carpet; feeling relieved that they had actually made it to the bedroom but *unsure* of how or when. Waiting until Bruce went to bed before rising, Andreas quickly dressed and leaving Angela still sleeping, he tiptoed out of the room and returned to the hotel. Reuben grinned as soon as he walked in and not trusting himself to speak, Andreas merely shook his head in mortification. Reuben remarked, "Don't beat yourself up; I saw the sparks flying when we were all at the office together and what happened had an air of inevitability about it. Come on; let's have breakfast; things will look different then!" A small breakfast and a cup of sweet tea later, Andreas *did* actually feel somewhat better about himself and telling Reuben that he was going for a walk in the park, he thrust his hands into his pockets and walked from the hotel.

Sitting on a bench underneath a tree boasting masses of yellow flowers hanging pendulous from it's branches and birds chirping loudly from the boughs and closing his eyes, he could have easily been back home in the forest, with the horrors of the past few weeks just a bad dream. The sun was shining warmly on his face and being lost in awe and wonder, he did not hear footsteps approaching, only sensing another's presence when he felt the bench move under a weight. Turning his head, he saw Angela at the other end of the bench, "Reuben told me where you were!" She informed him, "How do you feel?" Andreas replied, "Not so good; about myself anyway and I owe you an apology; I should not have taken advantage last night!" Moving close, she put a forefinger against his lips to silence him, "Don't feel too bad about it; I *wanted* it to happen; *you* were in a bad place and *I* took advantage of you; I knew all along that Bruce would not be coming!" Andreas smiled saying, "I didn't really stand a chance then, did I?" Walking back through the park hand in hand, they were aware that the previous night of passion was the beginning of a new dawn.

Deciding to use Bruce's apartment for convenience sake, the two lovers made the most of stolen hours together, spending the lion's share of the time in eating houses and bed, leaving Reuben to while away solitary hours in the El Matador. The fact that Andreas was spending little time in his hotel room was not mentioned by Reuben and with Bruce not commenting that his flat was being used as a love nest, it became easy to pretend that no other world existed outside of their cocoon and after all said and done, it was not a hard cross to bear, with her abandoned approach to sex reminding him so much of Jan, whom he had left behind in Stow so long ago. The rare times that they met in passing, Andreas asked Bruce how the investigation was going, always receiving the same answer in one form or another, "I don't think anyone's too bothered; as long as you keep your head down and don't attempt to leave, you will be fine. I'll let you *know* when it is safe for you to return home!" Andreas was aware that at some point he would receive the reply that he both sought and dreaded; finding that the uncertainty of the situation never allowed him to relax completely and when Bruce came home unexpectedly one lunchtime; Andreas quipped light-heartedly, "You're early, have you been sent home for being a naughty boy?" Standing silent for a few seconds, Bruce addressed the pair and Andreas in particular, "I've come home to let you know that you are now free to return to Britain. I could have waited until later and disturbed your noisy lovemaking but I thought I'd be *Mr Nice Guy* for a change. Frankly, I'll be glad when you're gone, perhaps I can have my home back!" Andreas jumped up saying with a huge smile, "Would you mind if I use my your phone to let Reuben know?" "Help yourself!" Bruce remarked "It's been practically *your* flat for the last few weeks anyway!" Andreas chuckled, "Bruce, it has been an absolute pleasure to make your acquaintance!" Picking up the phone, he dialled the El Matador's number and glancing Angela's way, he saw her crestfallen face. *She* was not happy and replacing the receiver, he muttered, "Reuben's not answering; he's probably watching cricket somewhere, I'll tell him tomorrow!" Bruce asserted firmly, "You would be better to tell him now and I'm quite sure that you know where he'll be!" Angela agreed gloomily, "Yes Andreas, it would be better to leave now!" Putting on his jacket, he walked to the door, turning back to speak, he saw Angela's despondent face and as he had always done at critical times, he said nothing and left in a taxi for the El Matador.

Turning round as the barmaid nodded in the direction of his compatriot walking down the stairs, Reuben remarked, "What the hell are you doing here? You're usually snuggled up to Angela's backside!" Andreas replied, "Bruce has just informed me that we can now go home!" Reuben commented, "That fact does *not* appear to be making you particularly happy!" Adding unsympathetically, "You *knew* this day would come!" "I know and I'm not sure of how I feel!" Andreas confessed, "Living in the pressure cooker of knowing what had to be done and why; sex was a release and it was easy to feel no guilt but these past few weeks have been different; I felt terrible cheating on Lu and even worse knowing that I was about to hurt Angela; I am so confused!" Reuben put a solicitous arm around his friend's shoulder, "Come on; let's get pissed!" Several hours later they staggered up the stairs after somehow managing to negotiate their way back to the hotel.

Ringing Angela in the morning, Andreas told her that they would be leaving for Melbourne the following morning and asked if she could be ready for nine o'clock, in order to reach Melbourne by early evening. She answered stiffly, "Andreas, I won't be going back with you; Bruce has offered to put up with me for a little longer and I think that it would the best thing in the circumstances!" Not knowing what to say, he replaced the receiver gently and sitting down, he informed Reuben of her decision, "She's not coming back with us!" Reuben muttered, "Perhaps it's just as well!" "That's more or less what *she* said!" Andreas remarked, "Do you fancy going back tonight? I can phone the office to book us into somewhere for tomorrow?" "I don't mind!" Reuben replied, "It would probably be better driving through the night without that relentless daytime heat and if we do get tired, we can always get our heads down for a few hours in the car!" Carrying the cases downstairs, they walked over to the desk, where the receptionist advised them that she had just received a message from Melbourne to confirm that a room had been booked at the Sebel Hotel.

28

Setting off for Melbourne almost immediately and not bothering with food at the refuelling stations, they managed to shave a couple of hours from the outward journey and arriving mid-morning, they parked the car at the rear of the hotel; heading straight for the bar for a welcome double. A few more doubles followed and belatedly toasting Ronaldo and their victory over the forces of evil, Reuben pointed out, "We owe a huge debt of thanks to that man and do not forget that you still have to repay part of that debt by fighting their champion!" Andreas's face fell, "Shit, I'd forgotten all about that; we'll go to the camp the day after tomorrow, that will give me a day to get over that bloody journey!" Waking in the morning, Andreas had the feeling that a massive load had been taken from his shoulders and opening the window, he took a deep breath, coughed and with his early-morning euphoria severely dampened by Melbourne smog, he turned to Reuben, "I'll be bloody glad when we're back home, breathing in the healthy fumes of cow dung. I'd better go down to the gym and put in some work if I am to fight for the British Empire championship!" Reuben laughed, "You'd better work all day then, you don't look fit enough to fight a schoolboy champion, let alone an Empire one!" "I've got to be honest!" Andreas averred, "I'm not really committed to this fight but I have an obligation and I'm sure my competitiveness will see me through. Come on, you can put me through my paces!" Entering the gym, they both applied themselves to serious training immediately, with Andreas feeling grateful at the end of it that it was not Reuben that he would be facing. Finishing the training with a mini session on the weights before going for a run, he felt ready for the coming fight; buoyant from his exertions and after a refreshing cold shower, he was actually looking forward to the prospect. Eating little during the day, he made up for his fast by indulging in a huge evening meal at the end of which, Andreas asked, "Did Ronaldo stipulate any particular time?" "No but I know it's to be sometime in the morning!" "Right!" Andreas resolved, "I'll have a couple of Tolley's and call it a day!" At ten o'clock, leaving Reuben in the bar, he went to bed where the tiring journey and the excesses of the run up to the event, eventually caught up with him and he was soon sleeping soundly.

Being surprisingly up and about before his friend, Reuben mocked Andreas's reluctance to quit his bed, saying, "It's six o'clock, I've already had a shower and changed so if your reluctance to rise from your *pit* means that you don't wanna go to the camp; I've still got time to call off the fight!" Growling, Andreas staggered from his bed to the bathroom and Reuben called through the door, "If we get an early enough start, you can have a run before the fight to loosen up your limbs and get your lungs pumping!" While the water was warming up, Andreas looked in the mirror, *I don't look* any different, he thought, *even though I've cheated on my wife and killed a host of people*. The steam was rising as he entered the shower but with the fierce cascade washing away his guilt, he was up for a battle and packing his gear into a holdall, he informed Reuben, "Right, I'm ready!" "No breakfast?" Reuben asked. "Nah!" Andreas replied. "I'll grab a sandwich and bottle of pop on the way!" Reuben shrugged, "Let's go then!" With the cheese and tomato sandwich looking and tasting as if it had been left over from the day before, Andreas was thankful that the ice-cold bottle of lemonade at least hit the right spot, "God that's good!" he exclaimed, as he wiped away the excess liquid from his mouth.

Setting off again, Andreas began to experience the first flutters of nervousness in his stomach but all that was forgotten when Reuben stopped the car a few miles down the road. Getting out of the car and opening Andreas's door he ordered Andreas out, "Come on, out you get!" Andreas protested, saying, "What on earth is going on?" Reuben repeated. "You can fight me over it if you want but even if you were to beat me, you would not be in a fit state to fight this champion of theirs. Out you get *now!*" Knowing that Reuben meant business, Andreas meekly climbed out of the car and began trotting but realizing after a few minutes that the car had not been restarted, he ceased running and turned round; Reuben was standing by the side of the car, laughing fit to burst. Andreas shouted, "You rotten bastard; I'll bloody kill you!" "I had you going though, didn't I?" Reuben's laughter was so infectious that in seconds they were both screeching with tears running down their faces. Getting back into the car Andreas swore at his comrade-at-arms, "You pure bastard!" With Reuben responding, "Now don't start me laughing again or I won't be able to steer this bloody car!"

Driving into the camp, they were immediately surrounded by a mob of screaming children until Ronaldo suddenly appeared and shooed them away, "Are you ready?" he asked; Andreas replied, "Have I got time for a run, just to remove the stiffness from my bones!" Ronaldo replied sternly, "I'll give you one hour!" "Fair enough!" Andreas answered and began to jog steadily in the opposite direction to which they had arrived. After a mile or so and stopping to look at his watch, he realized that he'd been running for twenty minutes, *time to go back* he thought and trotting back into camp, he found Ronaldo waiting to lead him to the same large clearing where the prisoners had been suspended, noting that hundreds of people had already arrived from the outlying districts to watch the spectacle. His opponent was already there, with his back turned to proceedings and perceiving that he was a huge specimen, Andreas realized that the fight would not be an easy ride. The referee asked Andreas, "You ready, boss?" Nodding, he stripped off his tracksuit and walked to the centre of a ring formed by statue-like spectators. There was a murmur from the crowd as the big man removed his hooded cape and flexing his biceps, he turned round slowly to begin his walk towards the centre of the ring. Andreas gasped in surprise as he recognized the grinning ape-like features of Lupe, Lu's ex-husband. Andreas declared, "Ronaldo, you are going to have to get another second for me, your champion is Reuben's brother!" "That's okay!" Ronaldo averred, "I'll second you myself!" Turning to Reuben, Ronaldo advised, "Come on, son, I'll take you to my van before it starts; it's better that you don't watch!" The crowd began to murmur once more, believing that they were about to be robbed of seeing blood spilt but Lupe enlightened them with the sly grin he invariably wore, "It's okay folks; we have history and the man who was his second is my brother!"

During the hiatus, Andreas thought back to a time when they had all been children; he and Lupe had fought to a standstill, with Lupe winning the altercation, courtesy of an untied shoelace and later, Lupe had married Lu in an arranged marriage ceremony, without realizing that she was pregnant with Andreas's son. When he discovered the truth, Lupe systematically beat and abused her in retribution but after Gunnar had beaten him in a revenge honour fight, he had been banished and Australia was where he had chosen to re-invent himself. *oh yes*, Andreas thought, *there is history all right*. Ronaldo returned and with the referee calling the two combatants to the centre of the ring, "Go to it, boys!" He shouted, "May the best man win!" Knowing that *he* was the faster of the two, Andreas was aware that Lupe would try by any means fair or foul to negate that advantage and deciding to conduct the fight at a distance, he resolved to finish the fight as quickly as he was able; *the punters can go to hell,* he thought.

Lupe moved round the ring warily and suddenly rushing forward, he was stopped in his tracks by a straight left from Andreas, that jarred his arm all the way up to the shoulder. Lupe reeled backward from the punch but suspecting trickery, Andreas resisted the temptation to follow up the punch. Rushing in once more, Lupe dropped to the floor and sliding between Andreas's open legs, he kicked out at his old enemy's limbs. Crashing to the floor, Andreas quickly jumped up, managing to avoid Lupe's kick to the head but having anticipated the move, Andreas caught Lupe's foot with both hands and twisted, trying to dislocate his knee. Going *with* the twist however, Lupe kicked out at Andreas's face with his other foot and smiled as he saw blood running down his opponent's cheek. Responding with a two-fisted attack of his own, even though most of the punches landed on Lupe's arms, Andreas drove him back with the ferocity of the onslaught but still being wary, knowing that Lupe would be like a wounded animal; more dangerous when hurt. Lupe rushed in again and letting him get closer, Andreas swayed away, feinted with a left and hit him with a right hook to the cheek. Lupe tottered and resisting the temptation to use the methods taught by Claire; realizing that doing otherwise would cost him Reuben's friendship, Andreas kicked the side of Lupe's leg and as he reeled away unsteadily, Andreas moved in swiftly, delivering a head-butt to the face. Quickly darting back out of range, Andreas noticed that Lupe's nose was pouring with blood but being disappointed, having been aiming for his chin, he *desperately* wanted the fight finished as quickly as possible and in a brief respite between skirmishes, Andreas thought back to the day that Gunnar and Lupe had fought. Gunnar had taken a beating but had administered a more severe one by fighting steadfastly through the pain and Andreas thought that perhaps therein lay the answer. To get close enough to finish the fight, he would have to let Lupe inflict damage on him but he had to get it just right, knowing that if he failed, Lupe's hatred was so deep-rooted that he would have no qualms about killing him. Standing in the middle of the ring, Andreas dropped his hands, giving Lupe the opportunity that he had been waiting for and coming at Andreas swinging both fists, he found Andreas waiting. Returning the blows with interest, they once again stood toe to toe, clubbing each other with blows that would have felled lesser men and through the mist, Andreas could hear the crowd going wild. Nobody had ever seen such a fight, with both men not giving an inch of ground and even though he was hurt, Andreas knew that he dare not weaken. Continuing to return Lupe's blows, he finally saw his opponent beginning to give ground and following him, he rained blows into that sly face until at last his hands began to lower. Sensing victory, Andreas seized the initiative, landing an almighty right to Lupe's jaw and watched as his lionhearted adversary fell to the ground unconscious. Standing over him, Andreas turned him over onto his back and staring down at his old adversary, he nodded in admiration at his bravery, "Wolf man, you fought well; now let that be an end to the enmity between us!" Staggering over to Ronaldo, he snatched a bottle of water from his hand and drinking deeply, he addressed Reuben, who had reappeared, "Tend your brother and I'll see you tomorrow at the hotel!" Reuben advised him, "You can't possibly drive back on your own, your eyes are almost closed already!" "Don't worry about me, you old woman, I'll be fine!" Holding out an open hand, he demanded, "Keys!" Reuben handed over the car-keys and walked to the prostrate figure of his brother, leaving Andreas to get into the car and return alone to the hotel.

As morning dawned, Andreas lay in the bed, being too sore to move and scarcely remembering the journey back, he thought wryly that he must have caused quite a stir when he arrived back at the hotel. Satisfied now that his debt of honour had been paid in full, the matter was now a closed book and smiling painfully at the irony of the situation, he eased himself up onto one elbow. Swinging his feet round, he managed to raise his body from the bed and reeling to the bathroom, he turning on the shower. Looking at the reflection in the mirror, he saw a different face to that which had smiled back at him twenty-four hours before; his face was black and blue, blood was still seeping from one or two cuts and his body was agony every time he moved *but* he was champion of the Empire and an old ghost had been exorcized. Gingerly easing his body into the hot spray, he winced as the almost scalding water eradicated any lingering germs lying dormant in the cuts and not tarrying too long in the relentless cascade, he gently patting himself dry but being dismayed, seeing the bloodied towel bloodied, he resolved to see the maid and pay her well for the inconvenience. Having always been a fast healer, he believed that in a day or so he would be fine, realizing that the healing process, could *not* prevent a delay in returning home.

Not leaving the camp until early afternoon, Reuben missed the spectacle of Andreas's inept attempts at feeding himself; with his arm agonizingly sore every time he lifted the fork and the inside of his mouth being torturous whenever the odd dollop of food managed to find its way into his mouth. Arriving as Andreas was leaving the dining room, he helped his friend into the lift, deeming the elevator an easier and more comfortable way of returning to the room. Capriciously asking him if he'd care to visit the gym for a session; Andreas smiled back gingerly through swollen lips and grinning, Reuben asked, "How abut a Tolley's instead, if you're feeling up to it!" Andreas's face lit up and he replied, "It could be just the thing to ease the pain!"

Finding Andreas's injuries to be the source of much interest and speculation when they entered the bar, Reuben declared, "Don't even *think* about all the attention you're getting; being such an ugly bastard, you should be used to it!" Painfully grinning at his friend, Andreas replied, "Thank you for that; *I think!*" "I know it may be hard to believe but Lupe's injuries are far worse than yours. You gave him the mother all beatings!" *A few rounds of Tolley's later and feeling much better, Andreas could not have cared less if people stared, nevertheless conceding, "I'm afraid my injuries will mean having to stay another couple of days!" Reuben smiled, "More like a couple of weeks by the look of your face!" Andreas asserted, "Book the flight for two days time and contact Viv to let him know when we will be arriving!" Feeling much cheerier after the Tolley's he retired early, leaving Reuben to take up a more familiar berth at the bar.

Reuben's company over the next couple of days was a pleasant balm to Andreas's spirit, with his constant banter buoying Andreas's dampened spirits and preventing him from seeking solace in drink. His body was now quickly recovering from the beating it had received, with the bruises now turning yellow and the cuts beginning to heal over; he hoped that by the time they arrived home, they would be indistinguishable from his sun-darkened skin. His ribs were still extremely sore however and when they went to the office to bid everyone in the office goodbye, he was grateful that not *too* many hugs were given. Angela, of course, was not there but having a quiet moment, he took Pauline aside and told her that he was sorry not to have had the opportunity to say goodbye to Angela but that he understood the reason why she had not come. She smiled and kissed his cheek, "Don't worry; I'll keep my eye on her!" Gripping her as tightly as he was able, he assured her, "I know you will and she's damned lucky to have a friend like you. You have my number and if I am ever needed, do not hesitate to call!"

29

Being ready and waiting at the airport well before the mandatory hour; Reuben took residence in the bar, while Andreas occupied himself doing the *Aussie* Times crossword, finding it however, difficult to concentrate, with the fear that at any minute they were going to be arrested. So it was with a deep sense of relief when they finally boarded the Sydney bound plane, with Andreas having a double-take moment when he saw someone remarkably like Angela, waving goodbye from a window in the observation room. Believing it to have been wishful thinking on his part, he waved back anyway and was relieved to see that the already sleeping Reuben had missed seeing him wave to a stranger. Leaning over, he strapped Reuben in and laying his own head back in the seat, he too mercifully fell asleep. Arriving in Sydney with an hour and a half to spare for the flight to Singapore, Andreas was once more plagued by the vision of being carted off to jail, so when Bruce came walking into the waiting room, he feared the worst but putting them at ease right away, he informed them, "I've come to say goodbye and to thank you both for ridding the world of a gang of vicious thugs. You won't be getting any medals but a line has been drawn underneath the episode and you are perfectly at liberty to visit Oz any time you wish!" Reuben went to the cafeteria for a Coke and taking advantage of his absence, Bruce told Andreas that Angela had gone back to Melbourne the day before but learning of Bruce's intention of seeing them off, she had asked him to wish Andreas the best of luck on her behalf. Andreas replied, "Thank you for that and thank you for all the help and many kindnesses extended to us and if you should ever want anything else sorted out…don't bloody call us!" Bruce laughed, shook Andreas's hand and left just as Reuben returned with his drink.

Boarding the plane for Singapore, they were relieved to be finally on their way out of Australia and as the craft sped over the runway, Andreas recalled the vision of the woman waving from the observation room in Melbourne and after the information that Bruce had just given him, he was convinced that it *had* indeed been Angela. After a couple of brandy and Cokes which came nowhere near being comparable to Tolley's, they both nevertheless fell asleep, waking when the public address system barked out the message that they were about to land at Singapore. Trudging their way wearily to the luggage carousel to pick up their luggage in preparation for the flight to Bombay, Andreas recalled the last time they had been in the airport and thought of the soldiers who were involved in a fracas in Bugis Street, missing their flight to Borneo. Falling asleep almost immediately, they were wakened when food was being served and asking when they would be arriving at Bombay, Andreas was shocked to find that they *were* in fact, en route for Aden. He was informed that whoever had booked the tickets, along with most of the other passengers, had asked for the fastest route and going via Aden was *it*. Andreas looked across at Reuben, grinning like a Cheshire cat remarked, "I don't think we'll be buying many souvenirs there!" Andreas responded hotly, "Christ almighty, didn't you think to ask the route?" Reuben said nothing but with both being relieved to be embarking on a plane bound for London and with only one more stop, the silence did not last long.

Finally landing at Gatwick Airport, they descended the steps onto the tarmac, with Andreas stopping to sniffed the air and loudly declaring, "Ah that's better; bloody good riddance to the morning petrol fumes of Australia and the heady miasma of the east!" Within seconds he was eating his words, having forgotten how cold it could be in December but despite the cold bite *and* a strong sense of foreboding in the chilled air, he was glad to be on home ground. Having cleared customs, they were collecting their luggage from the carousel when Reuben spotted a man holding up a piece of cardboard bearing their names in bright yellow ink and introducing themselves, they found that he had been hired to take them home. Being unimportant who took them home, as long as they had not been left to organize things for themselves after travelling for days practically non-stop, they both climbed into the rear of the spacious cab. The driver was a friendly sort, who chattered about things that no longer had the same relevance to the intrepid pair and as they left Gatwick Airport behind them, Andreas sat back and relaxed in the knowledge that they were now only a few hours from home and even though he was tired; his senses were racing.

Reuben was the first to be delivered home safely and Bill waved as the car pulled away from the house, taking Andreas home to an uncertain future but all of his fears proved groundless, as Lu came running out to greet him. Throwing her arms around his neck, she was followed closely by both boys holding Rosie's hands, aiding her faltering steps, *have I really been away that long?* he thought. Depositing the luggage in the hallway, the driver thanked Andreas for the generous tip and Andreas carried his baggage into the living room. Slowly unlocking the case containing presents, Andreas dragged out the suspense and there were squeals of delight as he brought out each gift, handing it over to the new owner. Lu kissed him warmly on the mouth each time he extracted a gift for her and he suddenly realized how much he had really missed her, with the recent past being just a dream; an overnight stop on the journey of life.

Fortunately the kids were in bed sleeping when Ma and Pa came visiting and Andreas could not help but notice the changes in their physical appearance. Ma's hair had become conspicuously more grey and Pa stooped over a little further but imparting all the recent family news, their faces became animated, giving their features a look of the Ma and Pa of his youth. He was particularly pleased to learn of Michael's successful re-routing of the river, having put his trust in him, despite the misgivings expressed by the firm. His brothers' situations were *virtually* unchanged, although Guaril was now a fully fledged member of the lautari, while Walthaar was busy with Ted Scamp in and around the whole of the West Country. Andreas remarked to Ma, "I hope you check on Walthaar at the flat just as you used to with me?" "He doesn't need it half as much as you did!" She replied, "He's a good boy, *unlike you!*" Andreas laughed but in his heart, he knew in that instant that she was well aware of what he had been up to in Australia and crossing to where she was seated, he kissed her cheek, "It doesn't matter where I am Ma, I always love and miss my family and in spite of all the grief you give me; that includes you!" She smiled, "I know that you love your family son, even if sometimes it may appear that you do not!" *Oh yes*, Andreas thought, *she bloody knows all right!*

When they had all left, he did not receive the expected rebukes from Lu, even though they would have been fully merited and with the matter of his infidelity not being mentioned neither then or at any time in the future; he knew that she had accepted what had happened and with typical Roma pragmatism, had cast it from her mind. When she said, "Are you ready for bed?" Andreas grinned, remembering the sight of her naked body as she waved goodbye to him from the window all those months ago when the Australian adventure began. Slipping between the cold sheets, he put his arms around her warm body and within seconds Australia was back where it always had been...*far away*!

THE END

AUTHOR BIO

Lloyd Ingle was born in Mansfield, England, in 1944; he moved to Dover in 1950. Ingle was educated at Dover Grammar School from 1955 to 1960, and he later joined the British Army, where he served in the Far and Middle East. He is divorced and has two daughters and two sons and lives in Caerphilly, South Wales. In 2014 he had pancreatic cancer and underwent a twelve-hour operation involving total pancreatomy. On release from hospital, he suffered traumatic hallucinations and many dreams, one of which became the basis of his first novel, *Gadjo*.

ABOUT THE BOOK

Andreas had been entrusted with the task of organizing a shindig to celebrate the completion of some construction work he had been involved in. The workforce had been given a generous bonus for their diligent role in the various ventures; now it was the bosses' turn to celebrate. Andreas's own contribution to the affair consisted of booking the gymnasium club, the only place big enough to host the vast number of guests, and organizing a tab behind the bar. All this was acquitted at his usual breakneck speed, enabling him to sit back and relax, so the last thing he needed was one of Viv's nefarious schemes!

Having delegated a sizeable degree of responsibility to Ma and Gunari; thus the lautari had been engaged to play at various times during the meal, and the catering had Ma's expertise bestowed upon it, ensuring, no doubt, that there would be a pot of her famous rabbit stew on the menu. Old grievances and vendettas had been put aside when they had been forced to coexist in their new housing estate. But the lavish get-together bringing the tribes together would prove one way or another whether the grievances rooted so deeply in the past were insoluble or not.